Annie

(how children are)

Annie
(how children are)

©2021
by
Billy Lee Harman
(All rights reserved.)

HI
www.hitrt.com
1210 First Street
Albion, MI 49224

Publisher
KDP

ISBN
979-8-762-37339-5

**for
each
and every one**

The greatest calamity is not knowing what's enough.
Lao Zi

Contents

Chapter 1	Friends	Page 5
Chapter 2	Home	Page 17
Chapter 3	Finding Her Footing	Page 30
Chapter 4	New York City	Page 45
Chapter 5	Return to School	Page 62
Chapter 6	Taming some Bullies	Page 78
Chapter 7	Thanks and Giving	Page 92
Chapter 8	Jehanne of Domremy	Page 109
Chapter 9	Making it Official	Page 125
Chapter 10	And Also All	Page 136
Chapter 11	East and West	Page 151
Chapter 12	War and Peace	Page 169
Chapter 13	Onward and Upward	Page 186
Chapter 14	Three More Steps	Page 203
Chapter 15	Diamonds and Forever	Page 220
Chapter 16	Closing some Circles	Page 239
Chapter 17	And Opening More	Page 255
Chapter 18	Beyond	Page 268

1

Friends

She was sitting alone in a corner. I looked at her, when I came in from the parking lot, but she didn't look at me. She was gazing into the space in front of her.

Her appearance wasn't particularly remarkable. Her jeans were frayed at their bottoms and a little dirty, and her sneakers were in a similar condition, and so was a backpack beneath her chair. But her T-shirt seemed to me to be in a condition more appropriate for a child.

And she wasn't leaning back in the chair. She was sitting erect with her hands in her lap, the left below the right, palms up. So, ordinarily, I'd have thought that showed thoughtful attention.

But she didn't seem to me to be happy. And, with her gaze toward nothing in particular, I couldn't discern any object of her attention. So, as I crossed the room to the reception window, I wondered what she was thinking sitting alone in that corner.

"How can I help you?" asked the woman behind the window, turning her attention from the computer in front of her.

"I'd like to see about becoming a foster parent," I said.

"I can give you the application form," she said, shrugging.

"I printed it from the Web," I said. "But I'd like to ask someone some questions before I fill it out. I don't want to waste anyone's time."

"Oh," she said. "OK. But Miss Walker has someone with her right now. Can you wait a few minutes?"

"Sure," I said. "That's fine. Just have a seat?"

She nodded. So I turned from the window. And then the child in the corner looked at me. So for a moment I thought I might talk with her while I waited. But she quickly returned her gaze to the space in front of her.

Chairs were along the walls on both sides of a small table beside her in the corner. But, while I wished to know what she was thinking and whether she was as unhappy as she seemed to me to be, I didn't wish to be an unwelcome imposition. So, instead of sitting in the chair nearest to hers, I sat in the second chair from the other side of table.

But, as soon as I sat, I reconsidered the possibility that she was as unhappy as she seemed to me to be and would welcome speaking with someone wishing to help her out of her unhappiness. So I moved to the chair between me and the table and shuffled through some magazines on the table. But I didn't select one.

"Hi," I said, and she glanced at me again.

She didn't turn her head, and she immediately returned her gaze forward again, but she spoke.

"Hi," she said quietly, after a pause.

"My name's Billy," I said. "What's yours?"

"Annie," she said.

But her pause before saying her name was longer than the one after the glance, and she said it as quietly as she'd returned my greeting, and she didn't glance when she said it.

"Nice to meet you, Annie," I said, but I also extended a hand to her across the magazines.

I was to her left. So, to put her right hand into mine, she had to turn from her posture and lean a little. But, after another pause before looking at the hand I offered and another while looking at it, she looked up at me and down again and did it'

So I shook the warm little hand she handed me.

And, though then she returned to her previous posture and her previous gaze, I persisted.

"Why are you here?" I asked.

Then she didn't shift her gaze. But, after another pause, she moved her hands to the arms of her chair, slid herself further into the chair and leaned against its back, and looked down at her knees. And, though she didn't look up to do it, she also replied to that question..

"I'm a troublemaker," she said, and then I had to pause.

I had to consider how to reply to her reply. But I decided to reply as I ordinarily tried to reply to any question. I tried to reply as simply and directly as she'd replied to my question.

"You don't look like a troublemaker to me," I said. "What kind of trouble do you make?"

"I told the foster parents I don't want go to Sunday school," she said, as quietly as she'd said all else she'd said to me.

But, for that, she didn't pause. So I again I replied as simply and directly as I could. But that reply required a little more thought.

"I quit going to Sunday school when I was about your age," I said. "Why don't you want to?"

"They said I'm going to hell," she said, "no matter what I do, if I don't accept Christ as my personal savior."

After saying that, she looked at her arms, first at the one nearest to me and then at the other. And then she shifted her gaze to the floor in front of her. But she continued.

"I don't think that's fair," she said. "Anyway I don't know who Christ is. They told me some stuff about why I should do that, and I tried to understand it, but I couldn't. And, when I asked them who he is, they said I'll find out if I'm not careful."

And then she looked at me, shrugged but hardly perceptibly, and returned her gaze to her knees.

"The Sunday school teacher told you that?" I asked.

"And my foster parents said she was right," she said after nodding. "So I told them I didn't want to go back there. So they said I'm a troublemaker and brought me back here."

And, after saying that, she sat up and slid forward again, returned her hands to her lap, and looked at them.. And then the door beside the reception window opened, and a man and a woman came through it and looked at Annie, but they didn't pause for a moment. They scowled, immediately looked away, and continued through the door through which I'd come in from the parking lot.

And Annie didn't return their look.

"That's about the reason I quit going to Sunday school," I said. "It sounds to me like some people are making trouble for you."

And then she looked directly at me, and also then the receptionist spoke, but then Annie didn't shift her gaze.

"Miss Walker can see you now," said the receptionist.

But, as I stood and turned to go to the window, Annie continued looking at me. So, before reaching the window, I turned back. And still she was looking at me.

"I'll see what I can do," I said.

I was wishing I could respond to her look by telling her I knew what I could do would be what she needed. But, hearing the door beside the window buzz, I turned back to the window. So, as the receptionist pointed toward the door, I pushed it open.

On the other side of it was another open door. On the other side of that door was a desk. And a woman was sitting at the desk.

She was looking down at a file folder open on the desk. But, at the sound of the door closing behind me, she looked up. And then she beckoned me into her office.

"What can I do for you?" she asked, gesturing to one of two chairs in front of the desk, one on each side of a name plate saying she was Miss Walker.

"I'm hoping you can help me do something for Annie," I said, sitting in the seat she offered.

"Who's Annie?" she asked.

"That little girl out there," I replied.

"Oh," she said looking down at the folder again. "What's your relationship to her?"

"A friend," I said.

"How did you know she was here?" she asked.

"I didn't," I said. "I came here to ask about becoming a foster parent. But, while I was waiting, we had a talk. So now we're friends."

At that, Miss Walker, pursing her lips, looked up at me for a few seconds, but then she looked down at the folder again.

"She has some problems," she said. "Her mother died of an opioid overdose a few months ago. We don't know where her father is or if she has any other relatives. And the foster parents we assigned to her said she's a troublemaker."

"She told me that last part," I said. "Sounds to me like they were making trouble for her."

"Why do you want to be a foster parent?" Miss Walker asked then, after another pursing of her lips.

"I have more time and money than I need," I said. "And I also have more room in my house than I'm using. So I'd like to put all that to some important use."

"But why foster parenting?" asked Miss Walker. "Surely you could find some other important use for your surplus resources."

I didn't know how to answer that question. I knew the answer, but I didn't know how to answer it in a way a social worker working for a government agency might understand, or be able to accept within her official responsibilities. So again I replied as simply and directly as I could, but the answer to that question of Miss Walker's took many turns, through man years.

"My sister," I said. "Peggy, my older sister. She was more of a parent to me than our parents were. She tried to teach me everything she knew, and that was a lot. She loved to read and had more imagination than anyone else I think I've known well enough to think that of anyone. And she gave me the sense of adventure that's taken me to thirty countries.

"But she never had a chance. An uncle molested her before she reached adolescence. And she fell in love with an eighteen-year-old boy when she was fourteen.

"He treated me about as Peggy did. And he also did lariat tricks, wore a cowboy hat and cowboy boots and played guitar, and could stick knives in trees by throwing them. So he was also a role models to me.

"But they tried to elope. So, because of their ages, Buzz went to prison for two years for statutory rape. That was his name, Buzz.

"But, anyway, about two years later, Peggy quit school, pregnant. She married the 27-year-old man who impregnated her. But he beat her after the marriage.

"Once, when she tried to get him to get up to go to work, he threw her down the stairs from their apartment and threw the alarm clock after her.

"She stayed with him long enough to have two sons by him. But, when she couldn't bear being with him anymore, she just disappeared. And she didn't have enough money to take her sons with her.

"I don't think anyone knew where she was going, and I'm not sure she had much of a plan, but she went to Fort Wayne. She found a job there working as a waitress in a bar, and she earned enough money to come back for her sons, but by then their father had divorced her and taken them to Angola.. The court had given him what it called full custody. I drove her down there to see them. But he didn't let her .

"She didn't go back to Fort Wayne. She found a waitress job in Coldwater, where all that started because it's where we grew up, and that job wasn't in a bar. It was in the restaurant of Coldwater's only hotel, and a few months later she moved in with its chef, and later she married him.

"He was a drunk, when she married him, but she made him quit drinking. And, after working in other restaurants in various other places and having a daughter, they bought a new little house in a suburban subdivision in Illinois and lived in that house long enough for a sapling in its front yard to become a respectable tree, but she never quit drinking and never quit smoking. So, at 56 years old, she died of her only heart attack.

"But, through all that, she never lost her imagination or her hope. By then, she and Bob were sleeping in separate rooms, but she had Star Trek posters all over the walls of her bedroom. And, in her early fifties, she reunited with her sons and became congenial with their father and stepmother. And, a few months before she died, she received her high school GED. Her newspaper obituary picture was of her in her cap and gown.

"And also in that mix are the misadventures of my life. I used the sense of adventure Peggy gave me to follow disparate paths of what people call desperados before I figured out that I was doing to myself and others what others had done to her. So I didn't graduate from college until I was in my thirties.

"I don't blame anyone for that. But I have to consider what my life might have been with more lasting displays of hope. I mean I can't discount how random obstructions can taint adventure.

"On my fifth Easter, instead of Easter baskets, our parents hid tin buckets with tin shovels in them in our apartment. They also had cellophane grass and candy in them, but Peggy and I preferred the more substantial tin and set aside the candy eggs and cellophane grass to take the buckets and shovels out to our back yard, to dig in sand around where our landlady's son burned trash. Less than a minute after we started, I dug into some blue paper and felt the frustration of the interruption., but Peggy didn't.

"'Maybe It's part of the sky of China,' she said.

"But she never made it to China. And neither did I until a few years ago. Except on R&R to Hong Cong from Vietnam.

"So the answer to your question is that I'd like to do anything I can to be sure that any child has a chance to be as wonderful as Peggy and to make her life as wonderful as Peggy's could have been. And now I'm hearing that those so-called foster parents called Annie a troublemaker and slammed their door in her face for being as wonderful as she is. So I'd like to be sure nothing like that ever happens to her again."

"How would you decide what opportunities would let her be as wonderful as she could be?" asked Miss Walker.

"I'd ask her," I replied.

"She's seven years old," said Miss Walker.

"Don't events have to be sequential?" I asked. "And also she told me why she didn't want to go to Sunday School. And her reasoning seems to me not only to be reasonable but also to show an excellently rational sense of fairness. And, anyway, children seem to me to be more reasonable than adults, until adults teach them to be like adults. I mean, until they learn what adults learned when they were children, from people who were adults then.

"Think of Annie's father deserting her, and think of those so-called foster parents evicting that brave and thoughtful child because they couldn't intimidate her, but you must see plenty of that sort of thing."

"I see far too many deadbeat dad situations," said Miss Walker. "And I also agree that events have to be sequential. But why didn't she want to go to Sunday school?"

"The Sunday school teacher told her she'll go to hell, if she doesn't accept Christ as her personal savior, no matter what else she does. And, when she asked who Christ was, trying to understand how that was fair, she told her she'll find out, if she isn't careful. And those so-called foster parents backed up the Sunday school teacher.

"The first part of that's the reason I quit Sunday school when I was about Annie's age. And the second part shows Annie's more responsible than either that Sunday school teacher or those so-called foster parents. Apparently responsibility's too much trouble for them."

"So you're not a Christian?" asked Miss Walker.

"No," I said. "I tried again a few years later, and I've read the Bible several times in several translations, cover to cover, carefully. But I've also done that with the definitive scriptures of each of the four of the six most popular religions other than Christianity and Judaism. So now I'm a Hindu Buddhist Daoist believing in Jesus but not in the apostles."

"Why don't you believe in the apostles?" she asked.

"They were Paul's disciples," I said. "The Book of Acts of the Apostles, which Paul's disciple and apostle Luke wrote, names fewer than half of Jesus' disciples. And, excepting three of Jesus' disciples the Book of Acts names, neither do Paul's epistles mention any of them. And all those references are in one epistle and refer to before Paul took charge of the church.

"And both that epistle and the Book of Acts refer to Peter more than to any other of Jesus' disciples, and the Gospels say not only that Peter denied Jesus three times on the morning of Jesus' crucifixion but also that Peter sank like a stone in the Sea of Galilee, for lack of faith. And they also say Jesus told his disciples to beware of the doctrine of the Pharisees. And Paul was a Pharisee.

"But doesn't the Bible say he repented being a Pharisee?" asked Miss Walker.

"No," I said. "It says he repented persecuting people for saying Jesus was the Christ. But interpretations of prophesies that God would anoint a descendent of David's to resurrect the kingdom of Judah to mean he'd resurrect everyone who either hasn't violated Mosaic law or repents having violated it is what makes Pharisees different from other Judaic people. The words 'christ' and 'messiah' are from Greek and Hebrew for 'anointed' and refer to those prophesies.

"And the only Gospel saying Jesus called himself the Christ directly is John's. And Matthew's and Mark's Gospels say Jesus told John he didn't know what he was talking about regarding that. And, as though Jesus didn't love all of his disciples and everyone else, John called himself the disciple Jesus loved.

"And Paul, in his epistles, undercut his own credibility in other ways. Examples are that he says slaves should obey their masters as they'd obey Christ and that women talking in church is a shame. And also, in one of his epistles telling his apostle Timothy how to be a bishop, he tells him to avoid foolish and unlearned questions.

"What, if not to learn, is the purpose of questions?

"And the Bible also says Jesus said loving one's neighbor is like loving God, and that's also fundamental to both Hinduism and Buddhism. Effectually, the monism Hindu and Buddhist scriptures express in various ways is the notion that your neighbor *is* God, because God is everything. And the defining premise of Daoism is the inevitability of all eventually realizing that unity.

"But more immediately pertinent to Annie is that the Gospels say Jesus said offending a child would be worse for a person than throwing the person into a sea with a millstone around his neck."

"Well," said Miss Walker after a few seconds of silence, "I don't know about all that, but this is a government agency, and we have separation of church and state in this country. And you seem to have taken Annie's interest to heart, and you'd save me and the system a lot of time and effort, if you're sure you want to do this. So my last question is whether you're sure."

"Absolutely," I said. "I don't think I've ever been more sure of anything."

"Then we have to do two things," said Miss Walker. "You have to fill out some forms, and I have to inspect your house, to be sure it's safe and sanitary. And a reason for both is to look for any indication that you're a criminal."

And then she looked at me with neither a smile nor a pursing of lips.

"Not as much as a parking ticket," I said, "in this millennium."

Still sternly looking at me, she leaned back in her chair and put her hands on her desk, but then she rose from her chair and pulled some forms from a file cabinet.

"How soon can you inspect my house?" I asked.

"As soon as we can get there," she said. "I have no other appointments today. If that's alright with you."

"It's fine with me," I said. "My house is in Albion. Is that too far?"

"No," she said, walking around her desk, "Let's go. After you."

"Can Annie go with us?" I asked. "It would be for her, and we don't want to leave her alone in that corner all that time, do we?"

"I don't see why not," said Miss Walker. "And no, we don't."

And she opened the door to the reception room. And, when I went through it, Annie looked up at me with her eyes wide in a questioning look. And I had to smile.

"Feel like going for a ride, little friend?" I asked, and she grinned and nodded and slid from her chair.

Then, after taking a couple of steps toward me, she stopped and turned around. But that was to grab her backpack from beneath her chair. So, after grabbing it, she turned around again. But then she stopped again. And her grin disappeared.

"Now?" she asked with a look suggesting much of her misfortune.

"If it's alright with you," I said, and her grin reappeared, and she stepped forward again and put a hand of hers into the hand of mine nearest to her.

At that, Miss Walker shook her head, but she grinned at the same time, and then she followed Annie and me outside, into the bright summer sun.

"Where's your car?" she asked.

"That black Mustang," I said. "Do you want to ride with me or follow me?"

"I'll follow you," she said. "So you won't have to bring me back."

"Can Annie ride with me?" I asked.

"I guess so," she said. "She'll need a booster seat. But I have one in my car she can use. I guess you probably don't have one."

So, as Annie and I continued on to our car, Miss Walker went to hers for the booster seat.

"Is this your car?" asked Annie when we reached ours.

"I'm hoping it'll be our car soon," I said.

"It's a convertible!" she said grinning again.

And its top was down.

So she threw her backpack into its backseat and pulled open the driver side door, climbed between its front seats into its backseat and accepted the booster seat from Miss Walker, and put it on the side of the backseat behind the front passenger seat.

And then, still grinning, she climbed onto it and fastened her seatbelt.

2

Home

Marshall was the county seat. So it was where the child protective services offices were. Albion was on I-94 about twelve miles further east.

During that drive, each time I looked in the inside rear view mirror, Annie was opening and closing her hands in the breeze above her head. And at home she was over the side of the car before I pulled the key from the ignition switch. But she waited in the drive until I came around to her.

"Is this your house?" she asked.

"I'm hoping it'll be our house soon," I said. "If you think you might like to live here."

Then she skipped up the steps to the small concrete front porch of the small concrete block and stucco Cape Cod house and tried the door handle.

 Finding that she couldn't open it, she stepped back and waited for me to open it, but then she continued through it and through the entranceway's inside door. Inside, after stopping and looking around for a moment, she continued on past the dining table and looked into the kitchen.. But then she returned to the dining table.

There, with her hands on the back of the chair at the end of the table nearest to the entrance to the kitchen, she waited for me and Miss Walker to catch up with her.

But then she continued her exploring.

Her next stop was a porcelain Buddha statuette I'd set on a Tibetan stool beneath a map of Earth between the dining room end of the main room and its living room end.

"What's this?" she asked, touching her right index finger to the statuette's *ushnisha*

"It's a Chinese imagining of the Buddha," I said.

"Who's the Buddha?" she asked.

"The Buddha was a prince," I said, "who left his father's palace to try to learn how to end all the misery in the world."

"It looks like a girl," she said after another of her pauses.

"People say he said everything's everything," I said. "So, if he thought that and was right about it, I guess he may have been both a boy and a girl."

"How can anyone be both a boy and a girl?" asked Annie.

"He said all differences are imaginary," I said. "and that the way to end misery is to realize that. But, anyway, I suspect that, if he met you, he wouldn't imagine telling you you'll suffer in hell if you don't believe in him. I think he'd say: 'Hi, little friend. Nice to imagine you.'"

Then, because she was looking at the statuette, I couldn't see if she smiled. And she was silent for the next few seconds. But then she looked up.

"What's that?" she asked.

"A map of Earth," I said.

"What are those little balls?" she asked.

"Map tacks," I said. "The red ones are for places I've spent at least one night. The green ones are for places I've planned to go but haven't gone yet."

"Is China on that map?" she asked.

"Yes," I said. "It's the big yellow place below the bigger pink place on the top right."

"Six red tacks and one green one," she said after another pause. "I want to go there."

Why?" I asked.

"Because you said that's where this imagining of the Buddha's from," she said.

"Oh," I said, "Well then I think you will. Maybe we can go there together and go where that green tack is. A lot of people who believe in the Buddha live there."

Another of her pauses followed that, and she touched the statuette's *ushnisha* again, but then she turned and looked into the living room end of the main room.

"Is that a piano?" she asked.

The room wrapped around the front and one side of the kitchen. So, from the end of the dining table where she launched her tour, she couldn't see the electronic keyboard I'd placed between a window to the backyard and the mud area inside the backdoor between the main room and the back entrance to the kitchen. So she didn't look into that end of the room until she turned from the Buddha statuette to determined her next step in her exploring.

"Sort of," I said. "It's a kind of electric piano."

And she continued on, between the TV and the coffee table and past the chair where I ordinarily sat to read until she reached the keyboard, and then she stopped and touched one of its keys.

"It isn't on," I said, following her to answer her questions. "The power button's the one the furthest to your left."

So she pressed the button and then pressed three keys in succession. But then she pushed the button again to turn the keyboard off, turned from the keyboard to look through the mud area, and continued her exploring into the kitchen. And there, as I continued following her, she slid a hand across the tops of the washer and dryer.

But, before stopping again, she continued through the front kitchen entrance to where Miss Walker was waiting for us with a hand on the back of the chair from which Annie had launched her tour.

And there, putting her hands on the back of the side chair nearest to the kitchen, she smiled up at Miss Walker.

"Where would she sleep?" asked Miss Walker, after returning Annie's smile with the second grin I saw from her.

"I'm thinking the front downstairs bedroom," I said also smiling. "Through there, across from the bathroom. It's the biggest downstairs bedroom, and I haven't furnished the upstairs. I haven't been heating the upstairs either."

And Annie followed Miss Walker there and looked around more than she did. I'd put a corner desk and a chair with a swivel base in the corner nearest the window nearest the head of the bed. And she pulled the chair from the desk, swiveled it around, and sat in it

Pushing on its base with her feet, she swiveled it around again and put her hands on the desk for a few seconds, but then she swiveled the chair around again and slid from it. And then, after swiveling it around again and returning it to where she found it, she stepped to the foot of the bed and looked at the folding doors to the closet. But she didn't open the doors.

She sat on the foot of the bed with her feet hanging from it and her hands in her lap as they were when I found her.

Then, lying back and spreading her arms out to her sides, she waved her arms as children do to make snow angels.

"Is that bed big enough for you?" asked Miss Walker.

It was queen size. And Annie stopped waving her arms, slid from it and turned around, and looked at it. But, instead of answering, she turned and looked at an occasional chair I'd placed in the corner of the room opposite the corner with the desk.

And then she turned and looked up at me.

"Where are the other kids?" she asked.

But I already had considered that question.

"It'd be just you and I," I said. "Would you be too lonely? A girl about your age lives across the street."

Then, looking down again, she shook her head.

"The other kids don't like me," she said, but what I'd already learned of her also gave me an easy reply to that.

"I think that'll change quickly," I said.

"How?" she asked, looking up at me again.

"I suspect," I said, "that soon you'll be more sure you're not a troublemaker. And I think that, when you go back to school and have more kids around you again, you'll see the troubles some of them are having. And I think you'll try to help them."

That drew a long look from her, but saying nothing in reply to it she returned to the dining table, to which Miss Walker already had returned.

"I just need to see the upstairs," said Miss Walker. "And the basement if you have one. I need to be sure you don't have any bodies buried or whatever."

And she didn't smile when she said that. So I showed her the doors to the stairways, and turned on the light for each, but I didn't go with her. And Annie waited with me.

I thought she might have gone with Miss Walker. But, as I pulled from the dining table the chair from which she'd launched her earlier exploration and sat in it, she did the same with the one to which she'd returned from the kitchen. So, as we sat there waiting for Miss Walker to finish her inspection, I asked her what I'd wondered since the first moment I saw her.

"What are you thinking, little friend?" I asked.

Then she smiled. But she shrugged and didn't otherwise reply. She sat there silent with her hands in her lap until Miss Walker returned.

"Water softener and filtration system," said Miss Walker. "That's a plus, and the place is immaculate, and orderly. I wouldn't expect that from a man your age."

"Ten years in the Army," I said. "A place for everything, for everything a place, clean as you go. That sort of thing."

"I'm not sure it'll stay that way," she said, "with your little seven-year-old friend sharing it with you."

"I can live with that," I said.

But, though Annie looked at us as we spoke, she showed no reaction to what we said.

"Alright," said Miss Walker, picking up the forms from between Annie and me on the dining table, where she put them when she came into the house. "We just need to fill out the forms. You need to fill out these, and I need to fill out the inspection forms, but I left my purse in my car. Do you have a pen?"

But I had a question for Annie.

"What do you think, Annie?" I asked. "Do you think you might like living here?"

And then she grinned and nodded.

So, also grinning, I grabbed two pens from a mug beside our TV. And Miss Walker sat in the chair at the end of the table opposite the chair I'd left. So, with Annie still watching and listening from the side chair, I returned to the end I left.

Still I wondered what she was thinking. But I thought I might be beginning to feel how she felt. And I felt reason for hope that she'd find ways to find far more doors than I could ever imagine for her.

"Why do you need this bank information?" I asked miss Walker.

"For direct deposit of the stipend," she said. "The state will pay you what it thinks taking care of Annie will cost."

"Did you hear that, little friend?" I asked. "The government's going to contribute to your college fund."

Neither did she speak in reply to that. But she grinned, slid from her chair, and pushed it back to where she'd found it. And then she went to the keyboard and began to teach herself to play "Twinkle, Twinkle, Little Star".

"I have a savings account I'm not using," I said as I left the table to find the information for it. "I was using it as an escrow account for a rental property I sold on a land contract. I haven't used it since the guy paid off the contract. So I'll use it for escrow for Annie."

Then, after we completed the forms, Miss Walker asked me to sign both sets and looked at the set I completed.

"You're ten times as old as she is," she said, shaking her head and grinning again. "You two are going to make quite a pair."

And then she offered a hand for shaking. And, after shaking the hand, I followed her outside. And Annie followed us.

"Oh," said Miss Walker. "I should have told you. The backpack she brought has everything she owns in it. Those other people said they bought clothes for her, but they said their other foster children can use them. So, well . . . ."

"Well," I said. "Then I guess we'll have to do some shopping."

"Then you can keep the booster seat," said Miss Walker smiling again. "You'll need it for the shopping. We have more."

And, still smiling, she bade farewell to Annie, climbed into her car, and drove away. And Annie retrieved her backpack from the backseat of our car. And we went back into our house.

"Can I put this in my room?" she asked.

"Sure," I said. "It's yours and your room."

And, grinning again, she took the backpack to her room.

"Are you hungry?" I asked her when she returned.

She didn't speak in reply to that, and neither did she grin or smile, but she nodded.

"I only have food I eat," I said. "But I guess we have to do some other shopping today anyway. So how about if we eat at a restaurant and then drive to Jackson and buy you some clothes and groceries and whatever else you need?"

And again she nodded but neither grinned nor smiled. So I drove us to the only restaurant between our house and the freeway that wasn't fast food. I thought we might do well with a little conversation to slow down the day a little and give us a chance to learn a little more about one another.

"Is this alright?" I asked her in the parking lot of the restaurant. "Or would you rather go to McDonalds or Pizza Hut or someplace like that?"

"This is OK," she said.

Still she didn't smile, but I turned off the engine, and she unfastened her seatbelt.

"Please seat yourself," said a sign inside the restaurant.

"Where would you like to sit?" I asked her.

"Over there?" she asked, pointing toward a table at a window to the street. "Is that OK?"

"It's OK with me," I said. "I like windows."

And then she smiled. So we sat at the table. A waitress brought menus to it and gave me one. She didn't give Annie one then, but she looked at her for a moment, and looked at me again. And she didn't turn away.

"How's your reading, little friend?" I asked.

At that, with no smile, Annie shrugged and looked out the window. But the waitress responded by putting a menu in front of her. So then both she and the waitress smiled.

"Can I get you something to drink?" asked the waitress.

"Do you have chocolate milk?" asked Annie.

"Yes, ma'am," said the waitress.

"Is that OK?" Annie asked me.

"Anything you like is OK with me," I said.

"And you sir?" asked the waitress.

"We'll have two large chocolate milks please," I said. "Thanks."

"Oh!" I said to Annie as we looked at the menus. "They have Belgian waffles. I think I'll just have one of those. I'm not as hungry as I think you might be, and I don't eat meat. I wouldn't want a cow to eat me."

"I wouldn't want a cow to eat me either," said Annie.

And she looked up and grinned but only for a moment.

"What's a Belgian waffle?" she asked looking down again.

"They're thicker than other waffles," I said. "And it looks like they put strawberries and whipped cream on them here."

"Oh!" she said, and then she picked up the menu and turned it toward me, and pointed at the picture of a Belgian waffle. "I saw that. I knew it was 'Bel' something, but I could read it. That looks good!"

"So that's OK?" I asked, and she nodded, grinning again.

"Have you decided yet?" asked the waitress, returning with two extraordinarily large glasses of chocolate milk."

"That," said Annie, turning the menu toward the waitress to point to the picture again. "A Belgian waffle."

"And you sir?" asked the waitress, smiling again.

"The same, please," I said.

"Anything else?" she asked.

"Not for me, thanks," I said, looking at Annie.

"Not for me either, thanks," said Annie looking at the waitress and smiling again, and she ate every speck of the waffle and its toppings and drank every drop of the chocolate milk, before speaking again.

"That was good!" she said, grinning again.

"Would you like another one?" I asked.

"Hm mm," she said. "I'm full!"

So then we drove to the Walmart in Jackson.

It was about twenty more miles further east.

"How about if we buy your clothes and other things first?" I asked pushing a cart from the parking lot to the entrance to the store. "Then bring them out to the car and go back in for the groceries? What do you think?"

Again, though she nodded, she didn't smile. So again I wasn't sure how she felt or what she thought. But we found our way to the kids' clothing department.

"See anything you like?" I asked. "How about if we buy enough for you to wear something different every day for a couple of weeks? So we won't have to do your laundry more than once a week?"

To that, she both nodded and looked around, but she didn't ask for anything. So I watched her eyes and asked her whether she liked things seeming to me to draw more of her attention than did other things. She didn't know her sizes, but we figured them out by holding things up to her, when she nodded. And, if still I wasn't sure they'd fit, I asked her whether she wanted to try them on, to be sure. And, each time, she nodded again and tried them.

So, in that way, in not quite two hours, with her not saying much but paying attention to everything, we collected into the cart some new clean T shirts and jeans, some shorts and other kinds of pants and some blouses and a couple of dresses, some socks and underwear and pajamas and a bathrobe, two pair of clean sneakers with no wear, two pair of other kinds of shoes, and a pair of bedroom slippers.

"Do you need anything else?" I asked when I thought we'd reached the goal of having enough for a couple of weeks, and then she looked into the cart, but I thought she might weep.

And, though she didn't, what she said told me more of what had happened to her and how she felt about it.

"A teddy bear?" she said quietly, lowering her head but looking up at me. "Do you think they have teddy bears? My mom bought me one, but I don't know what happened to it."

"If they don't," I said, nearly weeping myself, "we'll find one somewhere else."

But we found some there. And she went straight to a brown one about two feet tall with black plastic eyes and a black plastic nose. She looked at it for a few seconds and put a hand on its belly, and then she slowly picked it up, with both hands.

"Can I have this one?" she asked.

"Sure," I said. "Anything else?"

"Hm mm," she said, and I pushed the cart to checkout, as she carried the teddy bear in her arms.

"Looks like somebody struck it rich," said the checkout lady, looking at Annie. "Is he your grampa?"

But Annie didn't answer.

"The state calls me her foster parent," I said. "But I'm trying to be anything she needs me to be."

The checkout lady looked at me. But, saying nothing, she looked at Annie again, and Annie looked at me. And neither Annie nor the checkout lady was smiling then.

The teddy bear's UPC was on a tag on a ribbon around its neck. So I turned it up for the checkout lady and asked her whether she could reach it with her scanner. And she found that she could

So Annie carried the teddy bear out to our Mustang. And, before helping me unload the cart into the trunk, she set the teddy bear in her booster seat. And then was the first time after checkout she spoke..

"I don't know if I have a grampa," she said.

"We can try to find out," I said. "If you want."

Then she looked at me. But she didn't speak to that. And neither did she nod or smile.

"I think we should put the top up," I said. "I don't think we want anyone to take your new friend. We can put it back down after we buy the groceries."

And then I was glad she nodded. No way was I going to risk losing that teddy bear. And, as I pushed the cart back to the store, she put a hand onto one of mine pushing the cart.

"Oh," I said, "I should have asked you before. Do you have a toothbrush in that backpack, or a hairbrush or a comb, things like that?"

And to that, instead of nodding, she shook her head.

"What color of toothbrush do you want?" I asked in that part of the store.

"Yellow?" she said, questioning again.

So we found her a yellow toothbrush and a hairbrush and comb and headed for the grocery part of the store.

"Do they have strawberries?" she asked when I asked her what she liked to eat.

We found no fresh ones, but we found some frozen ones, and some frozen waffles and whipped cream. But she shrugged when I asked her what else she liked. So I asked her whether she liked cereal.

To that she nodded. And, when I asked her what kind, she said she liked Froot Loops. But, when I asked her whether she liked any other kind, she shrugged again. So I asked her whether she thought she might like Kellogg's Red Berry Special K. Then, looking at the box, she smiled and nodded. And so it went through every grocery aisle. But still she seemed to me to enjoy all that.

"We didn't buy any meat," I said as we unloaded the car at home after the twenty-mile drive back from Jackson. "I should have asked you."

"I wouldn't want a cow to eat me," she said grinning.

I was already sure adults and events hadn't spoiled her. But her grinning at that told me her mind was able to keep up with her heart. So, of course, I responded to that with a grin of my own.

"How about if I put the groceries away while you put your other things away?" I asked her as she looked at her things we'd piled on her bed, after she put her teddy bear on it with its head where the two pillows met, but then she began to weep.

"What's wrong, little friend?" I asked, dropping to my knees and taking her hands, not knowing what else to do but feeling she needed me to do something immediately in the face of the actuality of her sobs, from whatever her feelings were.

"I never had so much stuff," she said, looking down at me through her tears, but I had something to say to that.

"Well," I said, "that can only be because nobody's ever known what you're worth, or because they didn't have a way to give you stuff."

"What am I worth?" she asked, still sobbing.

"The three C's," I said. "Courage, curiosity, and compassion. You stood up for fairness to those people who threw you out, and you try to understand everything. And you wouldn't hurt anyone on purpose. Would you?"

"No," she said, her sobs beginning to subside. "But those people said I ask too many questions."

"I think that must be because they didn't have enough answers," I said. "I don't either, but I'll try to help you find the answers when I don't, and I have no doubt that you'd do the same for anyone. And I think that, as long as you're doing the best you can, no one can be better than you."

And then, after one more sniffle, she returned her attention to her new things and looked around the room.

"Some hangers are in your closet," I said standing up and removing one last tear from her face. "You can use them if you're tall enough I guess, or we can figure something else out I'm sure, if you aren't. But, for now, I'll be in the kitchen putting our groceries away and thinking about how wonderful you are. So, if you need me, you can just let me know. Alright?"

And she nodded and opened a drawer of her dresser.

3

Finding Her Footing

That was a busy day for both of us. I rearranged the kitchen to make things accessible to my new housemate. I opened a folding stepstool I had for no particular reason and showed it to her and told her she could use it to reach anything she needed in the kitchen or anywhere else. I cleared a drawer for her in the bathroom sink vanity for her not to need to use the stepstool to reach the medicine cabinet for things she'd use in the bathroom. And I moved the shower caddy from the shower head to a hook a previous owner of the house had glued to a lower part of the shower wall for no reason I knew. But she watched and asked questions and helped whenever she could. So more accurate would be to say we did that together.

But I didn't tell her to do anything with any of that. In all the years we shared our home I never told her to do anything. Instead, if I thought she might need to do something, I asked her what she thought. And, if I didn't understand her answer, I asked another question. And she did the same for me.

I was afraid my being no kind of cook might be a problem. But I solved that problem by learning quickly and asking Annie what she wanted to eat. And, to remember to buy things on my shopping trips, I was keeping a pad of notepaper and a pen on a stand beside the inside door to our entranceway. So I told her she also could use it for that if she wished. And I watched to see what she ate most.

And I asked her countless other questions to know her preferences. And, when I went anywhere, I asked her whether she wished to go. And she always went.

Still I was afraid she might find too little to do in the remaining weeks of her summer vacation from school. But she found much to do and asked me as many questions as I asked her. She found interest in everything.

"Well," I said after we put our dishes in our dishwasher and took our turns at brushing our teeth, after I ate a bowl of Froot Loops as she ate a bowl of Red Berry Special K, the morning after we set up housekeeping together. "Time for my morning *Taijiquan*"

"What's that?" she asked.

"Its's a Buddha kind of thing," I said. "It's a Chinese way of feeling how everything's everything. It's a way of feeling how the air and space inside you is the same as the air and space everywhere."

"You mean like soundwaves and music and dancing?" she asked.

"Yes," I said. "But always anywhere. How did you learn about soundwaves?"

"From my mom," she said. "She liked music. Do you have any kids?"

"Two sons," I said. "But I was a horrible father. So I never see them."

"I think you're the best father I can imagine," she said. "I'm glad I'm here."

"Thanks, little friend," I said. "I try not to be so horrible now. And I'm happy being here with you, too."

She asked no more questions then. But, after looking at the Buddha statuette, she sat at our dining table and watched as I went through the *Taijiquan* sequence. And she watched again the next morning.

"Do you do it the same way every day?" she asked.

"Yes," I said. "Each part of the motion has a name, and the series ends in its beginning position but three steps further forward. It's like taking something apart and putting it back together the way it really always is anyway, but more sure of what it is, and how it fits together. That's one way people talk about it."

"Do you think I can learn it?" she asked.

"I'm sure you can," I said. "If you'd like to."

"Can I do it over there?" she asked, pointing to the space between our entranceway and our kitchen. "So I can watch what you're doing while I'm doing it while you're doing it?"

And she did, every day we were at home from then until she returned to school, and in the beginning I also said aloud the names of the segments. Also in the beginning she often had to turn her head to see what I was doing, but the frequency of those exceptions to the flow quickly diminished, and soon she was ahead of me in saying the names. So, by the time she returned to school, we were doing it both simultaneously and silently.

And she similarly extended her curiosity to other regular habits of mine.

"What are you watching?" she asked, sitting beside me on our sofa after lunch the day she began learning *Taijiquan*, as I watched cable news while writing a posting for my social commentary weblog.

"The news," I said.

"Why?" she asked.

"To find out what's happening in other places," I said.

"Why?" she asked.

"To understand people," I said. "I think that, if everyone tried to understand everyone, people would stop hurting each other all over our world."

"And you're writing about that?" she asked, looking at the computer on the coffee table in front of us.

"Yes," I said. "To tell people on the World Wide Web what I learn, if I think it might be important to them."

"Who's that?" she asked, looking at the TV again.

"The President of Afghanistan," I said.

"Where's Afghanistan?" she asked, rising from our sofa and going to the map.

"It's the green country with a little part of the east end of it touching China," I said.

"Which way's east?" she asked.

"On the map it's to your right," I said. "It's to your left from here the way you're standing. Do you know the directions?"

"Hm mm," she said.

"Would you like to?" I asked.

"Mm hm," she said.

So I told her the directions on the map, how they related to the directions from our part of Earth, and how the flat map skewed the shapes and sizes of its representations of the countries.

"So," I said. "Russia isn't as much bigger than China as it looks on the map. Russia's that big pink part north of China."

"Two red tacks in Afghanistan," she said then. "Are China and Afghanistan really yellow and green, like a lot of things here are green like the United States on the map?"

"Not so much," I said. "Like the United States, they're a lot of different colors, in different places. A lot of China's desert, and I guess the sand in the desert is a kind of yellow, but more of China's green mountains. And most of Afghanistan's dry but not as dry as the desert in China. So most of it's more brown than green or yellow. But a lot of it's also desert or mountains.

"Those two tacks for Afghanistan are because I spent 21 months there a long time ago when I was in the Army. But most of the tacks for China are because I spent about 2 ½ weeks there just a few years ago. Do you want to see some pictures of China?"

And, of course, she nodded. So I showed her on the computer the pictures I took during that trip. And, of course, she had more questions.

"Why do they need such a big wall?" she asked, looking at the pictures I took of the Great Wall.

"They don't, now," I said. "They built it a long time ago, to keep out people from another country, but it didn't work. Now China and what was the other country are all one country."

She smiled at that, but I didn't have a ready answer for her next question, regarding a picture I took of some kids crouching beside a scattering of bright yellow ears of shucked corn on the pavement in front of some steps from a kind of patio or portico in front of a building in a village in China's central mountains.

"What are they doing?" she asked.

"I don't know," I said. "I'm trying to learn Chinese now. But I didn't know enough Chinese then to ask them what they were doing. And I don't know enough now either."

"I want to learn Chinese," she said.

"Well," I said. "Maybe we can learn together. I'm learning slowly, but I think I could learn more quickly, if I learned it with you. Then we could ask each other questions to use what we're learning and be sure we're thinking about it, to be sure we understand it and aren't only memorizing it, like rules."

"Yeah," said Annie. "I like to understand stuff."

So we started that the next afternoon. So, in the beginning of our doing *Taijiquan* together, I said the names of the segments in both English and Chinese. So, by the time she returned to school, she knew the names in both English and Chinese.

And the week after we set up housekeeping together, the first time we went to Albion's grocery store together, she announced the direction of every turn.

"Was I right?" she asked when we arrived at the store.

But, as we ate our breakfast of Red Berry Special K and Froot Loops on the day we talked about directions and colors of countries, I thought of a couple of housekeeping details we still needed to work out.

"I like how your new clothes look on you," I said.

And she smiled. But then I thought of the two more housekeeping details. So I asked her the question that made me think of them.

"What did you do with the dirty ones?" I asked.

"I put them in one of my dresser drawers," she said.

"A clothes hamper's in your closet," I said. "You can put your dirty ones in that if you want. Alright if I go into your room once a week to get them to do the laundry? And how about mornings to make your bed?"

"I made my bed," she said. "And I can do my laundry too. My mom let me help her do our laundry at the laundromat. I can use that step thing to reach the knobs. And I can clean my room too. Is that OK?"

"It's fine with me," of course I said.

And, after I showed her the pictures of China, she found another way to spend her time.

"That's all the pictures I took of China," I said.

So she leaned back from looking at the computer, but then she leaned forward and turned toward the bookshelves I'd placed on each side of our front living room window, and that look was longer than her look at the computer when she asked me whether I was writing about the news.

"Do any of those books have pictures?" she asked.

"The big green one does," I said. "The one on the left end of the middle shelf on the left side of the window."

So she slid from the sofa and went to the shelf. The book, the fifteenth edition of *Gardner's Art Through the Ages*, was more than a thousand pages and more than a foot tall. But she pulled it from the shelf and, returning to her seat on the sofa she left to go to the shelf, pulled it onto her lap.

"What's this book about?" she asked.

"It's a history of art," I said. "Some of the art's thousands of years old, and some of it's just a few years old."

"It has maps too," she said, opening it to a map of medieval Europe.

"Yeah," I said. "The art's from all over Earth."

And then she closed the book and slid from the sofa again, took the book to the chair where I ordinarily sat to read, and slid with the book to the back of the chair. Then she opened the book again and began turning its pages, from its beginning, slowly. And then I felt she felt at home.

And, as we did with our *Taijiquan*, she made a daily habit of reading her big book. But, the next day, she also expanded her horizon to our backyard, and she also readily made herself at home there, on a wooden playset previous owners of the house had left there. Just outside our backdoor we had a deck I'd furnished with a patio table and chairs, but she preferred the old playset, and not for its original purpose.

It was a frame for swings, a trapeze and a climbing rope, and a platform with a sandbox beneath it and a slide sloping down from it.

But the swings and the trapeze were gone when I bought the house. So, to make it a kind of arbor, I hung a kids swing where the trapeze had been, hung a porch swing and Moroccan lanterns where the other kids swings had been, and removed the slide. Then I tacked lattice around the frame below the platform and across the bottom of the frame on the other side of the porch swing. And then I planted roses to climb the lattice. And Annie didn't use the kids swing.

Instead, sitting on the porch swing between the roses, she used the playset to read her big art book. And, after our *Taijiquan*, every warm rainless morning she was at home, she did that for at least an hour. And she also read it some afternoons.

And she read it carefully. So she didn't do it quickly. No one had taught her to be in a hurry or that the only purpose of learning is to be able to do something else. To her, as far as I could tell, all she did was only because it was there to do wherever she was. So, while the words weren't her initial purpose for her attention to the book, she read them to learn why they were there. So she took all the time she needed for that. And she did it well.

I don't know how much of the book she was able to read the first day she did that. But, returning inside the first day she took the book outside, she asked me what some of the words meant. So I know she'd read some of it.

And she did that also on each of the next few days. So, the first time I didn't know the meaning of a word she asked me to define, I kept my promise to try to help her find answers to questions for which I had no answer. I looked the word up in our *Webster's New World College Dictionary* and told her the dictionary's definition.

But that was also the last time I did that.

"What's that book?" she asked.

"A dictionary," I said.

"What's a dictionary?" she asked.

"Well," I said, "It's a list of words. It's in alphabetical order, to make them easy to find, and it says what they mean. So how about if we look up the word 'dictionary' in this dictionary and see what it says 'dictionary' means?"

So, after her nod, in a few steps, with a few more questions, we did. So from then on, instead of asking me for the meanings of words, she looked them up in the dictionary. And, though she didn't take the heavy dictionary to the porch swing, she sometimes looked up several words after she returned inside.

And she grinned when she looked up some words. And, though, in the beginning, she frequently asked me questions regarding how the dictionary worked, she never repeated a question. So, as the days went by, the frequency of both her resorting to the dictionary and her questions regarding how to use it diminished.

But her reading led to more questions leading to more questions. And the first rainy day after she began reading *Gardner's* led to a question that led to her selecting a place other than my reading chair for her indoor reading. But that question was because, when she took the book from its shelf, I was reading.

"What kind of chairs are those?" she asked, looking at the Chinese corner chairs I'd placed between the bookshelves, with a small Chinese occasional table between the chairs.

"Chinese corner chairs," I said.

And she grinned at that. So after that, each rainy or cold day she read the book until she'd read every page of it, she sat on one or the other of the corner chairs to read it. But spirit was what filled her life.

To her, nearly everything, not only each picture or word, was a discovery or an adventure or both, and she showed me that one day in reply to my constant question regarding her.

She was on her way from her room to her book, but she stopped and stood gazing silently at our inside entranceway door's latch handle, until I asked her the question.

"What are you thinking about, little friend?" I asked.

"It isn't a knob," she said. "It's a handle."

"That's so you can open the door when your hands are full," I said. "You can open it with an elbow."

So she grinned and tried it.

"I like your house," she said. "I mean our house. I like the knobs on the other doors too. They aren't kind of flat like other doorknobs. They're round like balls. Like the map tacks.

" I like the floors too. I mean how there's no carpeting on it or any rugs on most of it. So you probably can slide on them."

Then, turning from the door, she stepped past our dining table and turned toward our Buddha statuette. Then she kicked off her shoes, gave herself a running start past the table, and slid on her socks to the statuette. And then, stopping with a hand on each side of its Tibetan stool, she grinned into its placid smile. And I had absolutely nothing to say. I was too busy grinning with her.

And, also facilitating with questions her learning to play our keyboard, she also extended her sense of adventure to that.

"Can electric pianos do stuff other pianos don't do?" she asked. "I mean because they're electric?"

So I told her some differences and showed her some of the electronic functions. And of course then she tried the functions I showed her. But she kept learning on her own.

She didn't approach that learning as methodically as she approached her big book. But occasionally, though I never knew what occasioned the occasions, she sat at the keyboard and applied some of its functions to melodies she taught herself to play. And soon she found a way to expand her social network.

One sunny afternoon, again on her way to the shelf for her book, she stopped at the little table between the corner chairs and looked out the window behind them.

"Is that the girl you said lives across the street," she asked.

So I went to the window to look where she was looking. The girl's parents, the first spring after I bought our house, installed a swing set at the end of their driveway. And, when Annie asked that question, the girl was playing on it.

"Yes," I said. "Do you want to go say Hi to her?"

"I think so," she said nodding, after one of her pauses. "Do you think it would be OK?"

"I don't know a reason it wouldn't be," I said. "If you look both ways before you cross the street."

That was the nearest I ever came to telling her what to do. And she said nothing in reply to it. But she complied.

As I watched from the window, she looked both ways as she crossed the grass between the sidewalk and the curb, but I didn't stop watching then.

I returned to my reading chair but wished to see how that adventure of hers would go.

The other girl was sitting in the middle swing of the three of the set. And, as she and Annie began talking, Annie sat in the swing nearest to the girl's house. But, a few minutes later, the girl's mother came out of the house, looked toward them, and spoke. And then the girl followed her mother into their house. And Annie returned to ours.

"Her mom said it's lunchtime," she said as she passed our dining table on her way again to her book.

But, before reaching the shelf, she turned to the Buddha statuette, touched the tip of its *ushnisha* as she'd come to do frequently, and looked up at the map.

"Her name's Beatrice," she said. "But she said everybody calls her Bee."

And then, having eaten her lunch already that day, she took her book to her own swing set. But she gave no indication of disappointment. So still I wasn't sure how it went.

Bee was African American. Interaction between African Americans and European Americans in Albion had been fractious since the Great Migration. Albion was a stop on the Underground Railroad, and during he Great Migration a foundry in Albion recruited African American employees, but Albion's municipal government responded to the foundry by enacting a statute proscribing anyone not European American from owning a home in Albion.

The foundry responded to the statute by providing housing for its employees, but it closed during the recession of the first decade of the 21st century, adding its employees to the victims of the recession. By then the city had repealed the statute, but that did nothing for people with no jobs, and then nearly thirty percent of Albion's population was African American. And results of all that became evident to me when I bought the home Annie and I were sharing.

Bee's parents didn't welcome me to the neighborhood. And most of the few conversations between them and me in the three years between then and when Annie and I began sharing our home were brief and not congenial. The longest and most congenial of them was from Bee's mother's ringing my doorbell, telling me her lawnmower needed a carburetor, and borrowing my mower. And that exchange was about a month before Annie and I set up housekeeping together. And neither of Bee's parents had spoken to me since her mother returned the mower.

So I had some reason to doubt that Annie, through that brief encounter, had found another friend.

But that doubt was a mistake. The next afternoon our doorbell rang. And, when I went to the door, Bee was standing there.

When I opened it, she looked back over a shoulder to her mother, who was standing on their porch. But her mother waved, and I responded in kind, with a smile. So Bee turned back to me.

"Is Annie at home?" she asked.

"Yes, Bee," I said. "Come in."

And, as she stepped through our front door, her mother stepped back through theirs.

"Annie," I said as Bee followed me inside, "Bee's here."

She was in her room. She'd just returned her book to its shelf after looking up a few words. Coming out, she looked at Bee and held her hands out to her sides in a gesture of surprise, but the gesture also expressed welcome and simple joy.

"Hi, Bee!" she said. "Do you want to see my room?"

And Bee nodded and followed her into it.

"This is pretty," said Bee. "You have a big bed."

So, smiling, I returned to my reading chair, and they were laughing when they came out, a few minutes later.

"Can we have some pop?" asked Annie.

"Sure," I said, and they went into our kitchen, came out with two cans of strawberry soda, and sat on the corner chairs to drink them.

"What's that?" asked Bee, pointing to the Buddha statuette.

"The Buddha," said Annie. "She was a prince."

"Princes are boys," said Bee.

"Yeah," said Annie. "But the Buddha said everything's everything. And I think she looks like a girl."

"How can everything be everything?" asked Bee.

"People say the Buddha thought everybody imagines everything," said Annie.

"Like maybe we're only imagining that you're white, and I'm black?" asked Bee after a pause like Annie's pauses.

"You don't look black to me," said Annie. "And I don't look white to me?"

"What color do you think we are?" asked Bee.

"I don't know," said Annie. "Maybe some kind of tan or brown or something. That's white."

And she pointed to the white porcelain Buddha statuette.

"And that's black," she said. "I mean the part around the outside."

And she pointed up at the frame around the map.

"My mom says princesses are black in Africa," said Bee.

So Annie slid from her chair, went to the Buddha statuette and touched its *ushnisha*, and pointed up to the map.

"That's Africa," she said. "The big place in the middle with all the different colors."

So Bee followed her, and stood beside her and also looked up at the map, but then she also touched the Buddha's *ushnisha*.

"I like her hat," she said.

"So do I," said Annie. But it isn't supposed to be a hat. It's supposed to be her curly hair. And the pointed part's supposed to be part of her head.

"People call it an *ushnisha*. Some people who say they believe what the Buddha said say curly hair and *ushnisha*s are ways you can tell if people are great.

"Do you want to see my backyard?"

And Bee nodded. So they headed toward our backdoor. But Bee stopped at the keyboard.

"Is that a piano?" she asked.

"Sort of," said Annie. "It's an electronic keyboard. It does stuff pianos don't do, but it only has sixty keys. Pianos have 88, and they have pedals, for changing how the keys work."

"Like what?" asked Bee.

"Like keeping the sound from stopping as soon as you take your fingers off of the keys," said Annie. "But you can make this do stuff like sounding like a trumpet or a violin or bells. But you still have to play it like a piano to make music with it. So I'm trying to learn how to do that sometimes. Do you want to help me?"

"I don't know how to play it," said Bee.

"But you can still help me," said Annie. "We can learn together by asking each other questions. Billy and I are learning Chinese together that way. What grade are you in?"

"I'll be in second," said Bee.

"I'll be in third," said Annie. "But we can still learn together. Billy's older than I am, and he started to learn Chinese before I did, too."

And then, with their strawberry sodas, they continued on out our backdoor.

A few minutes later I looked from our kitchen window. They'd found a way to climb onto the slide platform and, sitting beneath some begonias I'd hung in baskets above it, were talking among the roses climbing around them. And I never again doubted Annie's ability to befriend.

"I like your new friend," I said when she returned inside after Bee went home..

"So do I," said Annie.

"Have you thought about becoming Secretary-General of the United Nations?" I asked.

"What's the United Nations?" she asked, coming to sit beside me on our sofa.

"It's a kind of club for the countries of the world," I said. "They have a clubhouse in New York City and meet there to talk about the problems around the world."

"What's a secretary general?" asked Annie.

"That's what people call the head of the club," I said. "Most clubs call their leaders presidents, but the United Nations call theirs a secretary-general, because his job isn't to enforce rules. His job's only to try to help the members get along, instead of fighting each other all over Earth. And I think they need someone who's as straightforward as you are. I mean with your three C's."

"Courage, curiosity, and compassion," she said after another of her pauses.

And then she turned to look at the map.

"Where's New York City?" she asked.

"The tack that's the second-furthest east of here in the United States," I said.

So she rose from the sofa and went to the map.

"I have an idea," I said. "Your birthday's week after next. Do you think you might like to go to New York for that?"

And I'd never seen her turn her head so fast.

4

New York City

"Can we?" she said, looking at me.

And, taking her finger from the Buddha's *ushnisha*, she ran to our sofa and jumped knees first onto it beside me.

"I don't know a reason we couldn't," I said. "You don't start school again until more than a week after your birthday. So I think we can spend your birthday and two or three more days there before then."

Then she grinned, bounced around and placed her hands on her knees, and sat gazing into the space in front of her with a big smile on her face.

"We can see some art while we're there too," I said, looking at her with a big grin on my face. "Some museums there have some of the art that's in your book. If you'd like to."

"A lot of stuff there that I'd like to see," she said, nodding and again looking at me, and broadening her smile into another grin. "It says so under the pictures."

So, in the week and a half between then and that trip, she looked at every page of every chapter of her book for pictures and statues and buildings she'd like to see that were in New York.

But she also spent a lot of time learning to play the keyboard with Bee. And together they did that more methodically than Annie had begun to do it. They asked me how to read music.

I told them some of the fundamentals of how the keys and time related to the staffs and notes and other notation in the book of melodies that came with the keyboard. And, while I was doing that, I also showed them some of the programming in the keyboard to help with their learning to play it. But they neither asked nor needed help from me to develop a system for using all that.

For each melody sequentially, they let the display on the keyboard show them where to put their fingers for each note on the staff, and then they worked out how to use the book to play the melody.

And, while they were doing that, I made some arrangements for our trip to New York, beginning by calling my friend George, my editor at Scribner's. I'd written a book on the epistemological and behavioral variances in doctrine among the half dozen religions in which the most people claim to believe. And George, quickly coming to regard it as a welcome discovery for him, decided it should be for everyone. So he successfully promoted it as a text for courses in what universities call comparative religion. And his office was on Fifth Avenue.

"Hey, George," I said when I called. "I'll be in New York week after next. And I have a friend who'd like to see the United Nations' headquarters. Do you think you may be able to arrange some kind of access to the building for us? It's for my friend's eighth birthday. Her name's Annie."

"I don't know," he said. "But I'll see what I can do. Her being eight years old may help. At least I'd think that makes it important."

"Thanks, George," I said. "The whole thing's important."

I thought of taking Bee with us, but still I had no congenial relationship with her parents, and Annie didn't ask me whether we could. I thought that, beyond her disinclination to ask for anything, her reason for not asking for that may have been that she didn't think it reasonable, and that was essentially my reason. So I didn't mention it to her, and neither do I know whether Bee asked her anything about the trip, or what Annie told her of it.

But, excepting a few moments, Annie obviously enjoyed every waking minute of it, beginning with looking around at everything at the Kalamazoo airport, asking many questions.

"What are they going to do with our stuff," she asked at check-in.

"They'll put it on the plane for us," I said. "The part of the plane where the passengers sit doesn't have enough room for all the luggage. So they put the big bags in a part of it underneath the part for the passengers."

And she continued her obvious enjoyment through watching as the attendant put the bags on the conveyor belt, and on until those few moments, while we went through security.

"We'll have to take off our shoes," I said. "So they can X-ray them. That's an X-ray machine people are putting their things in up there."

"Why do they want to X-ray them?" she asked.

"A long time ago," I said, "a guy put some explosives in his shoes before getting on a plane, and someone caught him trying to set them off, on the plane. So, since then, governments have required airlines to require that."

"Why did he do that?" she asked.

"I don't know," I said. "The news on TV said he was a Muslim and was trying to kill everyone on the plane, to scare other people who aren't Muslims. But the book Muslims treat as Christians treat the Bible says we shouldn't kill anyone, except to defend ourselves. And it also says we shouldn't harm ourselves. So I don't know."

So, while attentive to everything everyone did during the security process, she neither spoke nor smiled again until we had our shoes on again.

But, though she showed some dismay as I told her all that, she gave no indication that her attention to the security process diminished her enjoyment of the flight.

"Do you want the window seat?" I asked her on the plane, and she nodded far more vehemently than she ordinarily did.

And, with her forehead against it most of the way, she made much use of that little window.

"I never saw so much white," she said as we flew over clouds.

But her next question was during our descent to JFK.

"Why are the cars going so slow?" she asked.

"I think they just seem to be," I said. "For the same reason they seem to be smaller than they are. Maybe for the same reason airplanes seem to be going so slow when we watch them from the ground. Maybe because all distances seem shorter from so far away, I guess."

"Yeah," she said. "I should have thought of that."

To say that, she turned her head from the window and nodded, but she quickly turned back.

"Is that the ocean?" she asked.

"Yes," I said. "Not much more than three thousand miles across it to Europe."

"And more tacks," she said.

She grinned when the wheels touched the runway. And she looked all around her as we found our way to our bags and the taxis and during our taxi ride to our hotel. But she didn't speak again until we were in midtown Manhattan.

"The buildings are so big," she said as we turned onto Seventh Avenue,

And she looked all around and up and down when we climbed out of the cab at our hotel, the Pennsylvania across Seventh Avenue from Penn Station,

"I never saw so many people all at the same time either," she said.

But, though she continued looking around in the lobby and exchanged smiles with the bellman and the young woman who checked us in, she didn't speak again until we were in the elevator.

"What does eighteen mean?" she asked when I pushed the button.

"Our room's on the eighteenth floor," I said.

Neither had she ever been in an elevator. And, as soon as I opened the door to our room, she ran to a window and looked down and laughed. And she stood there looking down until I asked her whether she was ready to go for a walk.

"One?" she asked as we entered the elevator.

And, when I nodded, she pushed the button.

The next stop in our plan was to be George's office. He'd called me, told me he was able to arrange a tour for us of the United States Nations' headquarters, and asked that we stop by his office as soon as we checked into our hotel. He said he had some visitor passes for us to take the tour that afternoon.

We walked the few block there, and Annie looked up and down and all around all the way, but we made a brief stop along the way. Some of the plans we made for that trip required reservations, and among those I suggested to her were seeing the city from the tops of the Empire State Building and World Trade Center One, and the Empire State Building was along that walk. So I stopped walking to point it out to her.

"That's the Empire State Building," I said, pointing across 34th Street, and Annie looked across the street, and then up.

"I knew it was big," she said. "But I didn't know it was that big."

"When it was new it was the tallest building on Earth," I said. "Still want to go up there?"

And then she nodded nearly as vehemently as she had when I asked her whether she wanted the window seat on the plane. And, in the elevator in George's building, she asked me the number of the floor where we were going there. And she also pushed that button.

"Hey, Bill," said George as we shook hands. "This is a surprise. I thought you'd turned your house into a one-Buddhist monastery and settled into seclusion for the duration."

"Annie's my Ananda," I said, smiling at Annie. "Or I'm hers."

"Or both," said George, also smiling at her, and also shaking hands with her. "Nice to meet you, Annie. I'm George. Happy birthday. What do you think of the city so far?"

"It's big," she said. "And I never saw so many people. And the cars' horns honking all the time. It's like music everywhere all the time."

"I never thought of it that way," said George, then grinning at her. "I'm hardly conscious of it anymore."

Then he turned back to me.

"Now I see why it's so important," he said. "Oh, and here."

He turned to his desk, picked up a business card and two laminated cards on cords, and handed the laminated cards to Annie and the business card to me.

"Those passes will get you past the guard desk," he said. "And, if you tell the guard you're there to see the woman whose name is on that card, he'll call her down."

So then Annie and I continued our walk to the United Nations' headquarters.

"What's an Ananda?" she asked on the way.

"Ananda was a friend of the Buddha's," I said, and she smiled and took a hand of mine again.

"Are those the flags of all the nations?" she asked when we were in sight of the headquarters building.

"Nearly, I think," I said. "I think a few nations may not be members."

So, for the remainder of our walk to the main entrance to the building, her looking was up at the flags.

"I'm Uma," said the woman who responded to the guard's call, offering me a hand to shake.

"Bill," I said, shaking the hand. "This is Annie."

Uma was young. She looked at Annie before greeting me and briefly looked at her again when I introduced her to her. But she didn't greet her in any way.

"The General Assembly's in session," she said. "So I guess we can start there, if you don't have a preference."

And, not waiting for a reply, she led the way.

But Annie quickly changed Uma's attitude.

"What's the General Assembly?" she asked.

"It's representatives of all the member nations meeting together," said Uma. "Or at least the ones that want to."

And Annie smiled. But, when we arrived in the General Assembly chamber, a man was speaking at the main podium in a language I couldn't identify. So that prompted another question from Annie.

"Does everybody here speak that language?" she asked.

"No," said Uma. "Come here. I'll show you how it works."

Then she led us to a table with no people at it but with microphones on it and headsets with earphones.

"Here," she said picking up one of the headsets. "Let's put this on you. Now push that button right there, and say into that microphone what language you want to hear, English or whatever."

"*Zhōngguó huà?*" said Annie into the microphone as she pushed the button, and then her eyes opened wide.

She turned and grinned at Uma, and Uma returned the grin and turned and looked at me, with her eyes nearly as wide as Annie's.

"She speaks Chinese?" she asked.

"She has many talents," I said.

"Now I see why they asked me to do this," said Uma, and she said nothing more to me until we returned to the guard desk, and the tour she gave us was nearly two hours with cheerful answers to each of Annie's further questions, and it included a visit to the offices of the Chinese delegation.

"I might get in trouble for this," said Uma. "But the Ambassador's probably in the General Assembly meeting. So you'll probably only meet the receptionist."

And, as she suggested, the only person we saw in the offices was a man in the outer office sitting at a desk near the door to the hallway.

"This is Annie," said Uma to the man. "She's visiting the U.N. and speaks some Chinese."

"*Hěn gāoxìng jiàn dào nǐ, Ān Nǔ,*" he said, standing and bowing to Annie and offering her a hand to shake.

"*Wǒ hěn hǎo,*" said Annie, grinning and shaking the hand. "*Xiè xiè. Nǐ hǎo ma?* Billy and I are learning *Zhōngwén*, but I don't know much yet."

"Fine, thanks," said the receptionist, offering us seats in some chairs in a corner of the office. "No matter. Most people who aren't *Zhōngguó rén* never try."

And, apologizing for the Ambassador's not being there to meet Annie, he offered her an almond biscuit from a plate of them on his desk and ate one with her as they talked about the parts of their countries that were their homes and about their interest in one another's countries.

He smiled at Annie's interest in *Taijiquan* and didn't frown at her interest in Buddhism, and that continued for nearly twenty minutes, until Uma thanked him and continued the tour.

"This has been a pleasure," she said when she returned us to where she found us, and then she shook hands with Annie.

And, though she didn't shake hands with me again, she gave me a big grin and turned it back to Annie and kept it as she turned to return to the elevator.

"Can we go in there?" I asked the guard, pointing toward the gift shop in the lobby, after Uma left us.

"Sure," he said, and he also grinned at Annie.

"How about a souvenir?" I asked her.

Then she shrugged.

But she grinned when we entered the shop.

"Can we get one of those?" she asked, pointing to a small United Nations flag on a stand.

"Sure," I said. "Anything else?"

Then she shook her head, but she exchanged waves and grins with the guard and held up her flag for him to see it, as we passed his desk to return to the street.

"Oh," I said. "You must be hungry. I should have thought of that. That cookie was all you've had to eat since our snack on the plane this morning. I saw an Au Bon Pain near the Empire State Building. They must have some no-cow sandwiches. What do you think?"

To that, she shrugged and nodded and smiled, but she didn't speak again until we were in the next block.

"What's an Au Bon Pain?" she asked.

"It's a sandwich shop," I said.

"Why do they call it that?" she asked.

"It's French for 'to the good bread'," I said.

"Do you speak French?" she asked.

"A little," I said. "I minored in French in college, but I never learned to speak it well."

"Can we learn French like we're learning Chinese?" she asked.

"I don't know a reason we couldn't," I said smiling down at her questioning look up at me. "I, I mean we, have some books and CD's we can use."

And then I thought of a question for her. Thinking of how she might feel in Albion after seeing New York already had reminded me of the song "How Ya Gonna Keep Him Down on the Farm After He's Seen Paree". But I asked the question anyway.

"So I guess you might want to go to France for your birthday next year?" I asked.

And she looked up at me again and nodded grinning wide.

"Well," I said. "I don't know a reason we couldn't."

But, as we ate our no-cow sandwiches at the Au Bon Pain, most of our conversation was of our plans for the remainder of that day and the first of the three more days of that trip of ours.

"Have you thought about what museums you'd like to visit while we're here?" I asked.

"The Metropolitan Museum of Art, and the Museum of Modern Art, and the Guggenheim Museum," she said after nodding while chewing. "But I'm not sure about the Museum of Modern Art. I don't know why they do it.

"But I like some of it, like that Jack-somebody's drip pictures, and that Mon-somebody's blue and red and yellow squares. When I looked at pictures of their paintings, I felt like they were supposed to be the way they are, but their paintings in my book aren't in the Museum of Modern Art. And I don't like that Alexander somebody's *Lobster Trap and Fish Tail*.

"It's in the Museum of Modern Art, but I wouldn't want to trap a lobster. And the picture of it in my book looks like the trap's trying to trap the fish. At least that's how it looks to me."

And then she took another bite of her sandwich. I never had heard her say that much with no pause. But, as she chewed, she asked another question.

"What do you think?" she asked.

"I think both the Museum of Modern Art and the Metropolitan Museum of Art must have more of Jackson Pollock's and Piet Mondrian's paintings than are in your book," I said. "And how about if we give MoMA a try and see how that Alexander Calder mobile looks in the space where it hangs?"

And, as she chewed some more, she nodded again.

"And I think we can probably see all of those museums tomorrow," I said, "and our reservations to see the *Lion King* are for tomorrow night, but how's this sound for the rest of today?

"Our reservations for seeing the city from the top of the Empire State Building are for later this afternoon, but we haven't planned to do anything else today. So how about if, during the rest of our time today, we just wander around midtown Manhattan? A lot of famous places are in this part of the city.

And she nodded and smiled. So, before we returned to the Empire State Building, we visited the New York Public Library, Grand Central Station, and Penn Station. And that took us nearly to the time of our Empire State Building reservation.

And there she walked all the way around its 86th floor and looked from every window of its 102nd floor observation deck.

"It's almost an island," she said on the 102nd floor. "It's like we're on an island. And it looks like this building's still taller than almost all the other buildings we can see. But maybe not that one."

And, though she didn't stop walking to look from every window, she did when she said that.

"That's the new World Trade Center tower," I said looking where she was looking. "Our reservation to see the city from up there's for the day after tomorrow."

And she smiled and continued walking.

"How about this?" I asked. "Our reservations for *Giselle* are for after supper the day after tomorrow, and our reservations for the World Trade Center are for late morning on that day. So I'm thinking we can spend the rest of that day riding the subway up and down the island seeing Manhattan's other neighborhoods. How's that sound?"

And she nodded again, but then she stopped walking again, to turn to another window..

"There's the Statue of Liberty," she said . "Look how little it looks from up here! When are we going there?"

"Our reservations for that are for the morning of the day after the day after tomorrow.," I said. "So I'm thinking we can spend the rest of that day just trying to make sure we've seen everything you want to see here. How's that sound?

"It sounds good," she said, and that time she grinned.

"See anything here you like?" I asked her in the Empire State Building's gift shop, and she pointed to a plastic replica of the building.

"Can we get that?" she asked.

So, on the street again, we were a couple of tourists, carrying the United Nations' flag and the Empire State Building, with horns honking all around us. Then, after dropping off her souvenirs at our hotel room, we found a restaurant for supper. But then we continued our exploring.

"All these lights!" she said looking all around her in Times Square, with her eyes wide and her mouth wide in a grin, as her eyes reflected the lights.

And then we wandered on to Broadway.

"The Lion King," she said, reading the marquis of the theatre where we'd see that the next evening.

At home, I'd asked her whether she though she might like to see some singing and dancing in a theatre while we were in New

York, and she grinned and nodded. So I searched the Web for possibilities and suggested *The Lion King* and *Giselle*, and she nodded and grinned when I suggested *The Lion King*, but she asked me what *Giselle* was. And, to my replying that it was a ballet and showing her some pictures of a performance of *Giselle* on the Web, she grinned and nodded again and said she'd heard of ballet and seen pictures of it before.

So, after Broadway, we wandered to the Lincoln Center.

"There it is," she said, pointing to a poster and grinning again.

But, though, next morning, we took a taxi to MoMa, we didn't stay there long.

"It looks bigger here," said Annie of the Calder mobile. "But I still think it looks like the trap's trying to trap the fish."

And, though we also found there some of Pollock's drip pictures and some of Mondrian's blue and yellow and red squares, nothing else we saw there caught much of Annie's attention.

So we moved on to the Metropolitan Museum of Art. And, for Annie to see Central Park, we walked the mile and a half there from MoMA. And much at the Metropolitan caught her attention.

But, though we found some of Pollock's and Mondrian's paintings there also, Monet most held her attention.

She stopped and grinned when she came to his 1919 *Water Lilies*, and she laughed when she turned from that and saw his *Bridge Over a Pond of Water Lilies*, before she looked to see whose work they were.

"He's French," she said when she looked. "Some of his pictures are in my book, but not those two."

And then she pointed to one of his series of paintings of light on the façade of the cathedral at Rouen.

"But that one, is" she said.

In the several hours we spent there, she also pointed out other paintings her book pictured, but she spent much more of that time looking at the two paintings of water lilies than she spent looking at anything else. So, after lunch there, we found in the museum's gift shop a book picturing Monet's works. And she held it to her heart as we left the museum.

"Frank Lloyd Wright," she said as we approached the Guggenheim on our half-mile walk there from the Metropolitan Museum of Art. "My book says it's shaped like a snail, but it looks more like a flowerpot to me."

"I hope you'll always say what you think." I said. "About your book and everything else. A lot of what the guy who wrote that edition of that book says in it is his opinions, and I've found that a lot of what he presents as though it's fact isn't. Maybe I should have told you that, but I suspect that you can figure it out, and at least the pictures are facts."

"You don't treat me like a kid," she said grinning again.

"That's because I don't think you're like a kid," I said. "I don't think anyone would ever be what adults say kids are like if adults didn't teach them to be what they think kids are. So I'm grateful that you're what you are."

And, grinning once more, she took my nearest hand again.

In the Guggenheim we took an elevator to the top of its ramp and walked down the ramp. But, because Annie spent nearly as much time walking back and forth across the ramp and looking down from it as she spent looking at the paintings, that took longer than it ordinarily may have. And, when I asked her whether she wanted a souvenir of that museum, she shook her head.

"That's OK," she said. "I just wanted to see the building. A picture of it's in my book. But I wanted to see it here."

And from there we walked across Central Park.

"This is nice," she said. "All these trees and everything and people doing stuff outside in the middle of all these big buildings."

"Do you want to take a subway back downtown?" I asked.

"I don't know," she said. "What's a subway? You said we can ride them up and down the island, but what are they?"

"They're underground trains," I said.

"Yes!" she said. "I've never been on a train either!"

So we took the Eighth Avenue subway back to Times Square.

"They have music down here too," she said of the musicians playing for tips in the tunnel."

Seats were vacant, but she held a pole and looked at the people, those on the train between the stops and those in the stations during the stops.

And, after seeing *The Lion King* that evening, she grinned and sang and danced all the way back to our hotel, as others on the street grinned at her, as she danced past them.

And the next day, beginning by riding uptown to stroll through Harlem, we followed our plan of riding subways up and down Manhattan.

"Most of the buildings aren't as big here," said Annie in Harlem. "And some of them are kind of messy. Is this where the poor people live?"

"A lot of them, I think," I said. "But a famous university's near here too. Do you think you might like to see that?"

"What's a university?" she asked.

"It's a big school," I said, "with a lot of different colleges where people can learn different things."

And, after she nodded to that, we walked to Columbia's main campus.

"This is nice too," she said. "It has trees like the park."

And next we rode downtown to Greenwich Village and spent about an hour in Washington Square Park just sitting and watching and talking.

"Some arches like that are in our art book," she said. "It says they're triumphal arches."

And that was Annie's eighth birthday. And from Washington Square we rode down to One World Trade Center. Our time in that park took us nearly to the time for our reservation to visit the tower.

"There's the Statue of Liberty again," said Annie on its observation level "It's further down from up here, but it's closer. So it doesn't look as small as it did from the Empire State Building."

And from there we walked to Wall Street and took a subway up to Chinatown. There, eating lunch and spending about another hour looking at the buildings and wandering in and out of shops, we impressed some more people with Annie's Chinese. And we bought some porcelain bowls..

"Those bowls look like ours," said Annie.

On our coffee table and on the little Chinese table between our corner chairs were some I'd bought in Boston's Chinatown.

"But they're not cracked," I said. "Think maybe we need some new ones?"

In the years since I bought the ones we had I'd broken both and done a poor job of gluing them back together.

"I don't know," said Annie. "I like these, but I like the ones we already have, too."

"How about if we buy a couple of these and decide what to do with all of them when we get home?" I asked.

So, after her shrug and smile and nod, we similarly decided which two to buy.

She was quiet during *Giselle*, and she said nothing in the taxi on our way back to our hotel from that performance, but she was attentive to every minute of it.

And next morning we took the ferry to see the Statue of Liberty.

"I've never been on a boat before either," she said.

And, in the statue, we climbed to its crown.

"There's the World Trade Center," she said. "And the Empire State Building. They don't look so big from up here, and hanging out over the ground like this is scarier to me, but it's fun. Like in the plane."

And then she looked down and grinned and then laughed.

"See anything here you like?" I asked her in the statue's gift shop, and she pointed to a statue of the statue.

"We have all the rest of the day for anything you like," I said. "Can you think of anything else you want to do while we're here or anything else you'd like to buy to take home? How about something for Bee?

"Can we get two of those?" she asked, smiling and pointing at the statue of the statue again."

"Can you think of anything else you'd like to see here?" I asked her after we bought them.

"Hm mm," she said. "I 've seen so much stuff here I never saw before already. I don't know what I'd do if I saw any more."

But I had a suggestion that showed what she'd do.

"Then how about if we just walk back uptown instead of riding the subway," I asked. "Just to see whatever's along the way?"

And she nodded and grinned again, and her talk along the way and the hours that walk took showed once again that everything to her was an adventure, including lunch outside at a café on the Lower East Side and supper at the Tavern on the Green in Central Park after dropping the two Statues of Liberty at our hotel room.

So Annie's birthday gifts that year, with the flight and all the exploring of the city we did, were a replica of the Empire State Building and a statue of the Statue of Liberty, the flag of the United Nations, and her Monet book.

And she decided not to keep the Empire State Building.

5

Return to School

"Can I give this to Bee too?" she asked, referring to her replica of the Empire State Building, as we unpacked at home. "We have the pictures we took, and I have enough stuff."

"Sure," I said. "We bought the stuff for you. So I want you to do with it whatever you want to do with it."

So she put the flag on her desk and her Statue of Liberty on her dresser. She put her program from *Giselle* in her Monet book and put the Monet book beside *Gardner's* on its shelf. And, with the Empire State Building and the other Statue of Liberty, she also decided to give Bee her *Lion King* program.

So the next question was what to do with our four Chinese bowls.

"What do you think?" I asked her, setting the new ones beside the cracked ones.

"I don't know," she said. "I still like the old ones, but I still like the new ones we bought, too."

"I like the new ones more because you found them," I said. "And the new ones aren't cracked."

"Where did you get the old ones?" she asked.

"Boston's Chinatown," I said. "Those corner chairs and that little table are from there too. I used to live in Boston."

"Did you like living there?" she asked.

"Yes," I said. "But I like living here with you more. How about if we put the new ones where the old ones are now, to make the house feel more like it belongs to both of us? And how about if we put the old ones upstairs, where we can find them later, if we want to?"

And, with no more discussion of the question, she handed the old ones to me and put the new ones where the old ones had been. And she spent about an hour giving Bee her stuff and telling her about the trip and showing her the pictures we took with my phone, and Bee listened and grinned and asked questions and said she wished she could have gone, and Annie said that so did she. But Bee, looking at her Empire State Building, asked Annie a question that wasn't directly pertinent to the trip.

"Why don't you have any toys?" she asked.

"I like things that do things," said Annie. "Toys are for pretending you're doing things. I like doing my laundry and ironing and playing our keyboard with you.

"And Billy would buy me toys, if I asked him to. He bought me my teddy bear because I asked him to, and that's a toy. But I asked him for my teddy bear because of my mom."

"Where's your mom?" asked Bee.

"She died," replied Annie.

"I had a little brother that died," said Bee.

"Why did he die?" asked Annie.

"I don't know," said Bee. "He was just born. My mom buys me a lot of toys. But I don't play with them much.

"And my dad likes to pretend. He wears shirts with numbers and names of football players and basketball and baseball players on them. And he hollers at the TV when he's watching sports. He watches sports a lot. I don't like sports.

"I don't like to watch people knocking people down."

And, after Bee went home, Annie asked me about that.

"Why don't you ever watch sports?" she asked.

"I don't like to watch people knocking people down," I said. "And the only way to win at sports is to make someone lose, and I don't like to make people lose, either.

"And sports are too much like war. The word 'sports' came from Sparta, a city in Greece that used athletics to train for war a long time ago, and the word 'Olympics' is from games Greeks played and named for a mountain where they said gods lived. And some of what they called gods are for war too.

"I spent ten years in the Army. So, instead of sports, I watch the news to see if people are doing anything to stop that sort of thing. But people seem to me to be trying harder to learn how to win wars than to learn how to keep from starting them.

"But maybe you can do something about that at the United Nations."

I was watching news then. And Annie was sitting beside me. And, after listening to all that, she looked at the TV and silently sat there to watch it a while. So, when I asked her whether she'd thought of being Secretary-General of the United Nations, I wasn't trying to be funny. I meant what I said to Miss Walker of letting children be as wonderful as they are, and Annie had proven herself wonderfully conciliatory from the day we began sharing our home, at least to me.

And, the evening we began setting up housekeeping together and the next morning, she proved her considerateness especially plainly and simply.

I thought I might need to be more flexible with my meditation schedule. I'd developed a habit of a half hour of *dhyana yoga* each morning and evening. And, for years, the half hours were the same half hours of each day. But Annie, that evening and morning, proved that worry unnecessary. And she did it entirely by her own initiative.

But that was partly her response to another step we needed to take in settling into our cohabitation.

"Do you want to take a shower tonight?" I asked her a few minutes before my meditation time, and she nodded.

So I showed her how to divert the water to the showerhead, the easiest way to adjust the water temperature before getting into the flow, and where everything was that I thought she might need.

"You can use that towel," I said pointing to a towel on the rack outside the shower. "It's clean. I've used the other one. And there's the soap, and there's some shampoo for you to wash your hair, if you want to. And more clean towels are on that shelf."

And, having hardly any notion of the bathing needs of seven-year-old girls and considering her disinclination to ask for anything, I watched her as she looked and listened while I told her all that. But neither had I yet learned whether her quietness was acceptance or reticence. So I tried to ask.

"Are you going to be alright?" I asked.

She looked around and nodded. But still I wasn't sure. So I tried again.

"Do you need anything else?" I asked.

"Can I go get my bathrobe?" she asked.

And then I was sure.

"Sure," I said. "It's your bathrobe, in your bedroom."

So she went to her bedroom for her bathrobe. And I returned to our living room for my *dhyana*. And less than a half hour later, in her new bathrobe and pajamas and slippers, she cane into our living room

I was in my reading chair with my hands in the *dhyana mudra* and my gaze through our front window toward the trees at the back of the vacant lot beside Bee's driveway.

"Goodnight," she said.

"Goodnight, little friend," I said, "Are you and your teddy bear going to be alright?"

And she nodded and smiled, and I didn't see her again until the next morning when, after I showered and dressed after my morning half hour of *dhyana*, I went into the kitchen for breakfast and found her there, pouring milk onto a bowl of Red Berry Special K.

"Good morning," I said, and she grinned, poured herself a glass of cranberry juice, carried her cereal and juice to our dining table, and pulled out a chair and climbed onto it.

And, excepting that after that she bade me goodnight before she went for her shower, so went nearly every evening and morning of all the years we shared that home of ours.

And on none of those mornings did I hear the clock radio I put in her room when I furnished it to make it a guestroom. I supposed she may have used my bathroom sounds to know when I began my days, but she seemed to me to be happy in whatever she was doing, and so I never asked her. And I asked her plenty of questions to be sure she was happy.

"What color of tack would you like?" I asked her as I sat on our sofa to catch up on the new after we decided what to do with what we bought in New York. "For New York, for the map."

"You already have a red tack for New York," she said.

"But I'm thinking we might get another color," I said. "For places we go together."

"Yellow," she said grinning and going to the map, "like our kitchen cupboards and how China looks on the map."

"What if we go to China?" I asked.

"You mean because yellow tacks will be hard to see on the yellow?" she asked turning to me but quickly turning back to the map. "Maybe orange, but I like yellow because of our cupboards and China, and people say the sun's yellow. But the sun looks more white to me, and sometimes orange, almost red."

"I think we might be able to see yellow ones," I said. "I'm thinking they might give a little shade to the other yellow."

She didn't grin at that, but she smiled and looked at the map again, and I grinned.

"I'll order some on the Web," I said. "I don't think Walmart has them. OK?"

But, after she nodded, I had another question for her.

"What are you thinking about starting the new schoolyear next week?" I asked.

That time she shrugged. But she came and sat beside me. So I continued my questioning.

"I'm thinking we might want to go to the school and find out if we need to do anything for that before then."

And then she nodded.

"How about now?" I asked.

And then she nodded and grinned.

Most of the European American parents in Albion sent their children to a charter school in the Marshall school district, but that school had a reputation for intending racial segregation, making it a sort of flagship of Albion's racial tension. And Annie's friendship with Bee told me both that she wouldn't have a problem learning with African Americans and that segregating her from Bee in that way would bely both their friendship and ours. So I didn't think asking her preference in that regard would be either necessary or productive.

So, with no questions in that regard, we drove to Albion's elementary school and found the Principal's office. A woman sitting at a desk behind a counter there rose from her desk and came to the counter. So I introduced us to her and asked her many questions.

Among them were whether a school bus would stop near our house, whether most third-graders there had cellphones or electronic tablets, and whether we'd need to buy books or other supplies. Answers were that the bus would stop two blocks from our house, that most third-graders at that school had neither a cellphone nor an electronic tablet, and that we didn't need to buy books but needed to buy supplies on a list the woman gave me.

But my last two questions were when Annie could enroll and what documents she'd need for that.

"She can do it now," said the woman. "If you have her birth certificate and your voter registration card or other official documentation at least as recent showing your address."

So, having neither with us and having Annie's birth certificate nowhere, we thanked the woman and returned home. But there I called Miss Walker to ask her whether she knew how we could obtain the birth certificate. And she said she had it.

"Can we come pick it up?" I asked.

"I can bring it to you," she said. "I'm supposed to check on Annie from time to time, and I'm overdue for that."

"When can you do that?" I asked.

"Now," she said. "If that works for you."

"It works for me," I said, remembering that she'd inspected our house with no delay, and appreciating her spontaneity. "We'll be here."

"Hello, Annie," said Miss Walker, when Annie answered our doorbell. "You look nice. Some new clothes, huh."

"We got 'em at Walmart," said Annie. "I washed 'em myself. Billy lets me do my own laundry. I use a step thing we have to reach the knobs and inside our washer. Billy doesn't treat me like a kid."

"And the house is still immaculate and orderly," said Miss Walker, still grinning at that as she shook hands with me, after following Annie inside.

"Annie's an excellent housemate," I said. "Calling her a troublemaker was crazy."

"So how's everything else going, Annie?" asked Miss Walker after smiling at that and responding to my offer of a seat by sitting at an end of our dining table. "Your birthday was last week. Did you do anything special?"

"We went to New York," said Annie, sitting in the side chair nearest to Miss Walker.

"New York?" exclaimed Miss Walker. "Now that *is* special!"

"We flew there in a plane," said Annie. "We went to the United Nations' clubhouse. They have a big room where you can hear people talk in any language you want, because they have microphones and earphones for that. They have 'em on all the tables, and all you have to do is put the earphones on and say into the microphone what language you want to hear. Then it sounds like the person who's talking's talking in that language. That's so they can understand each other so they won't have wars. That's what the club's for."

"That's a good idea," said Miss Walker, grinning again and looking at Annie as though she'd never heard anything so amazing.

"We went to some art museums too," said Annie, after nodding at that. "I'll show you."

And she slid from her chair, brought her Monet book to the table, opened it to the page where she'd put her program from *Giselle*, and pointed to the picture of Monet's 1919 *Water Lilies*.

"We saw that," she said.

"That's beautiful," said Miss Walker, smiling again.

"We saw that too," said Annie, nodding again and pointing to the *Giselle* program. "That's *Giselle*. It's a ballet. We saw *The Lion King* too."

"That must have been fun," said Miss Walker. "Did you save the program from that too?"

"Yes," said Annie. "But I gave it to Bee."

"Who's Bee" asked Miss Walker.

"She's my friend," said Annie. "She lives across the street. We're learning to play piano together. Want to see something else?"

"Sure!" said Miss Walker, and Annie went to her room and brought back her Statue of Liberty and United Nations flag.

"That's the United Nations' flag," she said. "And they have flags for almost every country out in front of the clubhouse. And we went up there too."

And she pointed to the crown of the Statue of Liberty.

"That was some birthday!" said Miss Walker.

"We went to the top of the Empire State Building and One World Trade Center too," said Annie nodding again. "We brought back a little Empire State Building too. But I gave that to Bee too.

"And we went to Harlem and Columbia University. A university's a big school with a bunch of different colleges where people can learn different things. And then we rode a subway to the other end of the island and went to Chinatown. We got those there."

And she pointed toward each of the bowls.

"Billy and I are learning Chinese together," she said. "And we ate lunch at an Au Bon Pain in New York. So we're learning French together too. Monet's French."

"What's left for you to learn in school?" asked Miss Walker, then laughing and shaking her head.

"They teach you how to read and write English and do arithmetic," said Annie. "Bee and I are going to study that together too. She's only in the second grade, but we can still learn together. Billy and I learn together, and he's been to college."

"Well!" said Miss Walker then turning to me. "Here's the birth certificate. You're doing wonderfully with her. I was a little worried about this situation. We try to place kids with married couples, not with single men driving Mustang convertibles, but you saved me a lot of time. And I'm not worried now."

"The car's because I love the openness of the sky," I said.

"As you love Annie's free spirit," said Miss Walker.

"Yes," I said. "So I'm just glad she's doing well. And all I'm doing is trying to be sure she can be as wonderful as she is. I think I told you that."

"You did," said Miss Walker. "And I'm glad it's working out. I'd never thought of that before, but now I'm going to think a lot about it."

Then she looked at Annie, grinned and shook her head again, and turned back to me.

"The United Nations, huh," she said. "And Columbia."

"We'll see," I said. "I'm just along for the ride."

And then she turned back to Annie.

"Well," she said. "I'm going back to work. This has been a pleasure."

And, rising from her chair, she shook hands with Annie.

"Alright if I come back from time to time?" she asked. "Not to inspect but just for the fun of it?"

"Sure!" said Annie, responding in kind to Miss Walker's grin, and we walked Miss Walker to her car.

"I have an idea," I said when we were back inside in the light of Annie's continuing smile from Miss Walker's visit, and she sat on our sofa and waited to hear it.

"You like to learn," I said, sitting in my reading chair. "And I think you can learn a lot faster than schools teach. So I'm thinking you might like to enroll in a school on the World Wide Web, and I think you could start the Web school in the fourth grade and may be able to skip the fourth grade at the school here. But I'm not saying you should."

"Do you mean I could use your computer?" asked Annie, looking at the laptop in front of her on our coffee table we never used for coffee.

"You can use that computer any time you like," I said. "But I'm thinking we might buy one especially for you. That way you could set it up especially for the things you'll do."

"When?" asked Annie.

"Right now," I said. "If you want. We have to go to Jackson for your school supplies, and tomorrow's our day for our Jackson shopping anyway. So we may as well do all that today I guess."

We'd been shopping for groceries together, and I'd developed a habit of driving to Jackson once a month, to buy things Albion's only supermarket didn't stock.

"I'll get the list," said Annie sliding from the sofa, and she pulled the top sheet from the pad and continued on outside.

"Oh, and something else," I said following her to our Mustang. "You're eight years old now. So you don't need that booster seat anymore. Unless you like to use it."

So she grinned, moved the booster seat to behind the driver seat, and sat where she put the booster the first time she used it.

"That's so we can talk better," she said. "Is that OK?"

"Everything you do is OK with me," I said grinning.

And we also bought her a cellphone, as much for her to learn how to use it as for her to call me for whatever reason, and we also bought her a new backpack and some clothes she'd need to be outdoors in the impending autumn and winter weather. And the next Tuesday, the first day of school there that year, I drove her to school and picked her up that afternoon. We'd decided against the bus.

With the school bus stopping two blocks from our house, I thought driving Annie to school would be as easy for me as would be walking her to the bus stop for her safety, and she liked riding in our Mustang. And, when I suggested that to Annie, she said Bee also might like riding in it more than she liked riding the bus. So she asked Bee, and I asked her mom the next time I saw her, and both accepted the invitation.

And Annie, as she and Bee climbed into the backseat that first day of school for them that year, considered and solved one more problem.

"You can use the booster seat until next year," she said to Bee. "Then you'll be eight."

Bee frowned, as she shrugged and buckled herself into the seat, but Annie also had an immediate answer to that.

"You can see more from up there," she said, and Bee looked around and grinned, and I was glad I'd put the top down."

But, dropping them off, I felt some trepidation.

"Are you two going to be alright?" I asked when we reached the school.

Both of them nodded, and they walked up the walk and into the school with no look back, but driving home I felt as though I may have thrown them into the mouth of a monster.

For various reasons, I'd attended six elementary schools, and I couldn't remember how I found my way to my classroom on my first day at any of them.

But, when I picked up Annie and Bee after school that afternoon, they were laughing. And both of them nodded again when I asked them whether everything had gone alright. So I stopped worrying about that also.

But then I remembered I'd told Annie we might be able to learn whether she had a grampa if she wanted. So, while she was at school that week, I tried to do that and began by calling Miss Walker to ask her whether she had Annie's mother's last address. And she did and gave it to me.

And, before driving to the address in Marshall to ask people in the neighborhood what they knew of Annie's family, I looked at her birth certificate for the names of her parents. But all the people I asked in the neighborhood told me they knew nothing of any relatives of either of Annie's parents and that neither did they know what became of her father. So, telling them I'd be back the next day, I asked them to ask others in the neighborhood what I'd asked them. But neither did two days of that and asking the landlord and their previous landlord help me. And the previous landlord had no rental application on file.

So I tried one more way. I tried to find her father on the Web. But neither did I find anyone with his name with any indication of any relationship to Michigan.

So that evening, as Annie and I sat at our dining table about to work on our Chinese, I told her what I'd done.

"That's OK," she said. "He never came to see us anyway, if I had a grampa."

But then I asked her a question I wasn't sure I should ask.

"How about your mom," I asked. "Has anyone told you what anyone's done with her since you saw her last?"

Then, she only shook her head, but I persisted.

"Do you think you might like to know?" I asked.

And then I was less sure I should have asked her that.

She looked down at the table for a few seconds and left her chair. She went to our sofa and sat on the edge of it, gazing down at the floor in front of her for several minutes, with her hands in her lap. And, when she returned to the table, she stopped at the corner of it between me and her chair.

"Maybe, I guess," she said. "But she isn't really anywhere, is she?"

Again, not knowing what to say, I told her my first thought.

"I think everyone's always everywhere," I said. "And I think that, whatever we imagine to be our bodies or anything else, all we love is always wherever we love it."

"Then," she said after standing silent for a few more seconds, "if we can find out where they put her, I guess we can go there once, to see what it looks like. But it's OK if we don't."

So then I was glad I asked her. And the next day I called the county's coroner. But he told me cremation was ordinary in such circumstance. And he said ordinarily no one kept records of such dispositions. And Annie simply nodded when I told her that.

So I was grateful for her responses to both of those failures of mine to resolve what I'd worried might be troubling her. But a few weeks later her teacher called me. And that gave me another worry..

"This is Mrs. Meredith," she said. "Annie's teacher. I have some concerns about Annie. So I'd like to talk with you if you don't mind, maybe after school today or at lunchtime, if that's possible. Or whenever's convenient for you."

"What time's your lunchtime?" I asked, and she told me a time and was at her desk when I arrived there precisely at the beginning of the time she told me, but her only greeting was a frown as she motioned me to a chair beside the desk.

"She has no problems academically," she said as I sat. "But I'm a little concerned about her socially. I don't know where to start, but . . . . Well, I'll start with this.

"For a half hour after each recess, I have the students work on problems in pairs, and Annie does that with the slowest girl in the class, every time."

"That doesn't surprise me," I said grinning, but Mrs. Meredith frowned at me again.

"Most children try to improve their academic and social status," she said. "But, anyway, there's another thing.

When the other children choose sides, to play games at recess and during their free time after lunch, Annie was going off and doing some kind of little dance by herself the whole time, before she settled in with her problem partner, and now they're doing the dance together. And, when I asked her what they were doing, she said it's a Chinese way of feeling you're part of every

"I told her she could be part of everything by playing games with the other kids. But then she said she doesn't like to make people lose. It's competition, for God's sake."

75

At that, I frowned, but she continued talking.

"And there's one more thing," she said. "Instead of writing her name on her papers, she draws some kind of little square pictures on them, two of them. And, when I asked her what they are, she said they're her name, in Chinese. Do you know what that Chinese thing she has is?"

"I know enough not to call it a thing," I said. "Can you show me one of her papers with the two little pictures on it?"

"I guess so," she said, and she shuffled through a stack of papers on her desk and pulled one from it and handed it to me. "But I don't see how it'll make any difference."

" 安 女 ", said the pictures.

"*Ān nǔ*," I said. "Every Chinese word is a one-syllable name for a picture English-speaking linguists call pictographs. And, because the Chinese language has no alphabet, the Chinese people write with those pictures. The names of those two pictures are *ān* and *nǔ*. And together they mean 'quiet girl'.

"Annie and I are learning Chinese together, and ordinarily each Chinese family name is one pictograph, and most of the names Chinese parents give their children are one or two pictographs. The Chinese write proper nouns from other languages by drawing pictographs with names that sound somewhat like the pronunciation of the nouns or names in the other language. And a Chinese person we met pronounced Annie's name that way.

"So I looked for pictographs with those names and found those two and told Annie I thought they might be appropriate for her, and this tells me she agreed, and you must know why.

"And what you called a little dance is the *Taijiquan* sequence. *Taijiquan* is a Chinese alternative to martial arts a Buddhist monk originated about fifteen centuries ago. And, in a martial situation, rather than trying to defeat any enemy, the *Taijiquan* practitioner tries to establish harmony with opponents, to eliminate the enmity making them opponents.

And doing the sequence alone is an approach to *yoga*. *Yoga*' is a Sanskrit word meaning 'union' Hindus use to refer to realizing the unity of all. And that notion of universal unity, of everyone being part of everything because all is all, is also the basic premise of Buddhism. So doing the *Taijiquan* sequence alone is a way of paying attention to one's breathing and posture to realize that the air and space inside one's body is the same as the air and space outside it.

"So *Taijiquan* is absolutely social, and the origin of the English word 'competition' is Greek for 'walking together', not walking or running against or trampling one another. And compassion and social responsibility are the reason Annie prefers not to make people lose, and it's also why she befriended the girl you called slow, and I suspect that soon she'll accelerate. So I suggest that you pay attention to that."

"Well," said Mrs. Meredith, "I don't know about all that voodoo business, but we have separation of church and state in this country, and I've done my job. I've made sure you're aware of the problem."

"Voodoo," I said, "originated as an African reaction to Christian missionaries' preaching, and Buddhism and Hinduism originated in India, long before Christianity was anywhere."

"Well, anyway," said Mrs. Meredith, "I trust that you won't tell Annie of this conversation."

"Annie trusts me to be her friend," I said, rising to leave. "And that doesn't mean keeping secrets from her, or taking anyone's side against her compassion, or her curiosity or courage."

And, since Mrs. Meredith hadn't offered to shake hands with me, I didn't offer to shake hands with her. But, as I turned to go, the children were returning for their afternoon classes. And Annie came in with a little blonde girl..

And that changed my whole mood.

6

Taming some Bullies

"Hi, Billy," said Annie. "What are you doing here?"

"Hey, little friend," I said. "Mrs. Meredith just wanted to talk about how wonderful you are."

But Annie looked at Mrs. Meredith and back at me with no smile. So I knew I'd have to tell her I meant the literal meaning of the word "want", and not its colloquial meaning, to wish. But, as I was deciding that, Annie smiled.

"This is my friend Suzy," she said, and she turned her smile to the little blonde girl, who was standing beside her and looking up at me with her eyebrows up in curiosity.

"A pleasure meeting you, Suzy," I said, offering a hand for her to shake. "Any friend of Annie's is a friend of mine."

And, grinning as Annie often did, Suzy shook the hand.

"See you at three, *Ān Nǔ*," I said.

And then all three of us were grinning together.

So, proud of Annie and happy for both her and her new friend, I left their classroom smiling but wondering how we should respond to Mrs. Meredith.

I thought of telling the Principal of that conversation. But I decided that doing that before asking Annie what she thought of the situation would be not only a violation of her trust in me but also contrary to my belief in her. And, after hearing Mrs. Meredith exemplify such failure, that was prominent in my mind.

So, that evening, after Bee went home for supper, I told Annie what Mrs. Meredith and I had said about her, and I asked her what she thought.

"Suzy isn't slow," she said. "She's like me. She just likes to understand things. Mrs. Meredith doesn't tell us how things make sense. She only tries to make us memorize what she says. She doesn't do what you said about Chinese. I mean about questions."

And, of course, but one response to that made sense to me.

"What do you think we should do?" I asked her.

How she put things together had become a constant wonder to me. So that question wasn't a grope in the dark but a reasonable expectation of a straight path from it. And Annie delivered.

"I don't know," she said. "But Suzy and I are alright. Her mom died too, some kind of sickness or something, but her dad loves her. And we're friends, and we're asking each other questions, so we can understand things, like you and I do, like Bee and me. The slow kids are the ones who only try to memorize things. The fast kids are the ones who try to understand things.

"That's how it seems to me. Maybe Mrs. Meredith'll figure that out if enough kids show her. That's what I think."

And I understood from what she said that she and Suzy would resolve the problem. So, while glad I asked her, all I did about the situation was to ask her more particular questions after school each day after that, and a week later she proved further how well she understood what was necessary. But I learned that by asking her a general question.

"Anything special happen at school today?" I asked.

"The bully tried to bully me," she said.

But, because she grinned when she said that, I couldn't not grin when I asked her a more particular question.

"How did that work out?" I asked.

79

"He told me I'm stupid," she said. "During recess. That's why the other kids call him the bully. He talks like that to everybody.

"But I asked him why he said it. And he said he said it because the dance I do is stupid. And he said I wouldn't hang out with Suzy if I weren't stupid.

"So I looked at Suzy, and I could tell that made her feel bad. I mean she was looking at me like she was afraid of what I might say. So I said the only thing I could think of.

"I asked him, if he's so smart, why didn't he study with Suzy and me after recess and help us be smarter. And he grinned at me and said OK. That's all, just OK. And he did.

"And Suzy grinned, when I said that, too. So that made me happy and glad I thought of saying it. And, when he studied with us after recess, I asked him some questions I thought were easy, and he answered them and asked me some I thought were harder, and I answered them.

"So, before the problems half hour was over, he said I wasn't as stupid as he thought I was. And then he asked me if he could study with us after afternoon recess too. And then he asked us if he could keep doing it.

"But I don't know if Mrs. Meredith will let us. I didn't think she would today, because we usually do it in pairs, but Bobby usually studies alone. Nobody wants to study with him.

"That's his name. Bobby."

"Sounds to me like he's not such a bad person after all," I said. "Do you have any idea why he's been so mean to people?"

""Mm hm," she said. "I asked him. He said it's because the other boys don't pick him for sports teams. He said that's because his parents divorced when he was little, and his dad never comes around. So he hasn't taught him how to play sports. So I asked him why he wanted to. And he said he didn't.

"And he said he didn't really want to be mean to people either. He said that's what people do to the other team when they play sports. But he said he wanted to have friends, and he thought he might make the other boys like him, if he was tough.

"But then he said he didn't care anymore because he'd rather be friends with Suzy and me."

And then she shrugged and grinned.

"You're a wonder, little friend," I said. "I can't tell you how happy I am that you're my friend. You're everyone's friend."

Then she shrugged again. But then she grinned again, and I resolved to ask her more particular questions after school, from then on. But, the next day, she didn't wait for me to ask.

She and I had set up her computer on our dining table. So, when we finished doing that, I asked her whether she wanted to leave it there for awhile for me to help her with it, if she needed help. She needed nearly no help, but she and Bee established a routine for working together on it there, and so they kept it there.

Each afternoon, after I drove them back to our house from school, they poured themselves some chocolate milk and filled a plate with cookies. Then, for an hour or more, they worked on the Web school together, before working on learning to play piano or finding other things to do, until time for Bee to go home for supper. Then Annie and I shared the supper I prepared while they were busy together.

I might have expected Bee's being a year behind Annie in the Albion school to be a problem with their working together at the Web school. But that would have required both underestimating Annie and her friendship with Bee and forgetting what Annie told Bee and Miss Walker about our learning together. And it also would have required ignoring how Annie and Bee worked together at the keyboard.

"I guess it works like letters and numbers," said Annie when she and Bee began learning to play it by themselves, after I told them some music theory and the relationship of the keys to the annotation in the keyboard's book.

"Yeah," said Bee. "Like reading and arithmetic."

"Maybe you can understand anything if you can read and count," said Annie.

"Yeah," said Bee. "Maybe the Buddha was right when she said everything's everything."

So Bee had little difficulty applying her second grade literary and mathematical skills to the fourth grade lessons of the Web school, and Annie was in no hurry and showed no interest in being ahead of Bee or anyone else, in anything.

But, the evening after Annie told me Bobby tried to bully her, the question she asked that forestalled any questions of mine changed that routine. When I picked up her and Bee after school that day, they were talking as they walked from the school to our car, but they stopped talking when they reached it. And they didn't speak again until we were in our house.

But then, before they gathered their cookies and milk, Annie asked the question that changed their routine.

"OK if Suzy and Bobby come over after school tomorrow?" she asked. "So they can meet Bee and see my computer?"

"It's OK with me," I said smiling, and she and Bee looked at one another and grinned.

"We can't all fit in our Mustang's backseat," said Annie. "But we can ride with them on the bus. That way we can tell them which bus stop is ours. Bee knows because she rode the bus to school last year. Is that OK?"

"That's OK with me too," I said grinning, and Bee and Annie grinned at one another again, and that was the last day I drove them home from school.

After that evening Suzy and Bobby joined them in their routine at our house. And, with little change, that routine continued until all of them finished the eighth grade in the Web school. But that evening Annie and Bee followed the routine they'd established.

So I waited for our supper talk to learn more of how things had gone that day and would go through those years.

But Annie also started that conversation.

"Can you take Suzy and Bobby home before suppertime tomorrow?" she asked. "They want to be home before their parents get home from work. I have to use my phone tonight to call them and tell them if that's OK and find out if it's OK with their parents if they come over after school. I mean Suzy's dad and Bobby's mom."

"Sure," I said. "Sounds like you and Bobby are friends already. You and Suzy have been friends for weeks I guess, but wasn't yesterday the first time Bobby talked to you?"

"Yeah," said Annie. "But you told me I'd have friends when I went back to school. Bee was my friend before, and now I've made two friends at school, and I have other friends too. I think George is my friend, and the lady at the United Nations, Uma. And I think Miss Walker's my friend.

"So that's six friends. And you've always been my friend. So that's seven, and I never had any friends before, except my mom. And Mrs. Meredith didn't stop Bobby from working with us today either. She looked at us a lot, but she didn't stop us.

"And the other kids don't make fun of me anymore. They still don't talk to me much. But they don't make fun of me."

"I think you may be right about Mrs. Meredith too," I said. "I think she may be your friend soon, if she isn't already."

And Annie grinned and after supper made her calls.

"Hey, Bobby," she said. "I thought your mom would answer. . . . So you already asked her? . . . That's great! Billy said it's OK with him too! . . . Great. See you tomorrow. Bye."

And, excepting one part, her call to Suzy was like that.

83

"I called Bobby first," she said, "because I wasn't sure his mom would let him, and I wanted to be able to tell you if he could make it or not."

"It's OK," she said to me, grinning after hanging up.

"Well," I said. "I guess I'll have to go to the store tomorrow for some more cookies and chocolate milk."

And she grinned again, and the next afternoon I heard the four of them talking and laughing, before they opened our front door.

"This is Bobby," said Annie. "You already met Suzy. This is Billy."

"Nice seeing you again, Suzy" I said grinning at her and then turning to Bobby. "Nice meeting you, Bobby."

"Nice to meet you," said Bobby shaking the hand I offered.

And then, after Annie and Bee led them into our kitchen to gather the cookies and chocolate milk, they followed Annie and Bee to our dining table.

"Wow," said Suzy looking at Annie's computer. "My dad doesn't have a computer, and you and Billy have two."

"My mom doesn't have one either," said Bobby. "She says her phone's all the computer she needs."

"My mom has one," said Bee. "But she doesn't let me use it."

And then Annie opened a fourth grade lesson.

"This is neat," said Bobby. "You can take your own time and figure everything out in your own way."

"Yeah," said Bee. "And it's all the same stuff anyway. The only difference is how people talk about it. I'm only in the second grade, and Annie and I are figuring out the fourth grade stuff together. We just figure out how it makes sense."

"So how about if all of us do it together every day?" asked Annie. "I mean the Albion school days when we can ride the bus. Billy said I might be able to skip the fourth grade in the Albion school that way. But, even if we can't skip grades, wouldn't it be fun?"

"But how would we get home afterward?" asked Suzy.

"I could take you," I said from my reading chair, where I'd done little reading during that conversation. "As I will today. I wouldn't want to keep friends from being friends together."

And so began the four of them homeschooling one another. And Suzy and Bobby immediately became as much friends to Bee as Annie was. So, at our house, the fourth grade was simply something the four of them did together.

They didn't give much attention to the keyboard, but Bee and Annie adjusted their routine to begin doing that a little later each day, while I was driving Suzy and Bobby home.

And things also continued improving at the Albion school. The week after the four of them began studying together at our house, Mrs. Meredith called me again, but not to present a problem. She called to express gratitude.

"I apologize," she said. "You were right. Suzy's nowhere near as slow as she was! And did Annie tell you she tamed the class bully?"

"Yes," I said. "And she also told me that, because you were having the others work in pairs, she was afraid you wouldn't let the three of them study together, but she said you did. So I need to thank you for that."

"I think I need to thank you," said Mrs. Meredith. "That's why I called, besides to apologize. I took your advice and watched how Annie's doing what she's doing, and what she's doing is asking the others questions. They're asking each other questions until all of them understand a problem. Then they go on to the next one.

"I guess you could call it the Socratic method. Of course I heard of that in college, but I thought it was only an idea, not something practical. So I was only trying to make the kids memorize everything. But now I think I might try Annie's method. I'm supposed to be the teacher. But Annie's teaching me. So thanks."

"No need to thank me for that either." I said. "I'm the same way. I'm supposed to be fostering Annie. But I feel that she's fostering me."

And that evening during supper, when I told Annie about that conversation, she told me Mrs. Meredith was true to her word.

"Yeah," said Annie. "You were right. I think she's my friend now too. And today she started asking us and the other kids what we think."

And, of course, during all that, Annie and I were continuing our learning together, and her first question regarding Chinese was what the phrase "*tài jí quán*" means.

So of course, when I told her it means "extreme polarity fist", she asked how that means feeling how everything fits together. So, referring to how fingers are like poles, I used my hands to show her how folding them together into a fist brings them together and makes them one fist instead of different fingers. So then she grinned and opened and closed her fists as she had in the air over her head as we drove home the day we became friends.

And, after supper the evening she told me of Mrs. Meredith's change of method, we solved another problem that had worried me a little.

"Annie," I said as we sat on our sofa watching the evening news, "I know you don't like to ask for things. So I've been thinking you should have some money. So I looked up allowances on the Web and read that eight-year-olds ordinarily have a weekly allowance of between five and ten dollars. So . . . ."

And I went to the stand where we kept our grocery list, took seventy dollars from the drawer in it where I kept my keys and wallet and pocket cash when I was at home, and brought it to the coffee table.

"Your birthday was seven weeks ago," I said putting the cash on the table in front of her. "So there's seventy dollars, and I'll put ten more dollars under the grocery list pad every Monday. You can do what you want with it, take it to school in your backpack, save some of it in your desk. Whatever.

"Is that alright?"

"I don't need it," she said. "You buy me everything I need."

"I try to," I said. "But I might not know what you need at school. OK?"

"OK," she said, and she shrugged.

But then she smiled, picked up the seventy dollars, and took it to her bedroom.

"I put some of it in my backpack and some in my desk drawer," she said when she returned. "I never had any money before."

But I had three more problems to solve concerning her that year.

Halloween was near. And, of course, Thanksgiving would follow that by a few weeks, and Christmas would be about a month later, and those were Christian holidays. Annie and I, the day we became friends, talked of a problem with Christianity we shared. But I had problems with each holiday that I thought we also might share. So, as they approached, I asked her what she thought of them.

"What do you think about Halloween?" I asked her during supper a few days before Halloween.

"I don't like to ask for things," she said after shrugging. "And I don't want to trick anybody. And I don't know why anybody wants to dress up like a monster either. Do you know?"

"No," I said. But I think it may come from what Christians call the resurrection. 'Hallow' means 'holy', and 'halloween' is short for 'all hallows eve', and resurrection is coming back to life.

So I guess some people may think of it as coming out of graves. Have you heard of zombies?"

"Yeah, on TV," said Annie, laughing a little but shaking her head. "But don't Christians say they're angels in heaven when they come back to life?"

"Yes," I said, smiling at her laughing. "But they also say dead sinners come back to some kind of life in that hell your silly Sunday School teacher talked about. They don't call those people holy, but the Bible also says the graves opened up on the day of Jesus' crucifixion for people they call holy to come out of them, but they say that was in spring. So I don't understand either.

"But what you said about tricking and treating is my main problem with Halloween. I don't understand why parents teach their kids to threaten people if they don't give them candy. We have laws against that sort of thing otherwise.

"I did it when I was your age. But that was because of my family's poverty. My sister and I had so little that we welcomed any way to have more. So we used to go out and fill a big paper grocery bag full of candy for each of us. Then we took those two bags home and went out and filled two more."

"Where's your sister?" asked Annie.

"She's gone," I said. "Gone beyond."

"Beyond what?" asked Annie.

"Beyond all these differences we call life," I said. "Most people seem to me to call it dying. But Buddhists call it being fixed beyond. *Paramita*."

"*Paramita*," quietly repeated Annie, turning to look back at our porcelain imagining of the Buddha on its stool beneath the map that then had two yellow tacks in it, one for Albion and one for New York City.

"It means 'fixed beyond' in the languages the Buddha spoke.," I said. "'*Para*' means 'beyond'. '*Mita*' means 'fixed'."

"What languages?" asked Annie.

"Pali and Vedic Sanskrit," I said. " Pali's a dialect of Sanskrit people spoke in what people now call Nepal. Nepal's a small country along the southern side of the Himalaya mountains north of India. Vedic Sanskrit was the main language of northern India, when the Buddha taught there, after he grew up in Nepal.

"A dialect's a form of a language."

So then Annie put her fork on her plate and left the table, went to the statuette and touched its *ushnisha*, and looked up from it to the map.

But I returned the conversation to my problem.

"So what do you think we should do on Halloween?" I asked her. "Do you think we should buy some candy and put a jack-o-lantern at the top of our front steps and turn on the porch light, or do you think we should keep the light off and do what we usually do, or what?"

She looked down at the Buddha statuette again, but she removed her finger from its ushnisha, and returned to her seat at our dining table.

"Get the candy and the pumpkin and turn on the light," she said. "In case some kids like you and your sister come by. What's her name?"

"Peggy," I said.

And then both of us smiled.

"Then do you want to go to the store when we're through eating?" I asked. "For the candy and the pumpkin?"

Her return to school had stopped our regularly shopping for groceries together. With the Albion school, the Web school and other learning and other things she did with her friends gave her plenty to do, and she hadn't stopped doing her laundry. When her Albion school classes began, I suggested to her that I do her laundry for her, but she said she could do it Saturdays.

So, when I asked her whether she'd like to go to the store for the candy and the pumpkin, she grinned and nodded.

"I'm through eating," she said, clearing her place.

"So am I," I said, and we put our dishes in our dishwasher, but she had another question.

"Can I pay for it," she asked, and she went to her bedroom and returned with some money, went to the stand where we kept our grocery list, and picked up the pad.

I'd seen that she hadn't taken the cash I put beneath the pad, and I'd begun to think she may not have understood what I said of it, but I was sure she at least knew it was there and was hers. And I already knew better than to expect any misunderstanding from her. So then I understood that she simply saw no urgency in its presence.

"I haven't spent any of this money you're giving me," she said. "Do you think it's enough?"

"You can if you'd like to," I said. "It's your money. And I think it's probably plenty."

So she picked up the cash, put the pad back in its place, and grabbed her coat from our entranceway coat closet, and I grabbed my cash and wallet and keys and coat, and followed her outside

At the store she treated that purchase as though she had a personal interest in both the obligations of the office she'd requested and in the happiness of any of its beneficiaries. She explored all the displays of Halloween candy and then went back and picked up a bag of candy in individual wrappers with Halloween images on the wrappers. But then she showed it to me.

"Do you think this would be OK?" she asked.

"I think so if you think so," I said.

"How many do you think we should get?" she asked.

"I don't know," I said, "No one's ever rang our doorbell on Halloween while I've lived in that house, and I don't remember seeing any trick-or-treaters walk past, but I haven't been doing this. I've been buying some candy each year for that possibility, but I haven't been carving a pumpkin, or turning on the porch light. So I'd have to guess.

"But still I don't see how a couple of bags wouldn't be plenty.

So she selected two bags. And we found a medium size pumpkin and a pillar candle for it   And, at home, we carved the pumpkin and put it out that night. And, on Halloween, we turned on the light. But no one stopped.

And, that evening, I thought of reasons for that. Our street was one block long and had but four houses on it, and no children other than Bee and Annie resided in any of them, and Annie had told me Bee told her that she had cousins in another neighborhood in Albion and trick-or-treated with them in their neighborhood. So, as Annie and I watched the evening news on that first Halloween of ours together, I asked myself what difference telling Annie that may have made. And, during the news, she looked toward our front window several times. And, after the news, she went to the window to look out several times.

But she said nothing of why until time for her shower.

"Oh, well," she said then, shrugging but smiling. "What are we going to do with all this candy?"

"You could eat it," I said.

"I don't want to eat all this candy," she said grinning.

But, before going for her shower, she ate the candy from one of the wrappers.

"I know," she said while eating it. "We can eat it instead of cookies while we're studying. Until it's gone."

And then she moved the bowl of candy from the stand at our entranceway to a kitchen counter and went to take her shower. And, excepting buying less candy the next year, we did that every year we shared that house. And that was by Annie's annual suggestions.

"Just in case," she said.

7

Thanks and Giving

But my Thanksgiving problem was more complex. It involved consideration of circumstances ranging from the Abrahamic notion of a "promised land" to the American notion of a "manifest destiny", and I had no wish to impose my ethical considerations on Annie, but she immediately solved that second problem. She reminded me that she already shared my ethics in at least one concern.

"What do you think about Thanksgiving?" I asked her during supper the Thursday before Thanksgiving.

"I wouldn't want a turkey to eat me," she said.

So I mentioned some manifest destiny history.

"I wouldn't want anyone to take our home from us either," I said. "But that's what people calling themselves pilgrims did to people they called Indians, and Thanksgiving celebrates that. The people calling themselves pilgrims were from England while the people they called Indians weren't from India but from this land. And Thanksgiving celebrates the people from England sharing with some of the people from here the first harvest they reaped from the land they took from them.

"And, when the people from here complained, when they figured out that the people from England came here to take their homeland, the people from England did worse. They took the land by force, and others did the same, all across this continent. And the force included killing for the land."

But Annie's beginning to frown made me lighten up a little.

"But I'm thankful that no one's trying to push us from our home," I said. "And I'm thankful that we have enough money to buy anything we need, and you seem to me to feel that way, and I'm thankful for that too. And I don't think a pumpkin would mind us eating it."

So then she stopped frowning and grinned.

"So what do you think about celebrating that?" I asked.

"I never heard of eating a pumpkin," she said. "Except in a pumpkin pie."

"I cut a little one in half once and baked it and ate its inside part," I said, "after I scraped the seeds out and put some brown sugar in it."

"That sounds good!" she said grinning again.

So, through further talk, we decided on a thanksgiving dinner of that and a *soufflé* of a mix of vegetables, some potato salad and a red bean and walnut salad with celery and pomegranate juice, and blueberry pie *à la mode* for desert.

"Boy!" said Annie on Thanksgiving day. "These beans are almost as good as that pumpkin! I can hardly wait 'til we get to that pie!"

So that left Christmas my only remaining holiday problem. And, though I expected that to be the most difficult of the three, we solved it in the same way. I mean Annie solved it.

"What do you think about Christmas?" I asked her the morning after Thanksgiving as she returned *Gardner's* to its shelf after using that day off from school to read it while I worked on my weblog.

And she came and sat beside me again.

"I remember we talked about it the day we met," I said. "I mean we talked about those people telling you you'd go to hell if you didn't believe in Christ. But those people were talking about Jesus. And I doubt that Jesus was the Christ."

"Why?" asked Annie.

"I've read the Bible," I said. "And, excepting one of its four books that say what Jesus said, it doesn't say Jesus said he was the Christ. And two of the other three of those four books say he told the person who wrote that book that he didn't know what he was talking about."

Then Annie grinned. But she didn't say anything. So I continued.

"And," I said, "the Bible also says Jesus said throwing someone into a sea with a big stone around his neck would be better for the person than if he offended a child. So I don't think he'd send you to hell for anything."

But then, instead of grinning, she frowned and looked toward our front window.

"But it doesn't say Jesus did that to anyone," I said. "And the guy who wrote that book saying Jesus called himself the Christ also wrote more about hell than any other writer of the Bible does, and some other things the Bible says Jesus said tell me he was more Buddhist than Christian."

So then, after looking back toward our Buddha statuette, she looked forward again with a smile.

"And one thing telling me that," I said, "is that it says he said loving our neighbors is like loving God, and I think that may be why people give things to one another on his birthday, or at least should be if people believe in him, or if they don't."

And then, broadening her smile a little, she shifted back a little further onto the sofa.

"But do you remember seeing people on TV fighting each other to buy Christmas gifts?" I asked. "They do it every year on the day after Thanksgiving. You may see some of it on TV this afternoon."

Then she nodded. But she also stopped smiling and shifted a little further forward on our sofa again. And already, as I had while telling her of the "manifest destiny", I was beginning to feel bad about putting her through those feelings. But I had but three more questions to raise in that regard. So I continued.

"And sometimes," I said, "people feel bad when someone gives them something more expensive than what they gave the person giving it to them. And some people seem to me to think the people who give them less owe them something. And the Bible doesn't say anything about Christmas trees.

"So what do you think?"

"I don't know," she said. "I'd like to use some of the money you give me to buy presents for Bee and Suzy and Bobby. But I don't think they have as much money as we do. And I don't want to make them feel bad."

And then she turned her head toward the window again for a few seconds, but then she turned back and looked directly at me, with no frown.

"I know," she said. "I'll talk to them about it, like you're talking to me."

And then I was smiling.

"How about a Christmas tree?" I asked.

"We have our Buddha," she said.

And then I was grinning.

"If you want," I said, "we can go to Jackson next Saturday for the presents. That might give the other shoppers time to settle down after today's fighting and give the stores some time to restock. And I was already thinking about buying computers for Suzy and Bobby.

"So, if you think that would be OK, we could buy the computers then too. I don't think kids think they have to buy adults presents no matter what adults give them. I think they know it's adults' job."

And Annie grinned wide at that, but then she frowned.

"But what about Bee?" she asked.

"Well," I said, "I wasn't going to tell you yet. But, well, you and Bee aren't finding much time to learn piano together lately. Since the four of you started working on the Web school and doing other things together during some of the time you were doing that. So I've already ordered a new keyboard for you, a full-size one with 88 keys, and three pedals.

"That way we could give that other one to Bee for both of you to be able to practice when you're not together what you learn together. I also ordered a pedal for that one that's supposed to do different things. I couldn't find a three-pedal set for it.

"And I'm thinking Bee's mom might let her use her computer now, if Bee tells her why."

And then Annie's frown disappeared into another big grin.

"And waiting until next Saturday will give me time to talk to Bee and Suzy and Bobby too," she said.

I didn't hear her conversations with Bee or Suzy or Bobby about that. But, by the next Saturday, she'd decided what she wished to buy for each. And she told me as we drove to Jackson.

"I want to get Bobby some gloves," she said. "He never wears gloves to school, and it's getting cold. And I want to buy Suzie a pink scarf to go with her coat, and do you think we can find a Rachmaninoff CD, for Bee?"

"I think we can find one somewhere," I said.

One rainy Saturday afternoon, while Annie was sitting on one of our corner chairs reading *Gardner's*, I put a CD of Rachmaninoff's piano concertos into the DVD drive of our home entertainment system and sat on our sofa to work on my weblog. And, less than a minute into the CD, Annie put her book on the other corner chair and came and sat on our sofa beside me. But she didn't speak immediately.

"What's that?" she asked after about another minute.

"Rachmaninoff's second piano concerto," I said.

She said nothing more of the CD that day. But she listened to all of it before returning to her book. And she plainly enjoyed it.

So that changed that shopping trip.

We went to the Jackson Crossing Mall to find a music store. Then, after finding one and the CD, we decided to go to the Target store there to see if it had the other things she'd decided to buy. And there she found some black nylon ski gloves for Bobby and a pink knit scarf for Suzy. Then we decided to go to the Best Buy store there to see what computers it had. And we found some there like Annie's and bought them.

So we didn't go to Walmart that day.

Annie decided to wait until the last Albion school day before its Christmas vacation to give those friends of hers the gifts she bought for them. And, though, until after the giving, I didn't know how they knew to do it, they also brought gifts for her and for one another to our house that day. So they did no studying at our house that day.

Instead, the four exchanged gifts at our dining table that had become also their study table, as I sat in my reading chair doing nearly no reading.

Bee gave a black knit cap to Bobby, a pink knit cap to Suzy, and a white one to Annie. Suzy gave a black knit scarf to Bobby and a red knit scarf to Bee and a white one to Annie. And Bobby gave pink knit mittens to Suzy and red ones to Bee and white ones to Annie.

"That's neat," said Bobby, "how we did that. I mean telling each other when one of us was away from the rest of us what we got the one that was away. So, except Bee's CD, we all got the same stuff. I guess that's because Bee already had a hat."

"Yeah," said Bee. "And I got you hats because I like mine."

She had a red knit cap she was wearing to school every day. So I thought of the verse in the Bible Christians call the Golden Rule. By then I was paying no attention to my book.

"And I think I started it." said Annie. "Because I didn't want any of us to feel bad about getting something more expensive than what we gave anyone."

So that told me both how Annie solved her shopping problem and how they knew when to bring the gifts to our house.

"So it's all neat," said Suzy. "and I love my stuff."

"Yeah," said Bobby. "Me too."

"Me too," said Bee looking at the CD box, and she read some of its cover notes. "Rach-ma-ni-noff. Piano music."

"I love mine too," said Annie, looking down at her cap lying on top of her mittens and scarf.

And then she looked up and at the Buddha statuette, and her eyes and mouth widened, her mouth into a grin.

"It's like the Buddha," she said, picking up the cap, and then she looked at the mittens, and then at the scarf. "And so is everything else."

The knit of the cap resembled the porcelain hair of the statuette, and it had a pom-pom where the *ushnisha* would be. And the statuette also had a porcelain sash over the Buddha's left shoulder. And no detail separated its fingers.

"Merry Buddhamas," said Bobby, grinning at Annie.

"We all agreed on that," said Suzy, grinning at Bee.

"That's great!" said Annie, still also grinning. "Thanks, you guys!"

And then she left her chair and went to the statuette.

"Oh!" she said. "This stuff's from Billy for you guys."

We'd wrapped the computers and the pedal and stacked them on the floor beside the statuette's stool. So, making three trips, Annie took the pedal to Bee and then took the computers to Bobby and Suzy. And the three looked at me, watched Annie make the three trips, and began opening what she took them.

"Computers!" said Bobby.

"And they're just like yours!" said Suzy, looking at Annie's computer in front of them in the middle of the table.

"I don't . . . ," said Bobby, looking at me again. "I . . . . I don't know what to say."

"Neither do I!" said Suzy, grinning at me. "Thanks!"

"You don't have to say anything," I said. "I feel like you're my family. You two and Bee and Annie. One big family."

But, while Bobby and Suzy were saying that, Bee was looking at the picture on the pedal box.

"What is it?" she asked, beginning to open the box.

"It's a pedal," said Annie. "For your keyboard."

"You mean your keyboard?" asked Bee. "I mean our keyboard. That one."

"It's all yours now," said Annie. "Billy bought a full size one with 88 keys and three pedals for when you and I play together. He couldn't find a set of three pedals for yours, but that one's supposed to do what all three regular pedals do, and some other stuff too. Do you want to hear your CD?"

Bee looked at her keyboard as Annie said that, but then she grinned and nodded and handed the CD to Annie, and Annie removed the cellophane from it and put it into the DVD drive of our home entertainment system.

"That's beautiful," said Suzy.

"Yeah it is," said Bobby.

"Yeah it is," said Bee.

"Do you want to set up your computers?" asked Annie.

"Yes!" said Suzy and Bobby simultaneously.

So, while Bee sat on our sofa listening to Rachmaninoff, Suzy and Bobby and Annie set up the computers on our Wi-Fi network.

Annie asked me a few questions, but she remembered most of what we'd done with hers, and she remembered that our Wi-Fi password was on the back of our router and read it to Suzy and Bobby as they entered it into their computers.

And, after smiling through all of her CD, Bee joined the others as they connected the two new computers to the Web school.

"We don't have a Web connection at home," said Bobby. "But I think my mom might get one now. She's just happy I'm not picking on anybody anymore."

"I think my dad will too," said Suzy. "He calls me his little genius now."

"I think my mom might let me use her computer now too," said Bee. "If I tell her why."

"That's what Billy said," said Annie.

"Then we can be on Facebook," said Bobby.

"Yeah," said Suzy. "But not like those people on TV and some of the kids at school. I mean I guess we could use it to tell each other stuff we didn't think of when we were together, if we need to before we see each other again, or something like that. But I'd rather do the stuff we do together when we're together."

"Yeah," said Bobby. "I don't see how it would be the same. I don't think I'd even want to use Skype. And my mom likes me to be with her when I'm with her, too. She likes to talk about the stuff I do when I'm not at home."

"Yeah," said Suzy. "My dad, too."

"And too much other stuff's always going on at our house," said Bee. "TV and stuff and my dad's friends."

But, when time came for me to drive Suzy and Bobby home, Annie and they carried the keyboard and its stand and power supply and earphones across the street, as Bee carried the pedal. And, as they gathered it all, Bee referred to part of that problem again. But all of that showed how they were.

"I'm glad it has those headphones," said Bee. "That way I won't bother my dad when he's watching sports."

"That way your dad's sports won't bother you when you're playing your music," said Bobby.

And all four of them laughed. They understood one another. They were good friends.

"Oh," I said. "Can you wait a minute?"

And I went to our basement for a stool I also bought.

"Those kitchen counter stools you and Annie were using for your keyboard are too tall for you to reach the pedal," I said. "This one's lower. So, when you set up the stand at home, you can make it low enough for you to be able to reach the pedal while you play. For when you two play together here, I bought a piano bench that's low enough, and wide enough for two."

So Bee put on her hat and mittens and scarf and carried the stool across the street with the pedal and the keyboard book and her CD.

And, on Christmas morning, beside the Buddha's stool, with some things I'd put there for Annie after she showered and went to her room the night before, were a hat and a scarf and a pair of gloves, and a CD of Wagner's instrumental music, for me.

I don't know how they managed the logistics of that. But Annie and I had talked about how instrumental music is essential to both ballet and opera. And I'd told her I'd listen to Wagner's instrumental music more if I didn't have to wait through the vocal music to hear it.

And a few weeks later all of us received another gift.

Mrs. Meredith never called me again, but I talked with her in January at our mid-year parent-teacher conference, and that conversation was much more congenial than our first conversation.

"I don't need to tell you how Annie's doing academically," she said. "But I don't know if you know Bobby's also doing that little dance with her and Suzy now, and some of the other kids have asked her about it, but they're not doing it. They just went back to their games.

"But they're talking to her more now. At first they mostly left her alone, because she was so quiet, and the same with Suzy. And a bigger change is that the other kids are also talking to Bobby now, and you know why they weren't talking to him.

"And an academic matter you may not know is that the whole class has improved its grades. And, if I'm busy helping other students while they're working on problems during the problem half hours, kids with questions go to Annie and her friends. And also I'm letting them decide for themselves how many work together for the problem-solving. So mostly now it's groups of three or four. And it's more lively that way."

But what Mrs. Meredith said of the dance made me think of Bee. The reason she wasn't doing the *Taijiquan* sequence at school with Annie and Suzy and Bobby was that the school scheduled recess and lunch by grade with two of the school's grades in each of three time periods. So, because Bee was in the second grade while the others were in the third, her lunch and recess times were earlier than theirs.

And Annie had told me of that schedule variance and also that, when I was picking up her and Bee in front of the school, Suzy and Boby were catching the bus behind it. So, together, those circumstances also explained why Suzy and Bobby didn't meet Bee before she rode the bus with them. So I told Mrs. Meredith about Bee and the Web school.

"All four of them are on track to finish the fourth grade in that by the end of this summer," I said. "So I'm wondering if Bee might move into your class to be with her friends. But I don't know the policies here.

"I don't know," said Mrs. Meredith with a smile, after a moment of apparently more serious thought. "But I don't see why not. We let kids skip grades sometimes. Besides academics, a concern is how the student would feel about leaving friends behind, but Bee would be doing the opposite of that."

Then she frowned and looked down at her desk for a few seconds, but then she looked up again, and straight at me.

"Anyway," she said. "I don't care about the policy. Let's go talk to the Principal."

So I followed her to the Principal's office.

"I'm happy to meet you," said the Principal shaking hands with me after Mrs. Meredith introduced me to her. "Annie's become quite famous in the teachers' lounge, and so has the Socratic method Mrs. Meredith has learned from her. She's started a bit of a revolution here."

And then Mrs. Meredith told her the question, and she answered it with less than a second's pause for thought, but she answered it thoughtfully.

"Oh," she said, "I don't see why not. Ordinarily a concern would be the student's leaving friends behind, but Bee would be catching up with her friends, and Bee's teacher has also told me about Bee. So I approve, and obviously Mrs. Meredith would welcome her into her class. So the only remaining requirement is the approval of Bee's parents.

"So do you want me to call them, or would you like to ask them to call me, if they approve."

"I think I should ask her mom," I said. "I think, if you call her, she may think I put you up to it. And I don't want her to think I'm trying to sneak her daughter away from her. Bee's already spending nearly all of her time between school and supper, and more hours weekends, at our house. Their house is across the street from ours."

"Oh," said the Principal. "That's good thinking. I think. Yes."

And she handed me her business card.

"That has my direct number on it," she said. "I'm here at least until five, school nights."

When I returned home, Bee's family's car was in their driveway, and I'd never seen her father drive it. So I supposed her mother must have been at home. But I wanted to be sure.

For various reasons, not only his continuing lack of congeniality to me, I had no wish to speak with her father. I'd seen that he spent nearly all of his time at home, and many cars stopped there and stayed but a few minutes, all day and into the night. So I suspected that he was in a commercial business one wouldn't ordinarily call working for a living. And what Bee said of his "friends" added to that suspicion.

But the main reason I preferred not to speak with him then was that I didn't wish to risk his extending his antipathy for me to the question at hand.

And I had a way to know more surely whether Bee's mother was at home. Bee and Annie, because of the parent-teacher conferences, had that day off from school. So, going inside, I found them working at their new keyboard.

Bee shrugged, turning to me to answer the question, but her answer made me sure enough.

"I think so," she said. "She was when I left a little while ago. Is her car in the driveway?"

But, because she didn't immediately turn back to the keyboard, that process required another decision. Still, though more congenial, my interaction with her mother seldom went beyond our waving to one another. So I supposed Bee was wondering why I was asking.

And, not being sure her mother would give the permission and having no wish to disappoint Bee, I didn't know how to answer the question I thought was in her mind.

When I was in the second grade, my mother told me my teacher told her I could skip the third grade, but then she told me the teacher also told her I might not be able to make friends with kids who weren't my age, and then she told me she and my teacher had decided against the skip, and I felt something had been taken from me.

Aside from my wishing then to shorten my number of school years, a consideration for me was that my family's poverty made making friends of any age difficult for me, but I didn't know how to tell my mother any of that. So, as I then ordinarily did to think through problems in my life, I silently went upstairs and sat on the bed my brother and I shared. And I found no solution to that problem.

So, having no wish to inflict such dejection on Bee, I responded more evasively than I ordinarily do to anything.

"I need to ask her something," I said, and then I turned back to our front door and walked across the street to knock on their front door to take the next step.

Bee's mother was at home and opened the inside door and then the storm door. But, instead of greeting me, she leaned across the threshold and looked at me with a questioning look and no words. So I supposed that, because I never before had knocked on her door, she essentially was asking me why I did then.

So I began that conversation in about the same way I replied to Bee's questioning look.

"Hi, Corinthia," I said. "I just need to ask you something."

I knew her name by looking it up on the Web. And, because I told her that on one of the few occasions on which I'd spoken with her, she knew that. On that occasion, as I returned from a walk downtown, she walked across the street and asked to use my phone. She told me she'd dropped hers in her toilet.

"Are you Corinthia?" I asked as I handed her my phone.

"How did you know that?" she asked.

"I looked up your address on the state's property tax website before I bought this house," I said. "I wanted to know who my neighbors would be."

"Oh," she replied. "I thought maybe I ran into you in one of those places I go."

And then she turned around and walked a few yards away to make her call. So remembering that as she leaned through her doors, and remembering that on that earlier occasion I wondered why she felt she needed to be so secretive, I continued more directly than I'd replied to Bee's questioning look. I decided that the last thing that situation needed was evasiveness.

"I guess you know about Bee and Annie and some friends of theirs studying on the Web at our house," I said continuing.

"Mm hm," she said. "She's using my computer for that."

"Well," I said, "it looks like all of them will finish the fourth grade on the Web this summer. So, when I was talking with Annie's teacher for our parent-teacher conference today, I asked her about the possibility of moving Bee into her third-grade class with Annie and the others. And she took me to the Principal's office to ask her, and the Principal said it's OK with her, if it's OK with you.

"So what do you think?"

And then Corinthia leaned back and laughed out loud.

"Are you kidding me?" she said. "I'm not going to stand in my daughter's way! What do I have to do?"

"Well," I said, grinning as I thought Annie might. "The Principal said you need to call her and tell her that. I don't know what else you'll need to do. I guess she'll tell you if you call her."

"I'll call her right now," she said. "Do you know her number?"

So I gave her the card, and she laughed again and began to turn away and close the doors, but she turned back.

"And thanks for that keyboard," she said. "Except sleeping, Bee spends almost all her time at home now with those headphones on her head, when she's not using my computer. I hardly ever get to talk to her anymore. I'm glad you moved in over there. She loves that keyboard."

"I'm glad too," I said. "Bee's a great friend to Annie."

"Well," she said. "Alright. Thanks."

And then she turned away and closed the doors.

Still I didn't tell Bee. I thought her mom might like to tell her. But, after Bee went home for supper, I told Annie. And that was the first time she hugged me and the first time I heard her giggle. And Bee was in the third grade the next day.

And, at the end of that schoolyear, all of them took such a step step.

A few weeks before the end of that schoolyear I called Mrs. Meredith with another request. I remembered when her lunchtime was and called her during one and asked her whether I could go there and talk with her during her next one. And she was ready for that call.

"Sure," she said when I called. "I was planning to ask you that. Is there a problem?"

"No," I said. "I'll see you tomorrow."

"No problem here either," she said. "I just want to ask you something. See you then."

And that time she smiled and offered a hand to shake and waited for me to begin the conversation.

"Well," I said, "I'd just like to ask you the question I asked you about Bee, but about all four of them this time. Now they're on track to finish the fourth grade on the Web by the middle of summer. So I'm wondering if they can skip the fourth grade here."

"That's funny," said Mrs. Meredith. "That's what I was going to ask you. I've already talked with the Principal about it. And she said she was going to ask me about it.

"And there's another thing. She told me the schoolboard's naming me teacher of the year this year. I told her Annie taught me everything I know, or at least how to be teacher of the year.

But she said the teacher of the year has to be a teacher. Semantics I guess."

"Policy semantics," I said, and she laughed.

"Well," she said. "Everybody knows it anyway, and I'll say so when they give me the certificate. But they're giving it to me mostly because of the improvement in the class's overall grade point average. So I guess it's a statistical thing too.

"I don't know if they know Annie tamed Bobby, and I don't know if they know the other kids in the class are also happier now, but I know it. And I'm grateful for it."

"I'm grateful for all of it. I was beginning to think my becoming a teacher was a mistake. I didn't feel I was doing the good I'd hoped to do.

"But Annie's taught me the key to that. I just need to be a facilitator. Not a preacher."

"Well," I said. "Congratulations on all counts. I don't think everyone could be such a facilitator. Or so receptive."

And that time, as I left their classroom, the four returned to it together. And Annie didn't ask me why I was there. But I told them all at once.

"So I hear you guys are going to be in the fifth grade in this school next year," I said.

But they said nothing. They grinned, but they went to their desks with no other reply, and I didn't think Mrs. Meredith would have told them before telling me and their parents. So I guessed all of them were learning their worth, all four of them, as a group.

8

Jehanne of Domremy

And they showed more of their worth that summer.

That spring, for Bobby's birthday and Suzy's a few weeks later, their parents gave them bicycles. So, when Suzy mentioned at our house that her dad had given her hers, Annie asked them whether they could ride their new bicycles to our house the next Saturday afternoon for her to see them. And that Saturday she had another suggestion.

"Billy and I do other stuff Saturday mornings," she said. "And that's when I do my laundry. But, if you're not busy doing other things, can you ride your bikes here more Saturday afternoons. So we can do more stuff together."

So, from then on, they made that ordinary each fair weather Saturday. And that summer, during their vacation from the Albion school, they also rode their bicycles to our house on weekdays. And, because Bee's parents bought her things to show they loved her, they bought her one that year to replace the smaller one they gave her for her sixth birthday.

So I bought Annie one. She hadn't learned to ride a bicycle, but she learned quickly with help from her friends, and the four went exploring. They rode all over Albion.

They rode to its parks and along the public access to the Kalamazoo River. They frequented the farmers market, that each summer was near Albion's central business district, and they attended the summer festivals in the main blocks of Albion's main street. And, putting to work the security cables they received with their bicycles, they also saw a Saturday matinee at the old movie theatre in the center of Albion's business district.

But they saw no more movies at that theatre.

I'd subscribed to Netflix since the year of its founding. So Annie already was watching movies with me and talking with me about them in ways showing she not only enjoyed the films but also thought of how they were relevant to circumstances in the world beyond them. So, when I heard the four talking about the movie they saw together in the theatre, I gave them my Netflix password and username.

So, Saturday afternoons after that, they returned from their exploring early enough to watch movies together in our living room and hear them through our home entertainment center's 5.1 surround sound system.

They decided together which to watch. And, after watching them, they talked about them and decided what to see next. But, in the beginning of that watching together, they watched them in the order of my Netflix queue. And, curious to know whether I'd appreciate *The Last Samurai* as much as I did when I saw it in Boston, I'd added it to my queue again. And their reaction to that film showed their character.

"I think he'll be happy now," said Annie, and Bee said that so did she.

"I don't think he'll do that other stuff again either," said Bobby. "Either the Samurai stuff or what he did before that."

"He doesn't need to," said Suzy. "He found his way home through all that, but now he's at home."

"Home is where the heart is," said Bee. "That's what my mom says."

And then they asked me whether I knew of any more movies about people making friends they didn't expect to be their friends and finding their way home.

So I suggested *ET*.

"I wonder why people think aliens would only attack us," said Suzy after they saw that. "That little guy has a big heart."

"Yeah," said Bobby. "And I think your mom's right, Bee. I mean about home being where the heart is."

So their question that led me to recommend *ET* became their main movie selection criterion.

But neither their exploring nor the movies kept them from their Web study. Having learned the value of scheduling, in assuring that they accomplish what they wished to accomplish, they continued to begin their Web study at about the same time each weekday afternoon. And they showed no indication that they enjoyed it less than anything else they did together.

So, apparently, nothing of what they did was a burden to them. And, from the beginning, they established methods to be sure all they did was equitable for all of them in all ways. And, also from the beginning, they did that both deliberately and easily.

"If we're going to do this every day," said Annie the day they began working on the Web school together, "shouldn't we take turns putting what we're doing into the computer, so we all can learn that too? Maybe somebody else tomorrow and somebody else the next day? Like that?"

"Yeah," said Bobby. "And we're friends. So we don't need any of us to be boss."

So how they did everything they did together was how Bee never needed to catch up with any of them in anything. And, during that summer, suggesting that they thought their study might be more important than other things they did, they extended their time for that through all the time they'd done other things together evenings after school. So, while they never hurried, they finished the fourth grade in the middle of July and started the fifth grade in the Web school the same day.

Yet, nevertheless, they looked further ahead.

The week after they started the fifth grade in the Web school, they asked me whether I thought they could skip it on the Web, and start the sixth grade on the Web then.

"We'll do the fifth grade stuff at the Albion school anyway," said Annie.

So I told them I thought they could do anything they thought they could do. So, with the Web school not requiring permission, they went from the third grade to the sixth grade in less than two months and never asked me for help with that transition. But, in August, Annie took a short vacation from her academic education but not from her exploring.

She'd finished reading her big book and lent it to Bee. And, though Bee's spending more time than the others with Annie at our house gave her the first opportunity to borrow it, Annie's mentioning things she learned from it had become an ordinary part of the study group's conversations. So it gave some cultural weight to their study of history and geography.

But the general interest in it among the group, with the references to France and other countries in it and Annie's also studying French and Chinese with me through that year, also had kept prominent in my mind my promise to her that we'd go to France for her birthday that year.

So, while Annie and I were working on our French at the study table the evening of the study group's asking me what I thought of the possibility of their skipping the fifth grade in the Web school, I reminded Annie of that promise.

"Do you remember we talked about going to France for your birthday this year?" I asked.

And, of course, she nodded.

"I want to see the Louvre and Versailles," she said. "If we go."

"I was already planning on it," I said grinning.

And then she grinned and wriggled in her chair.

"Then we need to take a little ride to the post office," I said after replying to her grin and wiggle by widening my grin. "You'll need a passport, and I need to renew mine. And I'm thinking that, if you'd like to do more exploring than that, we might also see some of France further from Paris than Versailles. I don't remember whether your book says anything about the girl people call Joan of Arc. Have you heard of her?"

And she shook her head.

"Well," I said, "She was French. So her name wasn't Joan. It was Jehanne."

And I told her Jehanne wasn't from Arc but from the tiny French town Domremy. But I also told her what she did for France when she was sixteen years old and what that bishop and his court of fifty priests did to her for that. So then she wept.

Annie wept. With tears flowing down her face. She put her elbows on the table, held her head in her hands, and sobbed. The only other time I'd seen her weep was when she was looking at her new belongings on her bed the day we became friends. So, again, I did the only thing I could think to do.

Reaching across the corner of the table between us I put my hands on hers and turned her face toward mine.

"She's in your heart," I said.

And she stopped sobbing. Immediately.

And, when I turned up my hands beside her face in surprise, she wiped the tears from it and smiled.

"And everywhere else?" she said. "Like my mom?"

"And we can go to her house," I said, smiling with her, in my continuing wonder at how she kept proving herself . "All that was nearly six centuries ago, but the house where she grew up is still there. So we can rent a car and drive to it. If you'd like to."

And, still smiling, she nodded. So, making one more use of her birth certificate, a few weeks later we received our passports in the mail. So, the next week, we were on another plane.

We were flying to France. We arrived at De Gaulle Airport on the morning of Annie's ninth birthday and rented a car at the airport. But, because Domremy had no hotel I could find on the Web, we drove from the airport to Coussey.

Not quite as small as Domremy, Coussey was about four kilometers from Domremy and had a little hotel on its town square, *La Place Jeanne d'Arc*. In the middle of the square was a fountain with a statue of Jehanne in the middle of the fountain. And parking for the hotel was also in the square.

"*C'est Jehanne?*" asked Annie as she climbed out of our rental car.

"Yes," I said, and she crossed the square to the fountain, stood looking at the statue several minutes, and took a picture of it.

Then she returned to me to check into the little hotel.

"*Nous sommes ici pour voir la pucelle*," she said to the woman who checked us in.

""*Tu es aussi une pucelle*," said the woman, and both she and Annie smiled.

And, after showing us to our room, she also served us our lunch in the hotel's small restaurant.

"*Tres bonne*," she said. "*Une petite fille Americaine qui parle Française. Tres belle.*"

Annie had slept a little on the plane and was alert to everything as we walked through the airport and during our drive to Coussey. And, when I asked her after lunch whether she wanted to take a nap before we drove on to Domremy, she shook her head and said she wasn't tired. So we returned then to the rental car and drove the four kilometers to the old farmhouse.

She smiled at the young woman who collected our admission fee in the reception building. But she said nothing to her, and neither did she say anything as we went outside and approached the house, or as she explored it. After about a minute of silently looking at it from outside, she went inside and stood just inside its front door, for about another minute.

The house had no furniture. But the front room was the largest and had a large fireplace, and beside the fireplace stood two large placards, telling of the house. One of them said Jehanne's parents slept in the front room, that her two brothers slept in the larger of the first floor's other two other rooms, and that Jehanne slept in the smaller with her younger sister. The house also had a second floor, but the placard said it was for chickens when Jehanne lived there, and a metal gate at the bottom of the stairs kept us from going up them.

So, before reading the placards, Annie went from the front door to the gate and looked up the stairs. But, after reading the placards, she placed a hand on each side of the fireplace for about a minute before going into the larger of the other two rooms and placing a hand on each of its walls. Then she went into the smallest of the three rooms, the one the placard said was Jehanne's, and there she did the same.

But she also looked from that room's window. It was less than two feet square, and Annie had to stand on tiptoes to look from it, but she stood that way with a hand on the wall on each side of it for several minutes. And then she turned from the window, looked around the room again, and went outside.

And then she looked back at the house.

It showed no indication of any renovation or maintenance since Jehanne lived in it. So I thought Annie might say something of that. And she did.

But what she said showed both the directness and the thoughtfulness I should have expected of her.

"It's dirty now," she said as we returned to the rental car. "But I think she liked it."

Then we drove on to find our way to the next place we planned to see in our exploration of the history of Jehanne's saving France from England.

But we hadn't planned our next stop.

"What's that," asked Annie as we passed a stone church at the intersection where we turned onto the road that would take us from Domremy.

So I stopped and backed up to see it more clearly.

"Is that where she went to church?" asked Annie.

I'd told her witnesses at the trial her mother instigated to invalidate the one that sent her to the stake said she went to church every day and more than once on many days.

"I don't know," I said. "But I think it looks old enough. Do you want to see if it is?"

I'd also told her Jehanne's parish priest said at the trial that he told her she didn't need to confess so often. And I'd also told her other witnesses were her childhood friends and that they said they thought she was too pious. But I'd also told her they also said they loved her.

So, in front of the church, Annie nodded. So I parked beside it, and we tried its front door, but it didn't open. So she shrugged.

But she placed her right hand on the old wooden door, placed her left hand on the wall on the left side of the door, and kept her hands that way for more than a minute.

And, as we walked to the corner of the church where we'd parked the car, she touched several more of the wall's stones.

I didn't think of it when she was touching the walls of Jehanne's house. But, as we walked back to our rental car, I remembered her gliding a hand across the tops of our washer and dryer her first day in our house. And then we drove the kilometer from Domremy to Greux.

"I think an uncle of hers lived in this little village," I said. "My understanding is that she walked here from Domremy and asked him for a ride in his wagon to Vaucouleurs. I read that her father said he dreamed she was a soldier and that he'd rather have her brothers drown her. So I guess that may have been part of why she didn't ask him for the ride."

Annie said nothing to that, but she shook her head and frowned, and we continued the eighteen more kilometers to Vaucouleurs.

And there she touched more stones. As we planned that trip, talking a little about how Jehanne did the two things she said God told her to do to save her homeland from a century of foreign invasion, I told her she talked the captain of the command post in Vaucouleurs into giving her an escort to Chinon to ask the Dauphin to give her command of France's armies. So the stones she touched in Vaucouleurs were of walls of the ruins of the command post.

I also told her that, because her father's farm was a sheep farm, the first horse she rode was one the people of Vaucouleur gave her for the three-hundred-mile ride to Chinon through enemy territory. And I also told her the Dauphin took her to Poitier for some clerical scholars and others to examine her for any reason he shouldn't accept her help. But I also told her nothing remained either of the palace at Chinon or of the original buildings of the University of Poitier.

So I also asked her whether she wished to see those two cities anyway.

"No," she said. "That's OK. I just want to see what she saw."

So, after breakfast next morning at the little hotel in Coussey, we drove to Orleans.

There, after again checking into our hotel at about lunchtime, we walked to that city's main square in search of a restaurant. A statue of Jehanne was also in the center of that square, and Annie stopped to take a picture of that statue also, but we didn't stop for lunch there. We continued on until, at an end of the city's main bridge across the Loire, we found a café and stopped for both lunch and the view of the bridge and the river.

"When Jehanne was here," I said as we ate, "the city had a wall around it. And that bridge was the main bridge across the river then too. So, for the river traffic, the main gate through the wall was here at this end of the bridge. But the English started the siege about six months before Jehanne arrived, and one of the half dozen fortifications the English were using for the siege was right over there, on that side of this end of the bridge. So, during those months, no one could use the gate that was here.

"So, for Jehanne and her army to bring into the city the food and other things they brought for the people here, they had to bring it through a side gate. But, in about ten days, they ran the English out of every one of those fortifications. And the last one they took was the one right over there.

"So can you imagine the cheers of the people when Jehanne and her soldiers rode into the city through the gate that was here?"

"How do you know so much about her," asked Annie, after grinning at that.

"I don't remember how I first heard of her," I said. "But, for a story I once wrote about some courageous people, I needed to base a character on a courageous woman and thought of Jehanne.

"So I read a book about her, and that book made me like her. So I read more about her, and everything I read about her made me like her more. And now she reminds me of you.

"You can do whatever you decide to do too. You're not a warrior, but she never killed anyone, and I think that by itself is wonderful. She had the sword I told you about, and she was at the front of every charge, but she never used the sword in battle.

"She led with her horse and her banner, and she wept the first time she saw the battle dead, and she let the survivors go if they promised to go back to England and not come back to France."

"Then why does that statue of her here have a horse and a sword but no banner?" asked Annie. "In the one in Coussey, she's holding her banner in one hand, and her other hand's on her heart. And she isn't on a horse, and her sword's in its . . . . What do you call those things people put swords in?"

"Scabbards," I said. "And I don't know why the statue here is like that, but the sword's pointing down. So I think the sculptor may have been trying to say she was trying to end the war. But I don't think that would explain why it doesn't have a banner.

"She designed her banner, with the names of Jesus and Mary on it and *fleurs de lis* in its corners, making it a kind of symbol of what she was trying to do and why and how."

"My book," said Annie. "I mean our artbook. It says sometimes artists try to make portraits look like what the artists want to say about the subjects instead of trying to make them look how they look to most people. So do you think Jehanne looked like the statue here, or the one in Coussey, or neither one?"

"I don't know how either could look like her," I said. "I've read that no one painted any portrait of her while she was alive. So I think those sculptors must have just imagined what she looked like, and I think your book is right, about that.

"And I don't think I've seen any two pictures of either Jehanne or the Buddha that look the same."

"I like our Buddha," said Annie.

"So do I, little friend," I said.

And from the café we walked to where the gate through which Jehanne brought in the food had been, and there we found a small park and sat on a bench, and talked a little more.

"So you like her so much because of her curiosity and compassion and courage?" asked Annie.

"And her faith," I said. "And I don't mean her faith in Christianity. Whether or not God told her to do those two things I told you she said he told her to do, we have no historical evidence that she said he told her how to do them or explained to her the military importance of raising the siege here or the political importance of escorting the Dauphin to Reims for his coronation, and I doubt that many adults then or now would expect any sixteen-year-old farm girl who couldn't read or write anything other than her name to be able to do what she did. But she did.

"And you're like that. If you think something's worth doing, you don't say you can't because you don't know how. You just jump in and figure out how to do it while you're doing it."

"Is that why you told me she's in my heart?" asked Annie.

"Yes," I said. "Because you have so much room in your heart, because you're you. And it's also why I asked you whether you'd heard of her. I thought you might like her too."

And the next morning we drove to Reims. We arrived there in late morning and parked about two blocks from the cathedral on the street ending at the square in front of it. And, in that square, we found another statue of Jehanne.

"A horse and a sword and no banner again," said Annie as we entered the square. "And that sword's pointing up."

"I don't understand it either," I said. "And this is a church."

So Annie shrugged. But then, when I stopped talking, she stopped walking. She turned her attention to the church.

"Pictures of it are in our artbook," she said. "Those are flying buttresses. And that's a rose window."

And inside she stopped at the beginning of the central aisle and said nothing for more than a minute.

"But the pictures don't make me feel like this," she said. "Look at those windows, the colors and the light. And it's so quiet in here."

And she said nothing as we walked around the ambulatory and returned to the square. And then a woman and two young girls were looking at the statue, as the girls held the woman's hands, as she talked. And Annie smiled.

And from there we returned to De Gaulle Airport to return the car. From there we took the *Métro* into Paris, and a taxi to the bottom of Montmartre, to check into our hotel. And then we climbed the hill to *la Basilique du Sacré Coeur* and surveyed the Paris skyline.

"There's the Eiffel Tower," said Annie.

But then she turned to the basilica and looked up at its bell towers and the statues over its entrance.

"There's another statue of Jehanne on her horse with no banner," she said. "And sword's pointing up too. And those cupolas on the campaniles in the corners look kind of like what our artbook says Muslims did to *Hagia Sophia* when they made it a mosque after they took Istanbul from Christians, after Romans took it from Greeks after Romans and Greeks fought over the world like all that fighting between Israelites and Philistines over the land of Canaan you told me about, when we were talking about the fighting between the Israelis and the Palestinians now."

"Out of the mouths of babes," I thought, smiling at my little friend *Ān Nǔ*'s departure from her ordinary quietness long enough not only to show the extraordinary vocabulary she'd developed through her conscientious curiosity but also to express the conscientiously comprehensive concept of about three millennia of world history she'd also developed through that caring attention.

"But our artbook says this church is newer than *Hagia Sophia*," she said. "Do you think they put those cupolas there to make it look like a mosque to get along with the Muslims?"

"Oh, little friend," I said. "A lot of Muslims live in this neighborhood now. But I don't know of any historical evidence of that either."

And we didn't spend much time inside that church. But we ate a late lunch at a nearby café before leaving the hill and exploring the neighborhood at the bottom of it. And next morning we took the *Métro* to the *Cathédrale Notre Dame de Paris*.

"Those are putti," said Annie as we looked at the *pietà* behind the alter. "They're supposed to look like angels, but I think they look like pictures of Cupid. Do you know if most Christians think angels look like that?"

"I doubt that most Christians think Michael looked like that," I said.

I'd told her the archangel Michael was one of the three saints through whom Jehanne said God spoke to her to tell her to do what she did to save France from England. So she smiled at my reply, and then we found our way to the chapel behind the *pietà*, where what the Roman Catholic Church says was Jesus' crown of thorns was in a translucent blood red box. But Annie said nothing of that.

And next we walked along the Seine to the *Louvre*.

Exploring it, through the remainder of that morning, we saw more of Monet's work. And, after lunch there, we continued exploring it through much of that afternoon. But what held Annie's attention most there was the *Nike of Samothrace*.

As soon as we could see it, she stopped and stood still to look at it standing on its stone ship at the top of a flight of stairs, at the far end of a long hallway. Then, looking at nothing else, she walked down the middle of the hallway until she came to the steps. And at their bottom she stopped and stood still again.

After several minutes, of looking up at it from there, she turned to go. But then she stopped again and turned back and stood looking up at it for several more minutes. And she did that twice more before taking a hand of mine for us to walk up the stairway. And she kept her silence until we passed the statue and turned into another hallway. And still she said nothing of the *Nike*.

From the *Louvre*, we walked to where an arrow hit Jehanne while she was laying fagots in the moat around Paris in hope of her troops' crossing it to scale the city's walls to take it back from the English, and that walk took us through the square with Paris' main monument to Jehanne, a large gold leaf *equestrienne* statue.

"A banner," said Annie grinning. "And her sword's in its scabbard."

But the only marker for the place where the arrow hit Jehanne was a small relief sculpture of her face between the first and second stories of the facade of a building.

So, after Annie took a picture of that, we returned to the Seine and walked along it to the *Champs-Élysées*. After supper, at a sidewalk café on the *Champs-Élysées*, we continued to the *Arc de Triomphe*. And, the next morning, we took a train to Versailles.

Annie wished most to see the gardens. But, after exploring them for about an hour, we explored the palace. So we found the huge painting of Jehanne at Orleans in its *Galerie des Batailles*.

"A horse and no banner or sword," said Annie. "But she's so famous here! Pictures and statues of her are everywhere! So I guess the French people haven't forgotten her anyway. And they still love her."

And, after lunch in the palace, we returned to Paris and took the elevators to the top of *le Tour Eiffel*.

"There's *la basilique*," said Annie as we waited in line for the elevator from the tower's middle observation level to its top. "It's as far as we can see the ground from here."

And she walked all the way around the top level.

"You can't see it from here," she said. "I mean the *basilique*. The horizon's further away from up here."

And the next morning we flew home and replaced three more red tacks with yellow ones on our map of Earth.

Annie bought but four souvenirs in France. She bought a small metal replica of *le Tour Eiffel* for each member of her study group. But, after copying to her computer the pictures she took there, she connected her computer to our TV through our wireless home entertainment system.

So, when the group gathered at our house the day after our return, she used our TV to show them the pictures.

"That's the Basilica of the Sacred Heart in the middle of the horizon," she said. "I took that picture from only about halfway up the tower. I couldn't see it from the top, because it was mixed up with the other buildings around it, and I couldn't find it. It's on a hill, but the tower's higher than the hill, a lot higher.

"From the top you can see roofs of buildings on the other side of the hill. Our hotel was on this side of the hill but was at its bottom. So I couldn't tell where it was from either level."

And then she clicked on the next picture.

"That's from the top," she said.

"I want to go there!" said Bobby.

"Who doesn't?" said Suzy, laughing.

And Bee's sudden inhale expressed her agreement.

"We came home the day after we went to the Eiffel Tower," said Annie after smiling but not laughing. "But we did this on our first day in France."

And then she showed them her pictures of Domremy.

"That was my favorite part," she said. "And it was on my birthday."

And she held their attention for more than an hour more, laughing and talking with them and answering their questions, from Vaucouleurs through Versailles

And the next day they returned to their routine.

9

Making it Official

But a few days later, while they were studying, Miss Walker came to see us. She hadn't come to see us since, at about the same time the previous year, she asked whether she might. And, because Annie was studying, I answered our doorbell.

Ordinarily, welcoming anyone, Annie did that.

"I wanted to come more often," said Miss Walker following me inside. "But the opioid epidemic is getting worse, and I could be doing other things now too. So I can only stay a minute.

"But I needed a break and thought of Annie."

"Hi, Miss Walker!" said Annie, and she left her chair to welcome Miss Walker with a handshake, and of course a grin. "These are my friends Bee and Suzy and Bobby. I told you about Bee the last time you were here."

"Nice to meet you Bee and Suzy and Bobby," said Miss Walker smiling at them as she had at Annie.

"This is Miss Walker," said Annie turning to them.

But then she turned back to Miss Walker.

"We're studying," she said.

"What are you studying?" asked Miss walker

"Sixth grade stuff," said Annie.

"Sixth grade?" asked Miss Walker with the intonation with which she'd said "New York?" on her visit the year before. "I thought you'd be starting the fourth grade this year."

"We skipped the fourth grade in the Albion school," said Annie. "We did it on the Web. So we'll be in the fifth grade this year in the Albion school. But we're in the sixth grade on the Web."

"And Bee skipped half of the second grade to catch up with us," said Suzy, smiling at Miss Walker and then grinning at Bee.

"That's amazing!" said Miss Walker. "You've got my head spinning! No troublemakers in this group, I'm sure."

"I used to be a troublemaker," said Bobby.

"You don't look like a troublemaker to me," said Miss Walker.

"Annie straightened me out," said Bobby.

"And then he helped us straighten our teacher out," said Suzy, then grinning at Bobby.

"And Billy and I went to France for my birthday this year," said Annie as Miss Walker grinned at Bee and Suzy and Bobby.

"She brought us little Eiffel Towers," said Bee. "Where's yours, Annie?"

"In my room," said Annie, and she brought it from her bedroom to show it to Miss Walker.

"We went up there," she said, setting it on the table and pointing to its top. "And we went to Jehanne's house too."

"Who's Jehanne?" asked Miss Walker.

"She's the sixteen-year-old girl who saved France from the English," said Annie. "People call her Joan of Arc, but her name wasn't Joan, and she wasn't from Arc. And she said God told her to save France."

"What do you think about that?" asked Miss Walker.

"I think everyone's everyone anyway," said Annie, looking at our Buddha for a moment before continuing. "But I like to call her what her name was. And she figured out how to do all that stuff she needed to do to save France, and she did it when she was still sixteen years old, and she's in my heart. So are you."

To that Miss Walker briefly frowned at Annie, and she didn't otherwise reply, until Annie spoke again.

"We saw the *Nike of Samothrace* too," she said. "She's on her stone ship at the top of some stairs in the *Louvre*."

"Now my head's spinning more," said Miss Walker, smiling then and shaking her head, as though she were awakening from some sort of trance. "You're a wonder, Annie. And you're in my heart too."

And then she turned to me.

"I don't know how you do it," she said.

"I don't do anything," I said. "That's just how Annie and her friends are. All I do is try to be sure no one stands in their way. Do you remember our first conversation?"

"I do," she said. "And I remember I thought that was a nice idea, but I also remember I also thought you'd change your mind, when you found out how seven-year-olds are. But I also thought that, because you seemed to me to be thoughtful and caring, you'd respond accordingly. And now I'm just glad I didn't stand in Annie's way."

"So am I," said Bee, grinning at Miss Walker, and Miss Walker returned that grin also.

"Well!" she said. "That's enough for me for now. Now I'm going to get out of your way and let you get back to your studies. But I'll try to stop by more often. If that's alright."

And all of the study group grinned and nodded.

"So she has room in her heart for both me and the patron saint of France?" asked Miss Walker as I walked her out to her car.

"And much more," I said. "As vast as this space around us is this space within the heart, and within it are contained both the earth and the sky."

"What's that from?" asked Miss Walker, stopping for a moment.

"The *Chandogya Upanishad*," I said. "Hinduism."

And then she looked down for moment.

"Well, anyway," she said, "in my job, I can't imagine better thanks than that, and that's a nice bicycle collection too."

And then she continued into her car and drove away.

But she kept her promise of coming back more often.

And that evening, as Annie and I sat at our dining table working on our Chinese, we talked about her life beyond the third grade. How quickly she learned Chinese made evident how she decided all she did. So that was an appropriate time for that talk..

In the beginning of that learning, having nearly no knowledge of academic opinions of how English or any other language operated, she had no prejudices obstructing her understanding the interrelationships of the Chinese language.

So, in that beginning, she learned it much as children learn their native languages. But, occasionally, she asked me the meanings of the English grammar terms the author of our Chinese grammar text used to try to explain Chinese grammar. And she easily applied those terms to both languages.

That is, responding to the Hindu Buddhist Daoist notion of the primal unity by continually giving nearly all her attention to understanding how things relate to one another, she gave nearly none of it to understanding how things differ from one another. And that was especially apparent in her regard for the fact that the Chinese people write with pictures. Her approach to semantics subordinated the abstract to visible relationships.

So, when she looked at *zì*, the pictures the Chinese people draw to represent meaning instead of writing letters to represent sounds, she tried to see what they represented before millennia of making them easier to draw simplified them nearly beyond recognition.

And, welcoming my suggestion that we extend our Chinese vocabulary beyond the examples in our Chinese grammar text, she also applied that to *Taijiquan*.

She had a Chinese-English dictionary on her computer. And I had a copy, in both Chinese and English, of the five short writings *Taijiquan* practitioners call the *Taijiquan* abiding writings. So we translated those writings together, and she applied her approach to zì directly to those in those writings, and especially to how they were pertinent to *Taijiquan*.

"*Sōng*," she said. "That's the most important word I think, and look at its *zì*. See how it looks like a tree and a human standing next to each other with their hair and leaves blowing in a breeze? The dictionary says it means 'loose', and its principal division means 'hair', and '*sōng shù*' means 'pine tree'. And that's how I feel when I'm doing our *Taijiquan*. Like I'm waving in a breeze."

"Principal division" was Annie's translation of a Chinese phrase English-speaking linguists ordinarily translate "radical". Part, and sometimes all, of each *zì* is one of the 214 *zì* that phrase designates, and Chinese dictionaries group the *zì* by those components of the *zì* and then by the number of pen strokes one needs to draw each, with the *zì* requiring fewer strokes preceding those requiring more. And the Chinese designation for that phrase is two *zì* with the first meaning "division" and the second meaning "primary".

So, considering a variance between Chinese syntax and English syntax, Annie called them principal divisions mainly because that was more literally what the Chinese called them. She was also attentive to English explanations, but her main method of translating Chinese into English was to seek literally sensible ways to understand both grammar and semantics either English or Chinese, and that also fit well with her general attitude toward all. But faith, because Annie made nothing a struggle, to her was simple fact.,

"Do you know why they call them radicals?" she asked.
"No, little friend," I said. "It seems radical to me."

129

"Me too," she said grinning. "And look. This *yú zì* means both 'to' and 'from', and its principal division means 'place'. It's like every place being everywhere at the same time."

But, also in that translating, before looking up a *zì* in her dictionary, we compared each Chinese sentence to its translation in the same book. And Annie quickly discovered that the book's translator's translation of the *zì* meaning "human" was "opponent" each time he ostensibly translated it. And she also asked me whether I knew a reason for that.

"One of the purposes of *Taijiquan*," I said, "is as an alternative to martial arts. But a lot of people use it as a martial art, instead of as an alternative to martial arts, or as you use it."

"You mean they use it for fighting?" she asked.

"Yes," I said. "Martial arts are for fighting. But, originally, when people used *Taijiquan* in fighting situations, they didn't use it for fighting. They didn't move against the opponent but with the opponent, for the two to feel as though they were moving together like what you said of the leaves and hair in that *sōng zì*, both flowing with one breeze. So the purpose was to feel they weren't opponents but one person."

"Oh," said Annie. "That makes sense to me. But I still don't understand why that translator used the word 'opponent' instead of the word 'human' or the word 'person'. I mean it still means what it means, and he could still treat people like opponents, if he liked to fight. Couldn't he?"

"I don't know," I said. "I guess he didn't understand as well as you do, or may have wanted other people to be like him, or both. And, if we found him and asked him, I don't know how we could believe his answer. I mean I think he must have done it intentionally."

"Yeah," said Annie. "And the principal divisions for '*tài*' and '*jí*' and '*quán*' mean 'big' and 'tree' and "hand". So I guess people could think of a tree and fingers as being like poles and not pay attention to how a fist is kind of round like that symbol for *yīn* and *yáng* flowing together like fingers folding into a fist. So I guess people can imagine ways to think words mean anything they want them to mean. But I still don't understand why anyone would want to think all humans are opponents. I mean I don't understand how anyone could only like to fight."

And she shrugged, and we returned to our study, and she continued looking directly at everything and everyone flowing around her. So, finding expression of that flow and unity to pervade those writings, she found in them no suggestion of anything martial. So, of course, she showed that care that evening as we talked about her life beyond the third grade.

"I'm not going to put my Chinese name on my fifth-grade papers," she said. "I don't want the other kids to think I'm trying to be smarter than they are, or different from them in other ways, either. When I started doing that, I didn't talk much with the kids at school, but now I do.

"And that was before Suzy and Bobby were my friends and before Bee was in our grade, and I don't want them to think I'm trying to think I'm smarter than they are, either.

"It's like those Republicans and Democrats on TV. They're always trying to get elected by telling people they're better than other people trying to get elected. And then they blame the other party for not getting anything done and call it congressional gridlock. At least that's what they seem to me to be doing.

"I looked those words up in our dictionary. It says a congress is supposed to be people working together. But it says gridlock's people keeping each other from getting things done.

"They need to try to understand each other. Look at all the stuff Bee and Suzy and Bobby and I get done by understanding each other. And, if I act like I think those politicians act, everybody'll think I don't make any sense either. And they'll think I think they don't either. What do you think?"

"I think you're going to be a great Secretary-General of the United Nations," I said. "If you don't find something else to do that you think is more important."

So her fifth grade teacher never called me. So my first conversation with her was for our midyear parent-teacher conference. But that conversation was remarkably different from that conversation with Annie.

"It's remarkable how four kids that intelligent happened to find each other in this tiny town," she said. "It's extraordinary."

"I think it's the other way around," I said. "People didn't think any of them were especially intelligent until after they found one another. Then they learned together."

"I don't think it works that way," said the teacher. "Intelligence isn't learning. It's the ability to learn, and studies show that it's established before school age, and probably before birth. IQ's don't generally improve with education."

"But think of those four kids," I said. "They have eight remarkably different parents, and their lives before elementary school were also remarkably different from each other's in other ways, extraordinarily different. Altogether, for different reasons, when they found one another, two of their fathers and two of their mothers were absent from their homes. And, half of the year the three with the absent parents were in the third grade, Bee was in the second grade. She's the one with no missing parents.

"And at least the other three had problems learning before they became friends. Some people called Annie a troublemaker, and Suzy's third grade teacher said she was the slowest kid in her class, and Bobby was the class bully. So isn't a question how none of them seemed intelligent until they became friends?

"And aren't they helping your other students learn?"

"They are," said the teacher. "But I think that must be because congeniality's a function of intelligence."

"You think being called a troublemaker or slow or being a

bully indicates congeniality?" I asked. "And at least those three, the ones with the missing parents, learned much of their congeniality by trying to understand one another because other people weren't congenial enough to try to understand them. And surely understanding and compassion are reciprocal causes, as they're also the foundation of the common decency of what Christians call the golden rule, but surely loneliness must also have been a factor in those three trying to understand one another. And haven't you noticed how much of what they say both to one another and to others is questions?"

"That's just politeness," she said. "Or curiosity."

I don't know whether that conversation led that teacher to learn more from her students during the second half of that schoolyear. But I know Mrs. Meredith was teacher of the year again that year and not only for the Albion school but also for all the public schools in the county. And I know the study group also skipped the Albion school's sixth grade.

And I also know the friendship between Suzy and Bobby had a substantial effect on their parents.

"I told my mom about your mom," said Bobby to Suzy at our house during the first schoolyear of the study group's friendship. "And she said she though that, because we're such good friends, inviting you and your dad to our house for dinner some night might be a good idea, but she asked me to ask you what you think, if it's OK with me. So what do you think?

And Suzy completed that process in the way it began.

"It's OK with me," she said. "If it's OK with my dad."

And about two weeks later I heard that Suzy's father had reciprocated by taking Bobby's mom and Bobby and Suzy to dinner at Win Schuler's, a restaurant in Marshall with a reputation for being the finest restaurant between Detroit and Chicago, but I didn't learn how close their parents became until more than year later. While the study group was at school, their last week in the fifth grade, our doorbell rang. And I found Suzy's and Bobby's parents, whom I'd never met, at our door.

"Nice to meet you!" I said grinning when they introduced themselves. "This is great! Come in!"

And, after accepting my offer of seats but declining my offer of something to drink, they told me why they were there.

"We're getting married," said Bobby's mom.

"And we're wondering if you'd be a witness at our wedding," said Suzy's dad.

"You must know Annie and Bee are Suzy's and Bobby's best friends," said Bobby's mom.

"And all this is pretty important to them," said Suzy's dad.

"So we're thinking of asking Bee's mom too," Said Bobby's mom, and I delightedly accepted, and both thanked me.

"Do you think Bee's mom's at home?" asked Suzy's dad.

"I think so," I said, looking out our front window. "Her car's there. I think her work hours are a little irregular."

And Corinthia also delightedly accepted. I watched from our front window as they walked across the street and knocked on her front door. And she reacted much as she did when I told her Bee could skip to the third grade.

Initially she leaned through her doors with a questioning look. And, about a minute later, she leaned back her head and laughed. But she also hugged them both.

So both Suzy and Bobby were to have two parents at home again and the same parents. And, the next Saturday, Corinthia and Bee rode with Annie and me to the wedding ceremony in a small church in Albion with Corinthia and me and the study group the only guests. Then, after the brief ceremony, Corinthia and I gave Suzy's and Bobby's parents the wedding gifts we took to the church for them, and Corinthia and I returned home with Bee and Annie.

But, of course, that marriage had some effects on all of us longer than the ceremony.

One, of course, was the combining of homes. Monday at our house Susie and Bobbie told Annie and Bee that Suzy and her dad had moved into Bobby's and his mom's home that weekend. They said the reasons for that were that Bobby's mom had received her and Bobby's house in her divorce settlement, that Suzy's dad had been renting the house that was Suzy's and his home, and that it was much smaller than Bobby's and his mom's house. And, of course, a result of that was simplification of my schoolyear evening drives. But, about two weeks after the wedding, Annie suggested another change.

"Why don't you adopt me?" she asked as we were eating supper. "You love me, don't you?"

"With all my heart and soul and mind," I said. "I just thought you might want to keep your mom's name."

"That isn't her name," she said. "It's my dad's name. And my mom told me he left us as soon as he found out she was going to have me. And I think you're already more of a dad to me than I think he ever would have been. Maybe more than anyone else is to anyone. And I like your name."

So I told her I'd see what we needed to do. So the next afternoon, while the study group was out exploring, I called Miss Walker to ask her what we needed to do. And she called the Judge we needed to approve the process, told me what the Judge told her we needed to do, and expedited the process.

So we completed it before our trip for Annie's birthday that year, and we'd decided to spend more time on that trip then we had on our previous trips together, to travel across China and Nepal and northeastern India.

So, when we flew across the Pacific together, we were officially a family.

10

And Also All

We spent the first three nights of that trip in Beijing. On our first full day there, because our hotel was less than a mile from the Forbidden City and Tiananmen Square, we walked to both. I knew the way because our hotel was where I stayed on my other trip there seven years earlier.

"Our artbook says only the Emperor could go through this gate," said Annie as we passed through the main entrance to the Forbidden City.

And in its first courtyard, to look at the buildings surrounding it, she stopped and turned all the way around.

"Look at all this red," she said. "I looked up the Chinese name of this place. It means 'purple forbidden city', but I don't know why. I guess they call it forbidden because most people couldn't come in here, but do you know why they call it red?"

"No, little friend," I said. "Purple's a mixture of red and blue, and it's a royal color in other countries, but I don't think that explains it."

"Well," she said, "I like it anyway."

And then she twirled all the way around again, and she also did that in the middle of each of its other two courtyards, before we explored inside any of the buildings.

"Our art book says only the emperor and his family and people they invited could come this far back," she said in the third courtyard. "But I guess they invited the servants."

And, after exploring the rooms around each courtyard as we returned to the main gate to leave, she twirled around in the center of each again.

But we spent fewer than fifteen minutes in Tiananmen Square. When we emerged into it from the tunnel beneath the street between it and the Forbidden City, Annie looked around at all the government buildings, but then she shrugged. And then she looked back across the street at the Forbidden City.

"Look at that big picture of Mao," she said, shrugging again, and we wandered on to explore the gardens and other imperial aspects of the neighborhood around the Forbidden City.

But we spent most of the next day at the Great Wall.

We went by bus to a section of it about forty miles north of Beijing, climbed to a watchtower and continued to another and on to one more. On my previous trip there, I climbed only to the first tower and stopped about a half dozen times on the way up, to sit on the steps. So I remembered the signs in English telling people to watch for people with heart problems.

But that was before my more than five years of daily *Taijiquan* and *dhyana yoga*. So, while I was there with Annie, I kept up with most of the others climbing the steps. But Annie skipped ahead and reached the first watchtower before I was halfway up to it.

Then she climbed the steps inside it and took a picture of me from its roof, and the next day we flew to Dunhuang to see the Mogao Grottoes, and the Gobi Desert.

Dunhuang was at a major fork in the Silk Road. So Bodhidharma, the Buddhist monk who formulated Zen and probably *Taijiquan*, may have stopped there on his way from Persia to the Shaolin Monastery, after trekking from India across the Himalaya's and west to the Buddhist community in Persia. And the oldest book in print with a date in print in it is a Chinese translation of the *Diamond Sutra* from Dunhuang.

The date is in 868, but in the grottoes are hundreds of Buddhist temples with imaginings of the Buddha, some of which Buddhists carved into the sandstone at the edge of the desert centuries before the fifth century birth of Bodhidharma. So, while seeing the Gobi Desert may have been plenty of reason for Annie to wish to go there, our conversations regarding the Buddha and Bodhidharma were why she wished to see it at Dunhuang. Her understanding of the Buddha was our main reason for that trip.

"You said the Buddha was from Nepal and taught in India," she said when she read of the grottoes in *Gardner's*. "And so does this book. So why is our Buddha and a lot of the art this book says is Buddhist from China? And why is *Taijiquan* Buddhist?"

And those questions and other situations relevant to the trip led to many other questions at other times and for other reasons. So all those questions together developed our itinerary for most of that trip through those three countries. But ordinarily she pondered her questions in her heart until she could ask them clearly.

And still she didn't ask them until circumstances might permit a careful response. And, when she had no reason to ask a question or share her thoughts, she didn't. And she never interrupted what others were saying.

So, during our tour of the grottoes with the group of other English-speaking tourists to which the caretakers of the grottoes assigned us, she said nothing. The tour was more than an hour, and Annie looked at everything to which the tour guide directed our attention, but she asked not one question. And, having learned what an *ān nǔ* she was, neither did I.

But she spoke in the desert the next day.

"I like Chinese architecture," she said as we climbed to the top of the pagoda at the Crescent Lake oasis.

But she said nothing as she looked around from its top. The next time she spoke was after I followed her over a high hill and up a lower one from which we could see neither the pagoda nor the city. There she stopped and turned all the way around, as she had in the courtyards of the Forbidden City, and then she spoke.

"Sand," she said. "As far as we can see."

But next morning, to join a tour group to fly to Lhasa, we flew to Chengdu. The Chinese government wasn't permitting tourists to visit Tibet individually, and I'd found on the Web a Chengdu travel agency that connected individual travelers to tour groups, but we flew to Chengdu three days before we were to fly to Lhasa. We did that to spend a day in Shangli.

I'd tried to go to Lhasa that way on my previous trip to China. But, because Buddhists then were immolating their ostensibly physical presences because of an escalation in the Chinese government's efforts to tell people how to behave in Tibet, the Chinese government was permitting no tourist travel there then. So changing my flight reservations left me in Chengdu for four nights with no reason to be there.

So, to see China's central mountains, I took a bus to Ya'an. And in my hotel room there, searching the Web for nearby places that might especially interest me, I learned of Shangli. So, the day between my two nights in Ya'an, I took a minibus there and took the picture of the kids playing with corn I showed to Annie while showing her pictures of China in response to her asking whether China was really yellow. So, in our planning our trip to China, she showed me that picture and asked me where it was and nodded to my telling her and asking whether she'd like to go there. So we took the same side trip.

"Look at those mountains," she said during the twenty-mile minibus ride from Ya'an to Shangli. "I thought the painters just imagined those watercolor pictures in our artbook. I didn't think trees could grow on the side of a cliff that's straight up like that. And the fog's like in the paintings too."

Streams surrounded the village. And the Chinese government had preserved the village for tourists and didn't permit motor vehicles in it. So the minibus left us across the road from a bridge to the village's entrance.

So we began our exploration of the village by walking across the bridge and then walking down the village's central thoroughfare with no particular destination in mind. But soon we came to where on my previous visit the kids were playing with the corn. And some kids were also doing that there then.

"This is about the time of year I was here before," I said. "I wonder if it's something they do every harvesttime."

And Annie shrugged. She also asked the children in Chinese what they were doing. But, though they looked up, they also shrugged.

"I guess shrugging's the same in Chinese as it is in English," said Annie, shrugging again but grinning, but then the only girl of that group of four little kids spoke.

"*Nǐmen shì Měiguó rén ma?*" she asked also grinning.

So Annie, replying affirmatively, grinned more widely.

The littler girl was asking Annie whether we were American people. "*Měiguó*", partly because it sounds somewhat like "America" and partly because it literally means "beautiful nation", is Chinese for "America". And the little girl responded to Annie's widening her grin by also widening hers.

But Annie didn't stay to talk further.

After some waves and more grins, we continued exploring and left the central thoroughfare to wander through byways, but we didn't wander far before coming to the southern edge of the village. And the stream along that edge of it had stone banks and stone bridges with a row of restaurants along its bank on its village side and rice paddies along its opposite bank. So, deciding to stop moving for a while to see how others moved around us, we sat at a table in front of a restaurant.

A man with a huge bundle of sticks on his back was walking toward us on a dike between two of the rice paddies. So Annie watched him until he looked toward us. Then she grinned and waved at him.

And he replied with a nod and a big grin of his own.

Then a woman sitting at a table beside ours also grinned at Annie. And, as the man turned down another dike, the woman looked at me and looked back at Annie and asked her in Chinese whether I was her grandfather. So Annie told her in Chinese that I was her father.

She'd continued calling me Billy, when she was talking to me or with people who knew our names, but she called me her dad when she was speaking to people who didn't. And then the woman looked at me again and grinned again, and then the others at her table also looked at me and grinned, but Annie asked them what we should drink. They recommended *suān méi zhī*, a cold plum drink that's traditional and popular in China, and we tried it.

And, after that, we drank it with our every meal in China. And, during the remainder of our exploration of the village, Annie spoke only Chinese. I'd become fluent enough in it to understand her and most replies to her in it, but she'd become far more fluent in it than I, and we didn't eat lunch at that restaurant. Our lunch that day was at a restaurant with a wooden terrace overlooking the stream at the northeastern corner of the village. There, after flowing toward the village from higher mountains before making of the village a kind of delta, the stream was shallow and rocky. And some people were using some stones in the stream as stepping stones to cross it. So Annie did to them what she did to the man with the sticks in the rice paddies. But, their hands being free, they responded with both grins and waves.

And no other customers were at the restaurant. So, after lunch on the terrace, Annie told the young woman who waited on us that her sitting and talking with us would please us very much.

The manners of *Ān Nǚ* in *Zhōngguó* were as impeccable as Annie's were in America.

So she and the young woman had a long pleasant conversation there, and Annie also talked with other passengers on the minibus, as we returned to Ya'an.

In Ya'an, as we explored the center of the city before supper, a statue near the river drew her attention. It was a large bronze statue of a man and a woman sitting with their feet beneath them and nothing of them other than their heads visible outside their robes while they kissed with nothing other than the tips of their lips touching. Annie stopped and stood silently looking up at the statue for several minutes, reminding me of my only remaining concern regarding her, how to tell her about puberty. But that could wait a year or two, and I was learning to take things as they came, as did Annie. So, with no conversation about that, next we found a restaurant for supper.

We spent most of the remainder of that evening on Ya'an's central bridge across the Qingyi River. The bridge, a wide mostly wooden footbridge with curving traditional Chinese rooves over it, also drew Annie's attention. And, as we sat among others relaxing in the evening on benches in the shade of the bridge's rooves, she talked with a grandmother and granddaughter.

The next day we returned to Chengdu to join the tour group, and the next morning we flew with the group to Lhasa, where we spent three nights. During our two full days there we did all the tour guides guided the group to do. But Annie didn't constrain herself to that.

She skipped up the 432 steps of the Potala Palace as lightly as she'd skipped up the steps of the Great Wall. Then, from that former seat of the Dalai Lama, she took a picture of me and the other members of the tour group before we were halfway up. And she added light to the others' visit in other ways also.

"I should have brought my granddaughter," said one.

And, exchanging grins with every monk we passed and greeting them in Chinese, she found some who spoke Chinese and spoke with them. She spoke with them at varying lengths but easily drew nods and smiles from each monk she passed. And from Lhasa we flew to Kathmandu.

But our purpose for visiting Nepal wasn't to see the Buddha's birthplace but to see Mount Everest. We didn't land on it, but we flew from Kathmandu past it and back, on a twin-engine propeller-driven Beechcraft aircraft. As we flew past it, a flight attendant conducted each of us sixteen passengers sequentially to the cockpit for the pilot to tell us what we were seeing, but the pilot gave Annie more of his time and talk than he gave to any of the other passengers.

"So we're on the mostly *yáng* side of it," said Annie to him when he told her Tibet was on the other side of the mountain. "And Tibet's on the mostly *yīn* side."

I'd told her, when we were translating the *Taijiquan* abiding writings, that "*yīn*" and "*yáng*" originally referred to how shade and sunlight shifted across mountains as each day passed but didn't divide the mountains.

But the next morning we flew to Varanasi. And that was for the Buddha, to see the deer sanctuary where Buddhists say he set into motion the wheel of truth, what the seminal *sutta* of Buddhism says he did there. But, on our way from our hotel in Varanasi to the deer sanctuary in Sarnath, Annie laughed at the cows in the streets.

And, all the way, showing once again that she was as fearless as she was congenial, as she had peering down from the crown of the Statue of Liberty and from the upper observation level of the Eiffel Tower, she laughed at the tiny old three-wheel open taxi lurching and swerving as its driver sped it and us through the other traffic as taxi drivers ordinarily do in India.

But she didn't laugh in the sanctuary. We spent a few minutes in the temple where Buddhists say the Buddha said and did what the *Dhammacakkappavattana Sutta* says he said and did there. Then we wandered the grounds and found the rusty old carnival ride there to symbolize the wheel of truth. But no one was there to operate the wheel. So we didn't ride it.

And, excepting at the temple, nearly no other people were in the sanctuary. But, near the gate to the enclosure with the carnival ride, a girl I thought may have been a little younger than Annie was standing with two women. And the three were in colorful but dirty traditional Indian dress.

The girl approached us holding out a hand. She held the palm of the hand upward. But she didn't speak.

"I think she wants some money," said Annie.

So I gave Annie the few rupees in coin I had. And, as silent as the other girl, she placed them on the palm. Then, not closing the hand, the girl looked at the coins and turned around.

And then, still silent, she returned to the women..

They were about fifty yards from us. And they hadn't moved from where the girl left them. But they were watching all the girl did.

Still silent, when she reached them, she showed the women the coins on the palm. Then, as one of the women closed the hand over the coins, both nodded to the girl and smiled. And we returned to the taxi.

Its driver had told us he'd wait for us. And, because Annie was sending her study group postcards from each country we visited on that trip, we asked him whether he knew where we could buy some. He didn't know what postcards were, but Annie was able to explain to him what they were, and he found some.

He lurched and swerved and inquired until he stopped at a small shop and led us into it.

"Post cards," he said, pointing to a wall of racks of them, and he waited inside with us until Annie selected and bought some.

Then, as Annie laughed some more, he lurched and swerved us back to our hotel.

Our hotel was two blocks from the Ganges. So, after supper in a restaurant next door to the hotel, we walked to the river to see it. Annie laughed at the cows along its concrete bank, but she didn't laugh at an old man splashing water from the river onto himself, and she exchanged grins with a man walking along the street along the bank with a monkey on his back. And the next day we took a train to Gaya and took another of those little taxis to our hotel in Bodhgaya. We went there to see the tree where Buddhists say the Buddha achieved *nirvana*.

"Look," said Annie, standing at the window of our hotel room the next morning, before we went downstairs for breakfast, before going to see the Bodhi Tree.

So I went to the window. And perhaps more than a hundred monks in saffron robes were walking in single file along the other side of the street in front of the hotel. So after breakfast we walked in the same direction.

We didn't see the monks again. But, by doing that and asking no directions, we found the tree in a compound where we found many people waiting to go in to see it. So we joined the line, left our shoes at the gate with theirs, and went in with them.

"It's so big," said Annie. "I wonder how old this one is."

I'd told her Buddhists don't say it's the tree under which the Buddha sat but a descendant of it by way of people planting sprigs of descendants of it when one dies.

And seeing it was the only item on our agenda for Bodhgaya. So the next morning we took a train to Allahabad to see the Triveni Sangam, the confluence of the Ganges and two other rivers where Hindus bathe *en masse*, considering that confluence to symbolize the unity of all. And, in front of the

Allahabad train station and during our short walk to our hotel, Annie laughed at more cows.

But the next morning we took another of those little three-wheel taxis to the *sangam*.

"What are those?" asked Annie as we passed a large herd of large black cattle with horns grazing in a large green field near the *sangam* with no fence between them and the road, and she didn't laugh at them.

"I don't know" I said. "I think they may be water buffalo."

"These must be nice people," said Annie, "letting them and the cows do whatever they want."

And, at the Ganges, we boarded a boat with some of those nice people. The boat took them and us to join other boats full of other nice people at the center of the *sangam*. And, on the way, Annie nicely talked with some of the nice people.

But, though she was silent as they bathed, she didn't bathe with them.

"I know it's another way to feel how everything's everything," she said as we returned from the river to our taxi. "But some of the others didn't do it, and I feel like that anyway."

"At some times in some years," I told her, "gatherings here for that bathing are bigger than any other gatherings of humans anywhere at any time. But this isn't one of those times."

She smiled at that but didn't laugh. And that *sangam* was the last place we'd planned to see in India. So, the next day, we flew back to Beijing.

We spent that night in the hotel near the Forbidden City, but the next day we took a train to Zhengzhou and a bus from there to Dengfeng, to see the Shaolin Monastery.

Annie had never asked me why the Buddha said everything's everything. But what she and Bee said of the relationship between numbers and letters and how they relate to music told me they were learning it for themselves. And it also told me another reason for her asking no questions in the Mogao Grottoes.

But, while asking why *Taijiquan* is Buddhist, she also asked me why our book of *Taijiquan* abiding writings doesn't say it is. So my answers to that question and my answers to her further questions in those conversations were why we visited the Shaolin Monastery. I'd told her Bodhidharma originated Zen there, and that some practitioners of what we now call *Taijiquan* say he also originated *Taijiquan* there, but that others say a Daoist monk originated *Taijiquan* at a Daoist monastery. So I'd also told her "zen" is a Japanese pronunciation of "chan", which is a Chinese pronunciation of "*dhyana*", which is Sanskrit for "meditation". But I also told her the Shaolin Monastery had become a school for what English-speaking people call kung fu.

And I'd also told her the Daoist monastery at which most people practicing *Taijiquan* say the Daoist monk founded it was on Wudang Mountain about three hundred miles from the Shaolin Monastery, but that many Taijiquan practitioners deny any relationship between those monasteries, or between *Taijiquan* and what some people call *Shaolinquan*.

"But both monasteries are in China," she said in response to all that. "So why don't we call Zen Chan?"

"Some monks took Buddhism to Japan," I said, "at about the time *Taijiquan* practitioners say Zhang Sanfeng, the monk they say was a Daoist and founded *Taijiquan*, founded it on Wudang Mountain."

And I also told her historians present no consensus of precise dates either of the transmission of Chan Buddhism to Japan or of the life of Zhang Sanfeng, but that they generally agree that both were during the twelfth century, about six centuries after the life of Bodhidharma. And I told her a hypothesis is that a shift of attitudes at the Shaolin Monastery led the monks continuing Bodhidharma's teachings to leave that monastery, and that Zhang

Sanfeng was a Buddhist monk and trekked the three hundred miles from it to the Daoist monastery on Wudang Mountain, while other Shaolin Buddhist monks sailed to Japan. And I told her I thought that, considering similarities between the Diamond Sutra and the *Dao De Jing*, reasonable is that the Wudang Mountain Daoist monks would have welcomed both Zhang Sanfeng and his teaching.

"So," I said, "I think an answer to your question may be that, for the same reason Zhang Sanfeng trekked to Wudang Mountain, more Buddhist monks sailed to Japan."

Yes, then Annie wasn't quite ten years old, but neither had anyone managed to impose on her sensibility the obfuscating irrationality of bigotry. So, for her, weeding through the complexities of more than a thousand pages of history of human culture few people read before college and looking up in a dictionary words with which she wasn't familiar, were but adventures in her effort to understand, to find sense in all she discovered along her way. And so, instead of taking any of the sides she found people taking in that book or anywhere else along her way, she tried to understand all sides in order to reconcile them in her mind.

So, listening to that long answer, Annie further confirmed the uselessness or counterproductivity of the form of patronizing adults absurdly call babytalk when they inflict it on children. And she also demonstrated her understanding of how things' relating to one another is evidence of everything being everything. And it also showed how her compassion related to her curiosity.

She listened quietly until I stopped talking, and she asked no more questions then, but she nodded. And she added a couple of comments showing plainly that her quietness wasn't because she didn't understand. They showed still more clearly her understanding of all being all.

"So Zhang Sanfeng could have become both a Buddhist monk and a Daoist monk," she said. "And your sword's from the Shaolin Monastery."

On my previous visit there I bought a *taiji jian*, a sword for the *taiji* sword form, and it was in our living room. It was in its scabbard leaning against an end of the credenza we were using as a TV stand. So Annie asked me why I had a sword.

So I told her I bought it at the Shaolin Monastery before I learned nearly as much as either of us knew then of *Taijiquan*. And I told her that since then I'd come to suspect that the development of the *taiji* sword form was after people started using *Taijiquan* as a martial art instead of as an alternative to martial arts. But, showing her the sword wasn't sharp, I told her I kept it because still it was a souvenir of the monastery. So, when we were planning our trip to China, she said she'd like to see for herself what was happening there. But still I didn't know how she'd approach that discovery.

I didn't learn that until we were in the monastery..

From our hotel in Dengfeng, we took a taxi to the tourist attraction the monastery also had become, since it became a kung fu academy. Then, from its concrete parking lot for taxis and buses, we stepped up the broad concrete steps to the large concrete plaza in front of the monastery's tall concreate main gate. But Annie didn't speak again until, after we came to a row of shops selling swords and other souvenirs along one side of the concrete plaza inside the gate, she looked into one of the shops.

"Is that where you got your sword?" she asked of that.

"I bought it in one of these shops," I said. "But I don't remember which one."

But, though she looked into another shop, she didn't go into any of them. We continued on to the temple and along a pathway into the grounds, but no monks were in the only part of the temple we were able to visit, and signs and caretakers kept tourists from leaving the pathway. So neither did we see any monks on the grounds.

So Annie found no opportunity to ask any monks what they thought of *Taijiquan*. So she said nothing from when she looked into the souvenir shops until we returned from our walk into the grounds. But in front of the temple, below a few more broad concrete steps, was another broad concrete plaza.

So she took picture of that and the misty mountains beyond it and stood silently gazing at all that for about another minute.

But then she spoke.

"Do you think they'll let us do our *Taijiquan* down there?" she asked.

"I think we can find out," I said, and we stepped down the steps and, after turning to face the temple from the middle of the plaza, went through the 94-segment sequence.

But, as we finished, before we stepped from our closing *wújí* stance, the form that begins and ends the sequence to symbolize returning to consciousness of the no polarity of the primal unity, after departing from it into the extreme polarity of the various *tàijí* forms, two young monks in saffron robes appeared at the top of the steps

And they descended them to join us. So, with one of the monks on each side of us, Annie and I went through the sequence again with them. And then, when we finished that repetition of the cycle, they left us as silently as they'd appeared.

But Annie stood silent and still and smiling until we no longer could see them. And then we left the plaza and found in a shop beside the temple some hanging bamboo scrolls with watercolor paintings of misty mountains. And then, after Annie bought four of them for her study group, we left the monastery.

And that was her tenth birthday.

11

East and West

And the next day we returned to Beijing, and the day after that we returned to the United States, but we didn't go home until two days later. I'd asked Annie whether she'd like to spend a couple of days in San Francisco to have a yellow tack on our map for each coast of the United States. So we walked all over the main part of the city, saw Fisherman's Wharf and the Golden Gate Bridge and San Francisco's Chinatown, and rode a cable car.

So at home, including the red tack for San Francisco, we replaced with yellow tacks ten more red tacks and one green one. The green one was for Lhasa, where I'd told Annie many Buddhists lived, when she counted the tacks for China on her first morning in our house. That tack had marked the failure of my plan to visit Lhasa on my trip to that region seven years earlier.

So, excepting the red tacks for my R&R to Hong Cong from Vietnam and my visits to New Delhi during my assignment to Afghanistan, we replaced all the tacks for the three countries we visited during that trip.

But, after we replaced the tacks, Annie mentioned but one.

"It's like a little sun for those kids and their corn," she said of the one for Ya'an and Shangli. "They're in my heart too."

But she had plenty to say as she showed her study group the pictures she took on that trip, projecting them onto our TV as she had her pictures of France, as the four sat on our sofa.

"Some monks did our *Taijiquan* dance with us there," she said when she showed them her pictures of the Shaolin Monastery. "That was on my birthday."

"I would have liked to be there for that," said Bee. "And these scrolls look like how I feel when we do our *Taijiquan*."

So Suzy and Bobby looked at their scrolls again and looked at Bee and smiled. And then, with that new sharing, they continued their usual sharing by their more ordinary means of discovery. So their summer schedule remained the same for the remaining few days of that summer vacation of theirs.

But, partly because Albion didn't have a middle school, they changed their schoolyear schedule.

The nearest middle school was nearly ten miles from our house. And, partly because they enjoyed riding the bus together and partly because Annie and Bee were two years older than they were when the safety of their walk to the school bus stop was part of my reason for driving them to school, all four of them rode the bus both to and from the middle school they selected. And they didn't select the nearest one.

A half dozen were between nine and fifteen miles from Albion, and the study group found each of them on the Web and easily selected Marshall Middle School, about twelve miles from our house. Their main reason for not selecting the charter school, which was also about twelve miles from our house, was its reputation for racial discrimination. And neither was their reason for selecting Marshall Middle School academic.

"It's old," said Suzy.

"Yeah," said Bobby. "It has more than one floor."

"Yeah," said Bee. "So it has stairs we can run up and down."

"Yeah," said Annie. "And the book stuff's probably about the same at all of 'em anyway."

"What do you think, Billy?" asked Bee.

"I think I like the way you four think," I said.

"Can we go see it?" asked Annie.

So we organized a two-car convoy to Marshall. Corinthia and Bee rode with Annie and me while Suzy and Bobby rode with their parents. And, excepting for Suzy's and Bobby's parents' wedding, never before were all of us together in one place.

Before going inside, the four stood grinning for about a minute, looking at the outside of the building. Then, inside, they found a stairway and ran up and down it, and then we found the Principal's office, for enrollment. They were sure.

And another change to their schedule was because of homework.

They elected a full courseload at the Marshall school. So at our house, before Suzy's and Bobby's time to go home for supper, they had hardly any time for anything other than the Web school and their homework for the Marshall school. So, when they finished the eighth grade in the Web school, they printed their transcripts and withdrew.

But their grades were perfect in the Web school. So, while the teachers and administrators in Marshall didn't know them as well as did those in Albion, that didn't keep them from skipping the eighth grade in the Marshall school. But, before they withdrew from the Web school, we took some steps to assure that.

One step was to enroll Bee and Suzy and Bobby in the Web school. They were completing the examinations separately, but officially Annie was taking each examination four times, and I thought the middle school administrators might not accept that as credentials for anyone other than Annie. So I asked the study group what they thought. They looked at one another and shrugged. But then they looked at me and nodded.

So, wishing to keep the process simple and remembering that Annie had told me she thought the others didn't have as much money as we had, I also paid for it.

"I thought this cost money," said Bobby.

"Not much," I said. "And it's easier this way."

"Thanks," he said with Suzy and Bee.

But that was only for the eighth grade..

So when we, the study group's parents, went to the Marshall School's Principal to ask that the four skip the eighth grade there, we also took letters of recommendation from Miss Walker and Mrs. Meredith and the Albion elementary school's Principal, but the Marshall Middle School Principal told us none of that was necessary. She said that, because some of the teachers there already had suggested that possibility, she already was considering it. So their adventure in that new environment was but one schoolyear.

At the end of their summer vacation that year, they enrolled in Marshall's newer high school, a school with no stairs to enjoy between classes.

But that was after Annie and I visited the lands of Canaan and Egypt together.

Annie's attitude toward TV fiction was like her attitude toward toys. She found no TV sitcom or drama with the unifying social messages of the movies she and her friends enjoyed on summer Saturday afternoons. So we used our TV only for watching movies and news, and that's how we decided where to go for her birthday that year, by talking about news as we watched it.

"Why don't they just share the land?" asked Annie as we watched the Prime Minister of Israel talking about terrorism and the Palestinian problem. "And why don't they want those people in Gaza to have any food or other things they need? I don't see how sending rockets out of Gaza is worse than what the Israelis are doing to the Palestinians, and the Israelis keep taking more of their land, and they're not ISIS."

"No," I said. "They aren't. And most of the people ISIS is killing are Muslims. And, excepting trying to defend themselves against what the Israelis are doing to them, I haven't heard of any Palestinian militance for any purpose. But the Israelis say the land's theirs because God promised it to them."

I never knew what effect my replies to Annie's questions would have on her, but I answered each of them as well as I could, as I promised her I always would.

"That doesn't explain why they can't share it," she said then. "At least it doesn't make sense to me! Are we going anywhere for my birthday this year?"

"I don't know a reason we couldn't go there," I said. "If you'd like to. So you want to go see the situation for yourself?"

So she nodded and smiled and went to the map.

"You have three red tacks there," she said. "Oh! You have two in Egypt too! Have you seen the pyramids and the Sphinx?"

"Yes," I said. "And we can go there too, if you'd like."

So she nodded and smiled again. And then she returned to our sofa, to extend her smile into a grin and gaze past our TV with her hands in her lap, as she ordinarily did when a decision we made especially pleased her. So, three weeks later, we landed at Ben Gurion Airport.

But, in those three weeks, we talked more about the Palestinian situation. I told her of stories in Judaic scripture of the Philistines invading the land from the southwest while the Israelites invaded it from the east. So she went to our map again.

"I guess that explains why the Israelis let the Palestinians have Gaza," she said. "But I don't see how it's a reason for how they treat them there. And I still don't understand why they can't just share the land."

In another conversation I told her a little of the Holocaust and the King David Hotel.

"But how are either the Palestinians or the Israelis German or British either?" she said.

And I told her some repercussions of 9/11.

"Were those people Palestinians?" she asked.

"No," I said. "They were Arabs."

"I still don't understand," she said shrugging.

But, upon our arrival at Ben Gurion Airport, she received a cordial welcome to that land.

"Welcome to Israel, little sister," said the young woman who stamped our passports at Passport Control, and she and Annie exchanged grins.

We arrived late in the afternoon and spent that night in Tel Aviv. So, after checking into our hotel, we spent that evening exploring the neighborhood around the hotel. It was between the Mediterranean and the city's main shopping district.

"Are those wedding dresses?" asked Annie as we walked past several bridal shops.

"Yes," I said.

"Why are so many stores for them here?" she asked.

"I don't know," I said. "But I think the Holocaust and what Judaic scripture says about that kind of thing may be part of the reason. It says the Israelites kept sinning, and it says God keeps punishing them by letting other people enslave them or kill them, or scatter them to other lands. But it says he always leaves a remnant of them, and that he'll forgive them and gather them together again and let them multiply again, if they stop sinning and ask him to forgive them."

"So you think they think the Holocaust was because they sinned?" asked Annie.

"I've thought of that possibility," I said. "But I haven't heard anyone suggest it."

She shrugged again and asked no more questions during that exploring or at supper. And neither did she ask any questions the next morning during our taxi ride to Tel Aviv's main bus station. But we had a long ride ahead of us that day for questions and answers.

We'd decided to see some of the places important to each of the three Abrahamic religions while we were there and to see the land both inside and outside the Israeli mandate. Tiberius was on Lake Tiberius, what the New Testament of the Bible calls the Sea of Galilee, and the Tiberius bus station was about fifteen miles from the hill where the Roman Catholic Church says Jesus delivered what it calls the Sermon on the Mount. So, because it was at the opposite end of the land from Tel Aviv, we went there that day both to see those places and to see the land along the way.

But, before boarding our bus, we began that seeing of sites by eating breakfast at the Tel Aviv bus station. The station had a row of food stands with tables in front of them, and we found scrambled eggs and croissants and jam and blueberry yogurt and orange juice and chocolate milk at one of the stands, and ate it at one of the tables. The variety of the breakfast was because Annie ate as adventurously and freely as she did everything else she did.

But that didn't explain why as she ate she folded the bag from her breakfast and put it into a pocket of her jeans. I watched her as she did that and was about to ask her why she did it. But she looked up and forestalled my asking.

"Suzy asked me to bring her back some of the holy land," she said. "Bobby's mom takes her to Sunday school. Suzy's not as much of a troublemaker as Bobby and I are. So she goes to church with Bobby's mom to make her happy while Bobby stays at home with Suzy's dad. So I'm thinking maybe I can put some dirt from the mountaintop in this bag."

But the only indication of the Palestinian problem we saw on that ride wasn't outside the bus but on it. About a half dozen Israeli soldiers with rifles with magazines in them were on it. And that was true of every bus we rode in that land.

But, because the Israeli mandate wrapped around the west bank of the Jordan through which the bus took us, Tiberius was Israeli. So we saw no soldiers as we walked across the Tiberius bus station's parking lot and checked into our hotel, and the hotel had a Christian name, the Casa Dona Gracia. So we received a cordial welcome there also.

But, after taking our bags to our room, we returned to the bus station and boarded another bus. And, on that bus to the Mount of Beatitudes, the soldiers didn't have all the firearms. The driver had a small pistol in a holster on the side of his belt toward the boarding entrance.

And, when I asked him to tell us when to deboard for the Mount of Beatitudes, he frowned and shook his head and motioned us aside.

But boarding behind us was a young female soldier who spoke English and had no rifle. And, after telling the driver in Hebrew what I asked him, she sat across the aisle from us to tell us when we arrived at our stop. And she also talked with Annie during that twenty-minute ride.

And she also congenially welcomed her.

"Welcome to Israel, little sister," she also said, as we left the bus at what she told us was our stop.

And she and Annie also exchanged grins.

A small sign at the bus stop said "Mount of Beatitudes" and pointed up a narrow sideroad. So we walked up the sideroad until we reached its highest point and could see the Sea of Galilee below us. But there beside the road was a tubular steel gate with a path like a tractor path on the other side of it.

And the path led further up the hill.

"Looks like that's the way to the top of the mountain," I said to Annie. "What do you think?"

She nodded and grinned. So we climbed through the gate and walked up the path to the top of the hill. And there we found ourselves between a grove of olive trees on the hill's slope toward the main road and the Sea of Galilee at the bottom of its slope away from the main road.

So Annie stopped and looked all around.

"Do you know what kind of trees those are?" she asked, looking at the grove.

"Olive trees, I think," I said.

And marking a triangle at the top of the hill were three tall eucalyptus trees. Annie didn't ask me what the eucalyptus trees were, but beneath them in the triangle they marked were three large boulders, and she sat on the largest of them. So I sat beside her on it, with the olive grove behind us and the Sea of Galilee in front of us, and no other human in sight.

"Where are all the Christians?" she asked.

"I don't know," I said. "The *Miqra*, the Judaic scripture Christians call the Old Testament of the Bible, says the king Christians say people said was an ancestor of Jesus' said in a song he wrote that because God was with him he'd fear no evil walking through the valley of the shadow of death. But most Christians seem to me to care more about Jesus' dying to give them eternal life than about what he tried to teach us about faith in the power and mercy of God. So I think they may be afraid to come here."

But, after shaking her head at that, she smiled.

"Look at all those flowers," she said gazing down the hill over the wildflowers all over its side toward the sea. "Do you think Jesus sat on this rock to give that sermon?"

"Makes sense to me," I said. "Consider the lilies of the field. Do you remember why the *fleurs de lis* were on Jehanne's banner?"

Of course, having told Annie of both the military importance of raising the siege from Orleans and the political importance of crowning the Dauphin at Reims, I'd told her of King Clovis I and Sainte Clotilde. So I also had told her Clotilde designed the *fleur de lis* in reference to Jesus' reference to the lilies of the field in the Sermon on the Mount. But I hadn't told her what Jesus said of them in it.

"That's what the Bible says Jesus said about them in that sermon," I said when she nodded. "Consider the lilies of the field, how they grow; they toil not, neither do they spin: And yet I say unto you, That even Solomon in all his glory was not arrayed like one of these."

"Who's Solomon?" asked Annie.

"A son of David's," I said. "David was the king who wrote that song about the valley of the shadow of death, and the *Miqra* says Solomon was the wealthiest of all the many kings of Israel."

"I like Jesus," she said. "If he said that about these flowers, or any flowers."

"So do I, little friend," I said.

And she scooped up some dirt and put it into her breakfast bag, took a picture of some flowers near us and put four small pink ones into the bag with the dirt, and looked into the bag

"They won't look much like flowers when we get home," she said. "But we can remember what they looked like. And we'll have the picture."

And then she folded the bag to close it and sat quiet a while with it in her lap as she gazed at the flowers and the sea.

"Do you know what those buildings are down there?" she asked.

"I think a convent," I said. "A place where nuns live."

"Will you still call me little friend when I'm bigger?" she asked.

"I'd like to," I said. "I call you that because I think you're the biggest person I've ever met."

And then she again sat quiet awhile. And then we walked back down the tractor path and again climbed through the gate. And, as we walked down the road to the bus stop, a nun was driving up the hill and gave us a big grin as she passed.

And that was Annie's eleventh birthday.

And, in Tiberius, we found a restaurant for lunch and then further explored the center of the city.

"Do you want to see if they have strawberry soda?" I asked Annie as we passed a sidewalk kiosk

A girl who may have been two or three years younger than Annie was leaning against the front of the kiosk beneath a window from which a man sold its offerings.

Annie nodded. And the man replied to the question affirmatively. So we bought two bottles of it and sat at one of the two tables in front of the kiosk to drink them.

"Your shoe's untied," said Annie to the girl.

The girl looked at Annie and smiled. She didn't otherwise reply, and neither did she looked down at the shoe, until the man said something to her in Hebrew. But then, after looking down and smiling at Annie again, she knelt and tied the shoe.

"Do you know what kind of tree those are?" Annie asked the man, pointing toward two eucalyptus trees beside the kiosk.

"Eucalyptus in English, I think," he said.

"Eucalyptus," Annie repeated quietly.

But then she gestured toward some people walking on the other side of the street.

"How can you tell if those people are Israelis or Palestinians?" she asked.

"This is Israel," said the man. "You don't have to worry about that."

"So they're all Israelis?" asked Annie.

"Yes," he said, as quietly as she'd said "eucalyptus".

But, a few hours later, we had supper in a small restaurant fewer than three blocks from the kiosk, and men drinking beer at other tables there were complaining loudly about the Israelis in English, while occasionally looking at us.

Annie didn't talk with them, but she talked about them to me, as we continued our exploring.

"I thought Muslims didn't drink alcohol," she said.

"A lot of people do things their religion's scriptures tell them not to do," I said. "I drank beer with people calling themselves Muslims in Afghanistan."

"When you were in the Army," said Annie.

"Yes," I said. "But before the war that's there now. I was there during the coup that ended the Afghan monarchy. The French phrase *"coup d'etat"* means a little rebellion that takes over a country's government. And they did it in one night, and that was all the war there when I was there, and I think we started it."

"How?" she asked.

"We spread a rumor that a prince was planning a coup while the king was in Italy for a sort of vacation. Then we advised the king to take the batteries out of all the tanks in the country before he left but to leave the batteries in the twelve that guarded the royal palace. But the commander of those twelve tanks was a lieutenant colonel my office had sent to Fort Knox for training.

"And those twelve tanks took over the country."

"Why?" she asked.

"I think we did it because the Soviets had more influence over the Afghan government than we did. They gave the Afghans all those tanks and other weapons, while all we did for their military was to train some of them, and that lieutenant colonel we trained was telling us of possible coups. He was also in favor of one faction, but we thought the Soviets would help pro-soviets swallow up any coup that wasn't pro-soviet, and we thought other Afghans would rebel against anyone who replaced the monarchy. So we let the lieutenant colonel know we wouldn't try to defend the king. And everything went as we expected.

"Then the CIA supported the rebellion against the resulting pro-Soviet government. So Afghanistan turned into the mess for the Soviet Union that Vietnam was for us. But the Soviet government wasn't as stable as ours and fell apart."

"So that's how the mess that's in Afghanistan now got started?" she asked.

"Yes, little friend," I said. "We need you in charge."

And she grinned at that, and the next morning we rode with the soldiers along the Jordan River and between Ramallah and Jericho, to Jerusalem.

"All this empty land to share," said Annie along the way. "I don't understand."

And, from Jerusalem's central bus station, we took a taxi to our hotel at the top of the Mount of Olives.

"Do you know a taxi driver whose name is Jamal?" I asked that taxi driver.

"My name is Jamal," he said, looking back at me.

"You look old enough to be the Jamal I'm asking about," I said. "My name's Bill. Did you take me from the Mount of Olives to Bethlehem when the Church of the Nativity was under siege?"

"*Allahu akbar*!" said Jamal, looking back again. "How are you? Yes, I remember you!"

"Yes, *Allahu akbar*!" I said. "I'm fine. This is my friend Annie, and also now my daughter. Great seeing you again."

"Hello, Annie," said Jamal.

"I don't know what to say," I said. "But can you take us to Bethlehem tomorrow morning? It should be easier this time."

"Of course," said Jamal. "*Inshallah*."

And, on the Mount of Olives, he stepped out of his taxi to shake hands with me.

"About nine o'clock?" I asked.

"I'll be here," he said.

And he waved as he drove away.

After checking into the Mount of Olives Hotel, Annie and I walked down the hill to explore Jerusalem, but before that walk we stopped in the restaurant across the street from the hotel.

"Alright if we go in there for a minute?" I asked Annie. "I want to see if some other friends of mine from the other time I was here still own it."

She nodded. And she also grinned. So we did.

"Sofian?" I asked the man behind the glass case displaying the food ready for the customers.

"Yes?" said Sofian with a look more questioning than my question.

"I'm Bill," I said. "I was here for a few days when the Church of the Nativity was under siege. I enjoyed some conversations with you and your brothers."

"*Allahu Akbar*!" said Sofian grinning, and he walked around the display case to shake hands with me. "What can I get you? Beer?"

"No," I said. "I quit drinking beer."

"Good," said Sofian, nodding while still grinning. "Are you a Muslim now?"

"More of a Buddhist," I said.

"Who's this?" he asked with no nod but still grinning.

"This is my friend, and now daughter, Annie," I said.

"How do you do, Annie," said Sofian, also shaking hands with her. "So what can I get you two?"

"Nothing now, thanks," I said. "We just stopped in to see if you're here. Now we're on our way down to explore the old city. But we'll be back for supper. If that's alright."

"It's fine with me," said Sofian. "*Inshallah*."

"Is that a pool table?" asked Annie.

I also had played pool with Sofian's brothers there on my previous visit.

"Yes," said Sofian, and Annie crossed the room to the table and sent the cue ball banking around it.

"I've never seen one before," she said. "Except in movies."

"My brothers will be here this evening," said Sofian. "They'll teach you how to play if you like."

So Annie grinned and nodded and came back to us. I bade Sofian farewell, told him we'd see him that evening, and accepted his handshake again. And Annie and I returned to the street to walk down the hill.

"That's the prayer garden," I said as we passed a garden of terraces. "The Roman Catholic Church says it's where Jesus prayed in the early morning before his crucifixion."

But, as we continued down the hill, a boy about Annie's age leaning against a wall a little further down the hill pushed himself away from the wall and walked up to us.

"Do you want to see the Garden of Gethsemane?" he asked when he reached us. "It has the biggest olive tree in all the land."

"Do we?" I asked Annie, shrugging.

"I don't know," she said, shrugging but smiling.

"I don't know a reason not to," I said to the boy.

So he led us to a door in the wall and opened it and motioned us through it.

"I don't think I've ever seen any kind of tree anywhere that big around," said Annie grinning at the boy. "But it isn't so tall."

The boy said no more to us of the garden, but he returned Annie's grin and led us the remainder of the way around the garden, before leading us through the door again.

"Do you want to see the tomb of Mary?" he asked as we returned to the road. "Everybody knows who Mary is."

"I don't think so now," I said, giving him the shekels I had in change. "Thanks."

So Annie and I continued down the hill, but I stepped up the steps to the entrance to the tomb, and Annie took a hand of mine as I turned toward it.

"That's the tomb," I said pointing down the steps inside its entrance. "Do you feel that air?"

"It's cold," she said. "I don't know if I want to go down there."

"That's how I felt the other time I was here," I said. "But I went down there on my way back up the hill, after I thought about it. We can do that if you want."

But she looked up at me with no nod and neither a shrug nor much of a smile. So we left that question at that and turned and walked on down the hill, across the highway between the hill and the city, and through the Lions Gate. It was the nearest gate to us of any of the gates through what was then the city's walls.

"This is the Via Dolorosa," I said of the narrow cobblestone street on which we then found ourselves. "That's Latin for 'way of sorrow'. The Roman Catholic Church says it was the path from Jesus' condemnation to his crucifixion. A church, the Church of the Holy Sepulcher, is at the end of it where the Church says the crucifixion was. Do you want to see that?"

"Hm mm," said Annie, shaking her head. "I'm glad we didn't go where they burned Jehanne too. What's a sepulcher?"

"A tomb," I said. "How about seeing the wailing wall? It's part of a wall Jews built around the city after Babylonians and Romans tore down earlier walls around it. Jews pray at it."

And Annie nodded to that.

"We saw those Christian places," she said. "But we haven't seen any Jewish places yet."

"How about the Dome of the Rock?" I asked her. "The wailing wall's part of a wall that originally went on to where two Judaic temples were, the one the *Miqra* says Solomon built and the one it says other Judaic people built after Persians let them come back after Babylonians took them captive and destroyed the first one. Muslims built the Dome of the Rock there after they took Jerusalem from Jews. I think it's in your art book."

And Annie nodded again.

"It says it's important for a lot of reasons," she said. "And we haven't gone to any Muslim places yet either,".

So we left the Via Dolorosa and next went to the Western Wall.

"Do you know what they call those hats?" asked Annie.

"They call the little ones yarmulkes," I said. "But I don't know what they call the other ones. I call them fedoras."

"Do you know why they wear them?" she asked.

"Some Judaic people say Judaic law requires men to wear hats all the time," I said. "But the *Miqra* doesn't say that, and I don't know what does say it, or why."

But the Dome of the Rock wasn't open to people who didn't say they were Islamic.

"That's alright," said Annie. "We can talk with your friends. Do you know what those words they said mean? '*Allahu akbar*' and '*inshallah*'?"

"'*Allahu akbar*' means 'God is great'," I said. "And '*inshallah*' means 'God willing'. '*Allah*' is Arabic for '*El*', and '*El*' is a Hebrew word for God, as in '*Isra-El*'."

"What does '*isra*' mean," she asked.

"It means 'fight'," I said. "The *Miqra*, in the Book of Genesis, the first of the first five books of it, the books Judaic people call the *Torah* that tell of the creation and the escape from Egypt to come back here, says God gave Jacob the name Israel when he wrestled with him on the other side of the Jordan River, after his family crossed it on his way back from Syria to this land.

"It says he went to Syria because he was afraid his twin brother might kill him because he tricked their father into giving him the brother's blessing. It says he fathered eleven sons and one daughter in Syria and fathered one more son on this side of the Jordan after he came back. The next book of the Torah says the twelve tribes of Israel descended from those twelve sons."

"Was that when they took the land from the Canaanites?" she asked. "I mean when he came back."

"No," I said. "The *Torah* says they did that after Jacob's great great grandson Moses led the tribes back from Egypt. But the Book of Genesis also says Jacob's son who was Moses' great grandfather started the Israelites' killing then with one of his brothers. So none of that killing was particularly Judaic, in its beginning, either. Those brothers' names were Levi and Simeon. So Moses's tribe was Levi.

"Judah was Jacob's fourth son. And 'Judaic' means descendant from Judah, and 'Jew' is short for "Jewish", or 'Judaic' or 'Judah'. Those brothers were Jacob's second and third sons."

"Why did Levi and Simeon start the killing?" asked Annie.

"The Book of Genesis," I said, "says a prince of the city nearest to the first place Jacob settled after he came back from Syria with his family married their only sister. It says they did it because they didn't like that."

"What was their sister's name?" asked Annie.

"Dinah," I said, and then Annie frowned and looked down at the cobblestones for a few seconds.

But she asked no more questions then or during our lunch at a small restaurant we found during our exploring, or until after we came upon another kiosk selling beverages, in our further exploration.

The kiosk's only seating for customers was stools at an inside counter along a wall opposite its service counter. But several men, one of them in a wheel chair, were talking on the cobblestones outside its open front. And I thought I remembered the one in the wheelchair.

"I think I may know that guy," I said to Annie. "The guy in the wheelchair. How about another strawberry soda?"

12

War and Peace

And she nodded. So we stepped up the step that was the kiosk's doorsill. And, finding that it had strawberry soda, we sat on two of the stools to drink some.

"I think I may remember you," I said to the man in the wheelchair. "From when I was here when the Israelis had the Church of the Nativity under siege."

"I'm quite memorable," he said. "But I also remember you. You said you think most people in the United States blame the Palestinians for the trouble here. And you also said you thought King Abdullah might fill the gap if Arafat lost his influence, but now the Israelis have poisoned Arafat, and Abdullah did nothing. And we've heard nearly nothing from him since before the Palestinian refugees started trying his patience. And now your corrupt President has moved your embassy from Tel Aviv to Jerusalem. Things are going backward here"

"Who's King Abdullah?" asked Annie when the man paused.

"The King of Jordan," I said. "That's the country south of Syria on the other side of the Jordan River. He was active in the region's diplomacy and made a lot of sense to me. But I've heard nothing of him in years."

"Is she your granddaughter?" asked the man in the wheelchair. "She's remarkably thoughtful and attentive for her age."

"This is Annie," I said. "She's a friend of mine and everyone's, and she's become my daughter. Yes, she tries to understand everything that seems to her to be especially important, and she isn't one of the probably more than a hundred million United States citizens calling themselves Christians and siding with the Israelis because Judaic scripture's most of the Bible."

"I'm a Palestinian Christian," said a man standing beside the wheelchair.

"I remember you, too," I said. "You told me that in 2002. You're a memorably exceptional Palestinian and a memorably exceptional Christian."

"How old are you?" the Palestinian Christian asked Annie.

"Eleven," said Annie. "My birthday was yesterday. We went to the Mount of Beatitudes and saw the lilies of the field. Have you been there?"

"No," said the Palestinian Christian. "The Israelis might not let me come back home if I went to the other side of their wall! So you're a Christian?"

"No," said Annie. "I think I like Jesus, but I like the Buddha too."

"How about Muhammad?" asked the man in the wheelchair.

"I don't know," said Annie. "Billy told me the *Qur'an* says it confirms the Gospels and the *Torah* and says Jesus was a prophet and that Mary was a virgin when she had him. And he told me it says the angel who told Mary she was going to have Jesus told Muhammad what the *Qur'an* says too. But I don't know what Muhammad said by himself.

"But I think God's everything. So I think everybody's everybody. I think we only imagine we're different from each other. So I think God and the angels and Muhammad and Jesus and the Buddha and you and I are all the same person. The Buddha said that.

"And Billy said '*Islam*' means 'submission'. And I think, if everything's everything, we have to submit to God whether we like it or not. And Billy said the *Qur'an* says that too.

"So I don't understand why ISIS says it's Islamic when it kills Muslims. I think we all should consider the lilies of the field. That's why I think I like Jesus."

"Yes," said another man standing on the cobblestones. "She *is* thoughtful and attentive, and she *is* everyone's friend."

"Of such is the kingdom of heaven," said the Palestinian Christian, and the proprietor brought Annie another bottle of strawberry soda."

"Happy birthday, little friend," he said.

And we talked no more of war there. And, before Annie finished that birthday strawberry soda, the men on the cobblestones bade us peace and went away. And, when she finished it, we bade the proprietor peace and returned to the Mount of Olives.

"Do you want to go down there again?" asked Annie as we passed the tomb of Mary again on our way back up the hill.

"Only if you'd like to," I said.

So we didn't. But we stopped at the prayer garden to sit for a few minutes on the stone wall retaining its lowest terrace. The view from there, beyond the Garden of Gethsemane, was of the newest wall around the old city.

"That wall looks like they don't want anyone to go in there," said Annie.

And, as she said that, the gardener came to talk to us. He was an old man in a turban and rubber sandals. And he told us he'd been to New York.

"But I live up there," he said pointing beyond the road toward a three-story house with clothes hanging from a line on a balcony of its top floor. "People in America don't know what it's like here."

Then the old man turned in the direction from which he came to us and, ambling on his walking stick, walked away.

But then I had no shekel coins. So I put a twenty-shekel note on the wall beside some steps up to the terrace and put a stone on it to keep it from blowing away. And then Annie and I continued to the top of the hill.

"Look," she said looking through the open entrance to a small tourist giftshop next door to Sofian's family's restaurant, and she went into the shop

She took a small wooden box from a shelf and, after looking at the carving on its lid, opened it and looked into it.

"Those are made of olivewood," said the shopkeeper, a boy about the age of Annie and the boy who showed us the Garden of Gethsemane, and Annie bought four of them.

"I have to go to the bathroom before we go see Sofian," she said as we returned to the street.

So we went up to our room. But, also before we walked across the street to see Sofian, she lined the boxes up on top of the dresser, took the flowers from her breakfast bag, and laid one beside each box. Then she emptied the dirt into the boxes, laid the flowers in them, and closed their lids.

Then she lightly tapped the lid of each box.

"For Bee and Suzy and Bobby and us," she said.

I thought of her habit of touching the Buddha's *ushnisha* to help her consider things. Then I remembered her touching the walls and stones in Domremy and Vaucouleurs. And then we walked across the street to see Sofian.

Annie, through her openness, had become a kind of Buddhist. But, if those people who called her a troublemaker had answered her questions instead of threatening her with hell, she as easily may have become a Christian. It could have happened as easily as her Buddhism began with her asking me what our Buddha statuette was.

So that made the statuette literally a kind of touchstone for her. And now she was befriending Muslims, people most citizens of the United States past elementary school thought were their mortal enemies, and she did both by the *dao* of being simply what she was. And the Muslims responded in kind.

"How did you like Jerusalem?" Sofian asked her as soon as we entered his restaurant.

"They wouldn't let us go inside the Dome of the Rock," she said. "But we saw some Jewish men in yarmulkes and fedoras praying at the wailing wall. And we talked with some Palestinian men at a little place that had strawberry pop. And one of them said he was a Christian."

"Well," said Sofian, smiling down to her looking up to him. "Speaking of Christians, I heard Buddhists don't eat meat. So I thought of things I can cook for you with no meat. If you don't."

"We wouldn't want a fish to eat us," said Annie smiling.

And Sofian, returning to behind his display case, laughed at that. And he hardly could stop laughing long enough to ask her whether she ate eggs. And he didn't reply to her affirmative reply by asking her whether she'd want an egg to eat her.

He had no other customers while we were there. So, after supper with an entrée of fried zucchini that made Annie smile, we talked more with him until his three brothers arrived and taught her to shoot pool. And her pool lesson involved a lot of laughing and no talk of war.

"She's a regular Minnesota Fats," said one of the brothers.

"Who's Minnesota Fats?" asked Annie.

"He was an American pool-shooter," said another brother.

"But he wasn't as good as you," said the other brother.

And the next morning, after our breakfast in Sofian's restaurant, Jamal drove us to Bethlehem.

"We won't have to sneak you in this time," he said. "I can drive you all the way to Manger Square."

"Yes," I said. "*Allahu Akbar* and *inshallah* for that too. How's your friend who drove me most of the way there after you snuck me into the city in 2002?

"He's fine," said Jamal. "I told him you were back. He asked me to convey to you his welcome back."

But, while the city's streets and the square were open to us, some buildings remained in rubble.

"Can you pick us up after lunch?" I asked Jamal as he dropped us at the square. "Right here at about two?"

"Sure," he said. "See you then."

"I like those old stones," said Annie of the Church of the Nativity as we walked across the square, and she stopped to take a picture of it before going on to touch some of its stones.

"The manger's under it," I said. "The Roman Catholic Church says the stable was a cave. Do you want to go down there? They built the church over it."

"Yes," she said. "If you want to. It isn't a tomb, is it? I mean isn't it where they say Jesus was born? So isn't it the most important part?"

So, after I replied to that with a nod and a smile, we found our way down to the cave. But she said nothing while we were in it, and she looked up at the August sun and smiled, as soon as we stepped out of the church. But she asked several questions as we walked through neighborhoods near the square to see how people lived in Bethlehem.

"Why do so many Palestinians live here?" she asked. "Do you think the Israelis let them live in Bethlehem because they don't care about Jesus".

"I think that could be a factor," I said. "But the *Miqra* says David's also from here, and it says he was the second of the four Judaic kings of Israel, the second of the three before his grandson who followed Solomon divided Israel against itself.

"That left the grandson King only of Judah while someone who didn't like Solomon was King of Israel. So all the rest of the *Miqra* treats David as a measure of how kings should be. So I don't think Jesus would be much of a factor either way.

"And the part of the Bible that's only Christian contradicts itself about whether Jesus descended from David or only from God through Mary, and the birth of Jesus was long after the writing of the *Miqra*, centuries later."

"But you said 'Jewish' means 'Judaic'," said Annie. "So, if the Kingdom of Judah and the Kingdom of Israel were two different kingdoms, why do the Israelis call Israel a Jewish state?"

"That, little friend," I said, "completely escapes my understanding."

And Annie grinned at that, and we continued that conversation during our lunch, in a Palestinian restaurant we found a few blocks from the square.

"You, little daughter," I said, "do not ask too many questions. I think, if more people asked the questions you ask and paid attention to the answers, this world would be a much more pleasant place for everyone. And the Israelis aren't willingly letting Palestinians live in Bethlehem.

"You know, from paying attention to the news, that the fighting didn't stop when the United Nations started calling Israel a nation, and that agreement was more than seven decades ago, when more Palestinians lived in Bethlehem.

"And the United Nations didn't agree to let the Israelis have it. But, after signing that agreement, the Israelis never fully abided by it, and they haven't abided by any of the treaties they've signed since then, and they were the first to break most of them, and a result of that has been a lot of war, and the Israelis have won most of it. And Islamic nations help the Palestinians, while Christian nations help the Israelis, making it a worldwide mess.

"Jordan administered Bethlehem for years, when the father of the king we talked about with the Palestinians in Jerusalem yesterday was king, but that was the longest Palestinian success."

"King Abdullah," said Annie. "The one you and the Palestinian in the wheelchair said wasn't doing what you said you thought he might do."

"Yes, little friend," I said. "And now the Israelis are trying to push Christians out of their homes here too. So does that make any of it make any more sense to you?"

"No," said Annie shaking her head. "Not to me."

"Not to me, either," I said.

And she smiled and shrugged. And, after our lunch and a little more exploring, our friend Jamal drove us back to the top of the Mount of Olives, where we spent the rest of that afternoon with our friend Sofian and spent that evening with him and our friends his brothers. And, the next morning, after our breakfast in their family's restaurant, Jamal drove us back to the bus station. And, from there, we rode with the soldiers back to Ben Gurion Airport.

From there we flew to Cairo. And from Cairo we took a taxi to Giza and ate supper at our hotel's rooftop restaurant with a view of the pyramids. And next morning we walked to the pyramids.

As we left our hotel, a boy perhaps a couple of years younger than Annie held a small package of Kleenex out to us and silently held his other hand out to us with its palm up, as had the girl at the deer sanctuary at Sarnath. As we continued our walk, after I gave the boy the change I had and let him keep his Kleenex, a man in a turban and on a camel rode the camel in front of us and stopped. So we stopped walking and looked up at him.

"Do you want to ride?" he asked us.

"What do you think?" I asked Annie.

"I wouldn't want a camel to ride me," she said, shaking her head but grinning.

"No," I said to the man. "But thanks."

"You're going to walk to the pyramids?" he asked.

"Yes," I said, and we walked around him and the camel.

But, after we bought our tickets and entered the necropolis, another man in a turban and on a camel asked us whether we'd like to ride the camel. And, to my also replying negatively and thanking him, he replied by asking whether we'd like someone to show us the insides of the pyramids. So I also asked Annie what she thought of that.

"Only if you want to," she said. "They aren't birthplaces, like under that church in Bethlehem, are they? I just wanted to see what they look like here, instead of only in the pictures in our art book, and I wanted to see the Sphinx."

"Me too," I said. "I didn't go inside them when I was here before either."

So, after I thanked that man for his second offer also but also declined it, we walked around each of the pyramids and around the sphinx, as Annie took pictures of each of those structures and of all of them together, with humans and camels between them and us.

"I know they're the great pyramids," she said. "But I didn't know they were this big. And I couldn't tell from the pictures in my book how big the Sphinx is. I mean in comparison to the pyramids.

"So the humans and camels in the pictures will show how big they are, and how big the camels are, too."

And from there we walked to the river. It was on the other side of our hotel from the pyramids and also further from the hotel than the hotel was from the necropolis. So the walk was a way to see more of how Egyptians lived.

"This country looks a lot poorer than Canaan," said Annie. "India looked poor too, but India has more grass and trees. I'm glad you gave that kid with the Kleenex some money."

But more trees were along the river. And our lunch was at a tourist café on the riverbank. So we stayed at the café talking and watching the river traffic until evening. Then, for supper, we returned to our hotel's rooftop restaurant. And, the next day, we flew home.

"This is beautiful," said Suzy as she looked into her olivewood box. "You bringing us these."

"The flowers don't look like flowers anymore," said Annie. "But I took a picture of them with some other flowers before I picked them."

"That's beautiful too," said Bee of the picture. "Can you email it to us?"

But a picture I took with Annie's phone drew more conversation.

"Only you, Annie," said Bobby. "Who else would fly to Israel and shoot pool with Palestinians?"

"I thought they were supposed to be dangerous," said Suzy.

"They're our friends," said Annie. "Those guys are brothers. Their family owns that restaurant. That guy standing over there watching is their brother too. He runs the restaurant for their family. His name's Sofian.

"And we talked with some Palestinians at a little place in Jerusalem too, and they weren't dangerous either. It had strawberry pop, and the guy who ran it gave me a bottle of it for my birthday. And some of the Israelis had guns."

"Most of the ones with guns were soldiers, but the bus driver who took us to the Mount of Beatitudes had a little one in a holster, and he didn't speak English."

"Didn't you talk to any Israelis?" asked Bee.

"Not many," said Annie. "But a girl who stamped our passports at the airport welcomed me to Israel and called me little sister. And a girl soldier on the bus to the Mount of Beatitudes didn't have a gun, and she talked to us and told us where we needed to get out of the bus, and she welcomed me to Israel and called me little sister too.

"And I asked a guy in Tiberius who was running another place with strawberry pop some questions. And he answered them, but I didn't think he wanted to, and he said no Palestinians were around there, but some were drinking beer in the restaurant where we ate supper, and that was only about three blocks away. But I didn't talk to them."

"I thought Muslims didn't drink," said Bobby.

"Those guys did," said Annie. "But not all Palestinians are Muslims. One of the men at that little place in Jerusalem said he was a Christian."

So Annie's transitioning from equitable childhood into equitable adulthood was a perpetual delight to me. But that Saturday, while the study group was out exploring on their bicycles, I remembered her curiosity regarding the wedding gowns in Tel Aviv and her asking me on the Mount of Beatitudes whether I'd call her little friend when she was bigger. So that reminded me of her attention to the statue in Ya'an and of her physical transition.

So then I remembered that her birthday among the wildflowers above the Sea of Galilee put her within a year of the ordinary range of years of puberty. So I thought the time had come for me to talk with her about it, but I wanted to be sure our conversation would be what she needed, and I wasn't sure. So I thought of Miss Walker and Mrs. Meredith.

But then I remembered that they wouldn't be at work on Saturday. I also thought of Corinthia, but still I hadn't developed any congeniality with her father, and I didn't think that was a time to risk an effort at that. So I decided to try Bobby's mother.

And, because telephones don't seem to me to be personal enough for important personal conversations, I drove to her house.

But that conversation was brief.

"I don't think you have to worry about that," she said. "I started to have that talk with Suzy a few weeks ago, and she said she and Annie and Bee had already looked it up on the Internet, to fact-check what some girls at school told them."

But still I wasn't certain. And still I also wished to have no secrets from my little friend. So, that evening, I told her of my conversation with Bobby's mother and asked her what she thought and how she felt about it all.

"Yeah," she said. "The girls and boys have different gym classes. And the girls talk about that stuff sometimes when the boys aren't around. And they all like us and try to take care of us because we're younger than they are too. So some of the girls told Bee and Suzy and me about that stuff once. And Bobby said the boys are like that with him too.

"So we're alright. But I think maybe we should buy a box of those things. They have machines for them in the bathrooms at school, but I'm thinking maybe I should have some here, for if it happens at home.

"I could put them in my drawer in our bathroom."

So, the next time I went to Albion's grocery store, I bought a box of "those things".

"How quickly they grow," said the woman at checkout.

"Yeah," I said. "She hasn't started yet, but her eleventh birthday was two or three weeks ago, and she thinks she should have some, for whenever."

"Her idea?" she asked.

"Yeah," I said.

"You know," she said, "when you started bringing her in here, we wondered what was up with that. But now everybody talks about what a great pair you two are."

"Well," I said, "she's the joy of my life."

"Well," she said, "I think she feels that way about you too."

"Thanks," I said. "See you next time."

At home I put the box of those things on our bathroom vanity for Annie to find it. She didn't tell me she did, but her supper conversation that evening suggested she had, and it also reminded me that I had her confidence. And it also told me a little more of her attitude toward the situation.

"Bobby's mom's teaching Suzy to use makeup," she said. "So Suzy told me she'll teach me too, if I want her to. What do you think?"

"I think you're a lily of the field," I said, and she smiled, and I never saw any makeup either on her or on Suzy or Bee.

And neither did I ever know Annie to change her hair, other than how she combed or brushed it or gathered it into a ponytail, for it to be out of her way. Suzy and Bee occasionally did but not by much, and I supposed Corinthia or Bobby's mom suggested those changes, and the occasions were seldom. And, every time I knew anyone to cut Annie's hair, I cut it.

"My hair's getting kind of long," she said to me one evening. "I was thinking of cutting it, but I don't know if I can see what I'm doing well enough, not to make it look jagged."

"I guess we can find someone to cut it for you." I said.

"Can you cut it?" she asked. "You can see well enough."

"I guess I could," I said. "Are you sure you want me to?"

"Yeah," she said. "You're good at figuring stuff out, and we have scissors."

"Then I guess I can try," I said. "How would you like it?"

"A girl at school say her haircut's a Dutch cut," she said, "and I like the way it looks, and I think it's short enough to be easy to comb, and I don't think it's short enough to make people think I'm trying to be different."

So, to be sure my notion of a Dutch cut was the same as what Annie acquired from the girl at school, we looked up images of Dutch cuts on the Web.

And after that, whenever her hair grew more than an inch or two below her shoulders, I asked her whether she thought she needed another haircut. I did that because her considering cutting it herself before asking me to cut it reminded me of her disinclination to ask for anything for herself. And, every time I asked her, she smiled and nodded.

So, while she generally enjoyed variety in everything, her most extreme changes in her hair were when I cut it, and her occasional changes in how she combed or brushed it or gathered it were never for longer than a day, and I never asked her why she made the changes or why they were so seldom.

I supposed her reason for both was that she was seeking a balance between convenience for various reasons and that she thought of her hair as being, like her ears or nose or knees or elbows, simply part of how she was. And I never intentionally suggested a change in anything she enjoyed. And plainly that included herself and nearly all she encountered.

So, the week after she put those things in her drawer in our bathroom vanity she never used vainly, the study group began enjoying high school.

That summer, discussing what elective courses they'd take in high school, they decided that each of them would elect one course different from the ones all of them took. They decided that, instead of participating in extracurricular activities, they'd use that time to share at our house what they learned in those various courses. But also, beginning with Annie's lending *Gardner's Art Through the Ages* to Bee, they developed an extracurricular reading program of their own. That, excepting our world atlas and dictionaries and grammars, was to read all the books on our shelves. And they already were using the atlas and the English dictionary frequently.

Their system was for each of them, upon finishing reading any of the books, to borrow the next in the books' order on our shelves that none of the others was reading. And then, when each of them returned a book, they all discussed it. So their schedule remained quite full.

But I didn't keep copies of print books I didn't expect to read again or use for reference. So the books on our shelves weren't too many for them to read all of them easily before they graduated from college. So, excepting the scriptures, translations of the definitive scriptures of each of the six most popular religions, treating that reading project as they treated all they did together, they read all of them before graduating from high school. And during the summers, with no regimentation from any school, they had plenty of discretionary time. But they didn't need any one to tell them what to do. Their curiosity filled their spare time.

I didn't discuss the books with the group. But Annie, as she had during her reading of *Gardner's*, talked with me about them as she read them. And she also talked with me about each of them when she finished reading it.

I was watching news when she finished reading *Gardner's*. So she closed the book, brought it to our sofa to sit beside me, and pulled it onto her lap as she had the day she began reading it. But then she didn't open it.

"A lot of politics and religion's in here," she said. "Wars too, and a lot of the wars were over religion, like when they broke Europe into different countries fighting over whether to put pictures or statues in churches. Do you know where the Second Commandment is in the Bible?"

"Yes," I said. "I'll get it for you."

I retrieved our copy of the King James Version of the Bible, opened it to the version of the Ten Commandments in the twentieth chapter of the Book of Exodus, and put it on top of *Gardner's* and pointed to the Second Commandment.

She looked where I pointed, read the commandment, and looked up. But then, after a moment of gazing past our TV, she looked down again and read more of that page. Then she looked at me.

"Is God supposed to be saying this?" she asked.

"Yes," I said. "That book of the Bible tells of the Israelites' escape from Egypt. So those commandments are from God to Moses to tell the Israelites how to behave to deserve the land it says he promised them."

"This says he told them not to make any image of anything anywhere!" she said. "Didn't they think God made everything, including them and everything they could make, or imagine making? And what about our Buddha?"

"I don't know," I said. "The Bible also says that. But, as far as I can tell, most Christians and Jews say that commandment doesn't mean any images other than what people use for that second part, the part about bowing down and serving. And a lot of people seem to me to say what they read in the Bible or anywhere else doesn't mean what it says.

"But, either way, I don't think most Buddhists think the Buddha was physically like how they imagine him. A Buddhist scripture says the Buddha said those who see him by form or follow him by voice engage in wrong efforts and won't see him. So I think Buddhist images of the Buddha must be only a way to help imagine how he thought and felt or thinks and feels.

"But I'm not so sure about images of Jesus in Churches."

"Yeah," said Annie. "I don't understand how those people saying they were fighting over the Second Commandment couldn't understand what this little part of this page means. And people in that church where those people took me to Sunday school were bowing to something. And a picture like some of the pictures this book says are of Jesus was up there. So . . . ."

And that was before our conversation in Orleans about Jehanne's sword and our Buddha. Annie's continual readiness to fit new analysis into the expanse of her synthesis, and her approaching each new question that raised with the same welcoming attitude and no rush to resolution, made me think Aristotle may have been a bit of a curmudgeon and Descartes a little sarcastic. And next she read *Bulfinch's Mythology*.

"Do you think the Greeks and Romans really believed in those gods?" she asked when she finished reading that.

"I don't think Socrates did," I said. "I think the people who made him drink the hemlock juice may have. But one reason I doubt that Socrates did is that the people who made him drink the hemlock said they did it because he didn't, and another reason is that he said he welcomed drinking the hemlock, to learn what death is. I think, if he believed in those gods, he'd think he already knew what death is because of stories like the story of Orpheus. But I have no reason to think the Romans believed in those gods. I mean other than that they said they did.

"What about the knights of the roundtable?" she asked. "Those Holy Grail stories don't sound like Christianity to me. But neither do the crusades."

"They don't to me either," I said. "The Bible says Jesus said he didn't come to bring peace but to bring a sword to divide people against one another. But it also says that, when he said loving our neighbors is like loving God, he also said only loving God is more important than loving our neighbors. And, anyway, it doesn't say he said anything about riding around on horses fighting for the fun of it."

"And those Holy Grail stories don't say anything about reading the Bible either," said Annie.

13

Onward and Upward

The next book she read was Holman's and Harmon's *A Handbook to Literature*

"Do you think most writers think about all that stuff when they're writing?" she asked. "I mean figures of speech and the technical stuff."

. "I don't know," I said. "And I've done some writing and thought about that question. English literature's what I mainly studied in college.

"I think many of them may try to. And I think you may think so when you read *The Norton Anthology of Poetry* and Norton's *World Poetry* anthology. But I doubt that many of them ordinarily think about that stuff.

"I learned it in college. And sometimes I've thought of it while I'm writing and done some of it then. But, more often, when I've done those things, I haven't known I did them, until I was proofreading. And sometimes, when I've found them, I've made them more obvious. But I've nearly never planned to do them.

"So I suspect that most writers learn to do that stuff in the same way little kids learn to talk."

"Literary allusions?" she asked.

"Sometimes," I said.

"Iambic pentameter?" she asked.

"Sometimes," I said. "And I've intentionally written some sonnets. But that feels ordinary to me, and it seems to me to be ordinary sometimes for other people too, whether or not they know what it is. So I think a lot of what we learn in schools is what people did long before anyone taught it in any school or had words for it. I think it's kind of like Socrates' saying we already know everything and that learning's only remembering. I mean I don't think it's quite like learning the meaning of words."

"I don't usually know where my thoughts come from," said Annie. "But I try to understand them after I think them, and then I try to use them for new thoughts, if they make sense to me."

And the next book she read was *Tess of the D'Urbervilles*.

"Is that what that book *A Handbook to Literature* calls irony?" she asked. "Calling that guy Angel?"

"I think so," I said. "I wouldn't call him an angel."

"Neither would I," said Annie. "And he was supposed to be a Christian too. What he and that other guy did to Tess may not be the most horrible thing I've heard of anyone doing to anyone. But I think its's the saddest story I've ever read, or heard or seen in movies or on the news, or anywhere. I hope he treats Tess's sister better than he treated Tess. But I don't feel like he would."

And the next book she read was Constance Garnett's translation of *War and Peace*.

"I think maybe he should have put those last hundred-and-some pages in a different book," she said. "I think the story ends with those people together at Pierre's and Natasha's house, and that's my favorite part, I think. They were such good friends after all that stuff that happened to them. But poor Sonia."

And the next book she read was *The Jungle Books*.

"I don't think other animals are afraid of humans because of the way humans look at them," she said. "I think it's because of what humans do to them, like eating them or chaining them up, or shooting them for fun. I like the story about the holy man getting along with the other animals because he sits by himself and doesn't bother them. But I don't understand why they would have helped him save the humans in the village.

"But maybe I do. I like what the book says is the law of the jungle: 'We be of one blood, thou and I.' That's like what you said the Buddha says."

"Yeah," I said. "Me too. And Kipling's other books have contradictions like that too."

And next she read the 1203 pages of the first edition of *The Norton Anthology of Poetry*. And after that she read the 1238 pages of Norton's *World Poetry*. But she said little of either.

"I think poems are more for feeling than for thinking or talking," she said. "I guess you could argue with them, but I don't think that's why poets write them, usually. I think maybe most of them are just the poets' trying to figure out how they feel. Like other art."

Next, though the grammars weren't in her study group's project, she read a short collection of French short stories I'd kept from one of my French courses and said nothing of it. But, whether or not that was because she recognized its purpose, next she read Régine Pernoud's *Jeanne d'Arc par elle-même et par ses témoins*. And, of course, she said something of that.

"She calls her Joan of Arc too," she said. "I mean Jeanne of Arc. And I don't understand why she argues so much about people who say Jehanne was a fraud. I think all she had to say was that she couldn't have done what she did if those people were right, and most of that book is what people said at the two trials. And the things she says Jehanne did that the transcripts of the trials don't say she did seem to me to be stuff she'd do too."

Next she read the book about how to paint with oils. But she said nothing of that to me, and neither did she say anything to me about the book about music theory, but she told Bee about the music theory book before she finished reading it. So Bee read it next, and then they tried some of it on their piano, but that was the last book Annie read before she began to read the scriptures. And, for Annie, that included reading the *Dao De Jing* in Chinese. And she said much if that.

But she and her study group friends were in their second year of college before all of them finished reading all of those scriptures. And Annie was in her first year of college before she read the *Dao De Jing*. And, before that, she and I visited Greece and Rome together.

"Greece," she said when I asked her where she'd like to go for her twelfth birthday. "I don't know why the Greeks said Athena was the goddess of wisdom if she was the goddess of war too. And I know the Parthenon's in ruins, because Turks bombed it when Venetians were storing ammunition in it, and I know Lord Elgin took most of the statues from it to London and sold them to the British Museum and said he did it to save them from the Turks. But I'd like to see what's left of its Doric architecture, and I'd like to see that big rock it's on, too.

"I'd like to see the Temple of Poseidon too. It's in ruins too, but a reason I'd like to see it is that it's on a promontory overlooking a kind of *sangam* of seas, where the Aegean meets the Mediterranean. So I'd like to be at the temple if only for that.

"I'd like to go to Rome too, because of all the art there that's in our art book, but I think I'd rather go to Greece. A lot of what's in Rome is because of Greece. So I think I'd like to see Greece first."

Beyond art, in the years since her eighth birthday, she'd learned a lot of history and geography, mythology and religion, and much else. And her saying all that so easily and quickly reminded me of that, and what she said of the site of the Temple of Poseidon being on a promontory overlooking a *sangam* also reminded me of how far she'd extended her vocabulary through her reading, and through her travels. And I was grateful for all of that both for her and for possibilities for all of us.

But I was most grateful for how what she said of what she learned showed how she learned it. It showed she considered how everything related to everything, and then spoke directly to the point, wherever that led her. So I was grateful that it showed she hadn't stopped being what she was.

But we went nowhere for her birthday that year. That was 2020, the year of the beginning of the COVID-19 chaos, the year of prohibition of nonessential travel. And the proscriptions didn't specify exploring among the categories of exceptions.

But, other than that, the chaos affected us relatively little. Bobby's mom worked in the Albion assessor's office, and Suzy's dad worked in maintenance, in Albion's largest remaining factory. And the virus didn't end the need for taxes or maintenance.

And neither did I see any reduction in the traffic of what Bee called her dad's friends or in Corinthia's going to what she'd called all the places she went. And, while many high school students may have found learning at home difficult, it was ordinary for the study group. And I already was leaving home only for what I thought was essential for Annie.

And Annie's heart took her a long long way.

"I hope those little kids with their corn are alright," she said. "Whichever little kids they are this year."

"I looked," I said. "Shangli's a long way from Wuhan."

"So did I," said Annie.

So, excepting doing no exploring on their bicycles, the main difference for the study group that year was that their schoolyear was much like their summers. Another difference was that Suzy's dad or Bobby's mom dropped them off at our house on their workday mornings. But Bee walked across the street as she ordinarily did.

Annie and I watched less news that year. But, because the President one of the Palestinians who spoke with us in Jerusalem called our corrupt President still dominated the news, the time we spent watching it already was diminishing. And Annie succinctly expressed the reason we didn't find the danger of COVID to be a reason to watch more news.

"Now he isn't the only one disagreeing with himself and not saying why," she said. "And some of them are supposed to be experts. So how can anyone know what to believe?"

"I don't know," I said. "I guess we just have to sort it out and do what makes sense to us."

"Yeah," said Annie smiling. "Like we always do."

But we continued to watch the evening news, rotating daily among the three main broadcast networks for balance, and we used our computers to keep track of the CDC's guidelines..

So, for the study group to be able to study as much as they could together but six feet apart, I bought each member of the group an electronic tablet. And, for them to be able to continue doing their *Taijiquan* together, I opened the heat vents to a room that was nearly half of our upstairs space. And, on the warm days with no rain, they used our backyard for that and other freedom of their spirit.

And Suzy and Bobby began learning piano that year. So their parents bought them a keyboard for that. And Corinthia bought Bee her own computer.

And the study group used much of their additional time together to discuss the books they brought home the day their school closed for the remainder of that schoolyear and working through the problems and questions in them. So, with the fullness of their interaction, they must have understood and remembered more than they might have in school. They shared their thoughts spontaneously. They didn't need to raise their hands. They were one another's teachers.

We also watched more movies. But we put masks on our faces for that and for most of our other interaction we couldn't do six feet apart. And that included much of their studying.

But they removed their masks for lunch. And Suzy and Bobby, on their parents' workdays, ate lunch at our house. And, at some lunches, the four took another risk.

That year was the first year all the members of the study group were together for each of their birthdays. So I baked and decorated a small layer cake for each of those days. And, on those days, Bee also stayed for lunch.

So the additional risk was blowing out the candles.

So my wish, as they did that, was that they and their remaining parents survive that time of physiological and psychological and political chaos.

And they did. Bee, because of her father's "friends" and her mother's "places", worried us most. But she and her parents and Suzy and Bobby and their parents and Annie and I survived all of that. So, with no death days for us that year, the study group from then on called it the year of the birthdays. And, the next year, things returned nearly to what had been ordinary for us.

"Are you ready to see sunlight on some more clouds, little friend?" I asked Annie on a sunny Sunday that summer.

With a book in hand, on her way from the shelves to the porch swing in our backyard, she'd stopped and looked up at the map. So, when I asked her that, her head turned toward me about as quickly as it had when I asked her whether she'd like to go to New York. She didn't jump onto our sofa, but she came and sat on it beside me, with a big grin on her face.

"I'm thinking," I said, "that, because we didn't go to Greece last year, we might want to catch up a little and go to both Greece and Rome this year. I remember you said you'd also like to see Rome."

So then, nodding and widening her grin, she gazed into the space beyond that side of our TV.

So, that year, on her birthday, on the Acropolis, by saying of the Parthenon what she'd said of the pyramids but in fewer words, she showed that still she hadn't lost her simple directness, that still she was what she always was.

"It's bigger than I thought it was," she said.

Then she walked all the way around it taking pictures of its columns and capitals and cornices. Next she spent nearly as much time looking at the Erechtheion and taking pictures of its caryatids. But next she looked beyond the Acropolis.

A flagpole was at its east end. And east of the flagpole was a nook with a stone wall around it on three of its sides. So Annie walked around the flagpole to the center of the wall at the back of the nook and looked over it over the city. But then she stepped back, raised her arms out to her sides and turned her palms up, and looked up and out at the sky. And she stood still and silent that way for several minutes.

"I wanted to see how the *Nike of Samothrace* felt standing on the prow of her stone ship," she said as we left the nook.

"Did you?" I asked. "I mean did you feel that way?"

"I don't know," she said. "But I felt like I was flying. And I felt like my mom was out there too. I felt like we were in each other's heart and flying everywhere together."

And she did the same at the Temple of Poseidon looking out over the *sangam* of the Mediterranean with the Aegean.

In Athens we also visited other ruins. But her Greek gifts for her study group were small stone replicas of the Parthenon. And our visit to Italy was more complex and wasn't only to Rome.

We flew to Venice, took trains to other cities, and walked to the places we visited in each city. In Venice, after having lunch on the *Piazza San Marco* and walking across the Bridge of Sighs, we saw some of Titian's and Tintoretto's paintings in churches. And in Pisa we climbed to the top of the leaning campanile.

In Florence, we saw Michelangelo's *David* and *Deposition*, but Annie showed little interest in anything else there.

"The Medici seem to me to be troublemakers," she said.

We walked all over the oldest part of Rome, and we spent much of a day in the Vatican Museums, but the statues that received the most attention from Annie there were Michelangelo's *Pieta* in St. Peter's Basilica and his *Moses* in the Church of St. Peter in Chains.

"Michelangelo's statues seem to me to feel," she said.

But she spent less than a minute looking at his paintings on the ceiling of the Sistine Chapel.

"That's Judith in the corner," she said. "She beheaded that guy while he was sleeping. That story isn't in the Bible anymore. But the picture's still here."

She spent several minutes standing still at the entrance to St. Peter's Square.

"It tells us it's important," she said. "But it welcomes us in with the colonnades too, like arms around us."

But the Roman building that received the most attention from her was the Colosseum.

"Look," she said as we approached it. "All three orders of Greek architecture. Doric on the bottom, Ionic in the middle, Corinthian on top. Basic Doric, then Ionic scrolls like for writing books, then Corinthian leaves like trees. I don't understand why Bulfinch used Roman names for the gods in his book. The Romans copied the Greeks."

And she also thought of her friends.

"I wonder if Bee's mom's parents named her after the Corinthians," she said.

And, inside the Colosseum, she said of it what she'd said of the Empire State Building, and of the Pyramids and the Parthenon, but in different words.

"I know it's the Colosseum," she said. "But I didn't know it was this colossal."

For Annie, art wasn't the ideas of Picasso or Rodin, or Polykleitos. For her, it was how it fit into whatever was or wasn't around it, how it fit into her life and how she felt about others' lives. It was what Holman and Harmon's *A Handbook to Literature* told her the New Critics called the affective fallacy. And I have no doubt that she thought about that as she read that book. But she didn't let labels limit her.

So her gifts from Italy for her study group were small stone replicas of the Colosseum, not because of its original purpose but because of what remained of it, what it had become.

"They don't do that gladiator stuff here or anywhere anymore," she said. "I guess football's about as much like it as anything, or maybe hockey or boxing or that mixed martial arts stuff, and they're not slaves. So doesn't that say something for the rest of us? At least that we're learning?"

And for her fourteenth birthday, for reasons beyond what she'd read in *Gardner's*, we went to Russia.

"I'd like to see the Hermitage," she said. "But I'd also like to see how people live there, after being serfs and then calling themselves communists, and how they live since the Cold War. And I'd like to see Tolstoy's estate, partly because he treated his serfs better than other landowners treated theirs, but mostly because I'd like to see what his life was like when he was writing *War and Peace*."

So we flew to Moscow and, on our first full day in Russia, walked from our hotel to Red Square and the Kremlin.

"This isn't like *Zǐjìnchéng* and *Tiānānmén*," said Annie as we returned to Red Square after visiting the Kremlin. "The Chinese government's offices aren't in *Zǐjìnchéng* anymore, and *Tiānānmén*'s a lot newer than *Zǐjìnchéng* and has some government buildings around it."

"And the name of Red Square doesn't mean 'quiet'," I said.

"I don't think the *tiān ān mén* across the street from *Zǐjìnchéng* is the sky's quiet gate either," she said grinning as we compared those memories of ours. "And Red Square doesn't look as red as *Zǐjìnchéng* to me."

But from Red Square we walked around the Kremlin to GUM for Annie to see Russians doing something they ordinarily needed to do beyond walking and eating. So, as we walked through it, she compared it to the United States. She'd read of it in her research for that trip.

"It's a mall," she said. "Look! There's a Gucci store. And there's a Calvin Klein store. The building's old, but I think it has more stores than Jackson Crossing, and it has more than one floor, like the malls in movies. I thought a national department store would be more like a big warehouse, and I thought almost all the people here were poor, but maybe they are. I haven't see any shoppers in most of the stores."

But, next morning, returning to Annie's appreciation for art, we took a train to St. Petersburg to see the Hermitage, and that surprised her somewhat similarly but also more complexly and broadly.

"Look at all these czars," she said as we walked through its long first-floor hallway for portraits of them.

But, turning though a doorway at the end of that hallway, we found a stairway and climbed it.

And, in the room at its top, she stopped and stared.

"Cezanne!" she said. "Cezanne! After all those czars! It's like we stepped into another world!"

And the next morning we took a train back to Moscow. And that afternoon she found her Russian gifts for her study group. In Red Square, among a variety of things venders were selling from tables, she found some Dymkovo toys.

"They'll like these, I think," she said. "They're more like art than like toys, but they're cheerful, too."

And that evening we saw the Bolshoi Ballet perform *Swan Lake*, and Annie remembered *Giselle*, and Bee.

"This is for Bee," she said of her program during intermission. "I gave her my *Giselle* program too after I saw how much she liked Rachmaninoff. And she likes Tchaikovsky's ballet music now too."

And the next day we took the special train from Moscow to Tula, to see Tolstoy's estate, *Yasnaya Polyana*.

"I feel like they're here," she said in the main parlor of the main house. "I mean Natasha and Pierre and their friends."

But that was her fourteenth birthday.

So, because her study group would enroll in college the next year, that was our last trip out of the United States together. To be able to graduate in three years, they planned to go to school through the summers, and they were too busy preparing to begin college for us to take a trip the last summer before they enrolled. But neither were they going far for that.

Since the third grade, their grade point average had been perfect, and all of their SAT scores were above the 99th percentile. So they could have acquired scholarships to nearly any university anywhere, but their academic record and their friendship already had made them quite famous, among Michigan academics. So the University of Michigan offered them full scholarships before they requested any scholarship from anyone. And its Dean of Admissions telephoned their parents to make that offer.

"The University of Michigan is interested in all four of them," she said when she called me. "If they're interested in us."

"Can we go see what it's like there?" asked Annie when I told her, after waiting for our supper talk, to leave telling Bee and Suzy and Bobby to their parents.

So, the next morning, I walked across the street to ask Corinthia whether anyone had called her, and she told me the Dean of Admissions had called her with the same message, and Suzy's and Bobby's parents said the same when I called them. So then, answering Annie's question, we agreed to make an appointment for all of us together to talk with an admissions counselor in Ann Arbor and to go there in a two-car convoy like the one we took to Marshall Middle School. So we arrived at our decision on that in about the same way we decided on Marshall Middle School.

To answer Annie's question literally, we arrived about a half hour early for the appointment to wander about the campus to look at it, and Suzy was the first to speak as she'd initiated the exchange that decided on Marshall Middle School.

"It feels nice here," she said as we crossed a grassy quadrangle.

"Yeah," said Annie. "I want to go to Columbia for graduate school, to be near the United Nations. But I don't know how we'd get along in New York City now. We're kind of young."

"Yeah," said Bobby. "We'd know what we're doing, but the eight million New Yorkers might not think so."

"And maybe we could use some time getting used to college before we have to deal with that," said Bee. "What do you think, Billy?"

I looked at the other parents. But they were looking at me as though they also wished to know what I thought. So I answered as well as I could.

"I think you four already take responsibility for your own education," I said. "So I think you can learn as well here as you could anywhere. And the University of Michigan has a strong enough reputation for your performance here to get you into graduate school at Columbia or anywhere else. But I think it's up to you."

I wouldn't have advised them as much as that, if what they'd said hadn't told me how they already felt, and their responding accordingly to the admissions counselor proved further that they felt that way.

But one more decision, a decision the four had somewhat considered in what they said in that short walk, remained essential to that move. We had to decide where three fifteen-year-olds and a fourteen-year-old would sleep at a university fifty-some miles from home. The admissions counselor said she thought she could find faculty members to take them in. But she also said she wasn't sure she could find a household to take in all four of them. And Annie demurred from that for another reason.

When we returned home, Bee and her mother walked hand in hand across the street to their house, and Suzy and Bobby and their parents turned toward their home before we reached our neighborhood. And that was before our suppertime and not at a time we ordinarily worked on our Chinese or French. So Annie had nothing on her schedule for then.

But, when we went inside, she sat at our dining table. And she didn't sit at her computer, where she and her friends had done most of the work that earned them their way into college, but at the end of the table where she sat to eat. So, wondering more than I ordinarily did what she was thinking, I sat in the side chair where I sat to eat.

"So, little friend," I said. "You're going to college."

Then she looked at me with a big smile and nodded. But, after a few minutes of talking about what college might be academically, our conversation turned to the agreement with Suzy about how nice the campus felt. And then she frowned a little.

"I know they wouldn't be foster parents," she said, not looking at me but straight ahead of her. "But I'd feel like they were."

I had an answer to that. What she and Bee and Bobby had said of New York in response to what Suzy said of the campus already had me considering an alternative. But Annie also had answers to my answer.

"How about this?" I said. "We could buy a house in Ann Arbor and sell this one."

"Oh," said Annie. "I didn't think of that."

But she put her palms on the table and looked down between her hands and stayed that way for more than a minute before speaking again.

"I've thought about living in New York," she said, slowly looking up but gazing straight ahead of her as she often did in silent thought. "But I haven't thought about not living here, and I love this house. It's my home, and it's been my only home since my mom went beyond, and think of all I've learned here with you and my other friends, and all the other fun all of us have had together here, and I wasn't anybody before I came here. I mean I didn't know who I was, and now everybody likes me and thinks I'm smart, and I'm going to college."

And then she looked down at the table again. But not as long before lifting her head again, and then she turned from her chair and went to our Buddha statuette and touched the tip of her right index finger to the tip of its *ushnisha*, as she still often did to consider especially important questions. And then she looked up at the map.

"And I've been to China," she said. "As you told me we might. And I feel like it's here."

But then she looked down at the statuette again. And, after standing that way for what seemed to me to be several minutes, she returned to her chair and put her hands on the table again. But then she didn't look down.

"But we have to," she said. "And we can take this stuff with us, can't we? I mean this table and my piano and our Buddha."

"Sure we can," I said, and then she began to grin.

But then she stopped the grin and frowned again.

"But what about Bee and Suzy and Bobby?" she said.

"They can move in with us if they want," I said.

And then she grinned.

And Bee and Corinthia gratefully accepted our offer.

"I can come see her there, can't I?" asked Corinthia. "She had those earphones on her head all the time the first couple of months after you gave her that keyboard. But now she talks to me more than she did before, and she's talking to her dad more too. Hell, I'm talking to him more.

"I don't know what's got into us."

And Bobby and Suzy and their parents initially accepted the offer. But, when time came to begin that buying and selling process, their parents changed their minds. They decided to do what Annie and I had decided to do.

"They said they're not quite ready to live without us," said Suzy.

"So they're going to look for jobs in Ann Arbor," said Bobby.

And they relatively easily found jobs there.

"They said they think they'll like their new jobs more than their old ones," said Suzy a few weeks later.

"They said they'll pay more too," said Bobby.

"And my dad said the guy who interviewed him for his new job congratulated him on his reason for quitting his job here," said Suzy, grinning. "He said he said he couldn't hold that against anyone. He said he said it was the best reason he ever heard for changing jobs."

"My mom too," said Bobby. "I mean she said the woman who interviewed her congratulated her too. And she said she said it showed an admirable sense of responsibility."

So only Bee moved in with us. But, before I learned of Suzy's and Bobby's parents' decision, I found on the Web a listing for a house I thought might be big enough for all five of us. And I made an appointment to see it.

It had three bedrooms and a bathroom upstairs and another bedroom and bathroom downstairs, and a study downstairs and a two-car garage, and woods were behind it.

So I thought it was more than we needed. But I told Annie and Bee about it and asked them whether they'd like to see it and decide for themselves. And they looked at one another and grinned and said they'd like to if it was OK with me. So their reply was what I'd learned to expect from them. So we kept the appointment.

But then I had another problem. That was the nearest I ever came to asking *Ān Nǔ* to be quiet. And that was difficult.

"If we like it," I said to her and Bee during that drive to Ann Arbor, "we don't want to tell the real estate agent how much we do while she's showing it to us. If we do, she might make us pay more for it than we might if we don't, but I don't think anything's worth lying. And I hope you know I don't and wouldn't ask you to lie about anything.

"So how about if we just don't say much while she's showing it to us. Then, if we like it, you can tell her and thank her after we decide the price. And, anyway, I'm sure we'll pay at least what we should."

They neither grinned nor smiled when I told them that. But, as I looked at Bee, and then back at Annie, who for that ride was sitting in the backseat behind Bee, they nodded. And they said nothing as the agent showed us the house.

They looked at one another from time to time as both I and the agent watched them to see how they felt, and the agent spoke cheerfully to them and asked them a few questions, but they kept their replies to nods or shrugs.

But, when the agent left us in the driveway, both they and I had plenty to say.

14

Three More Steps

"So what do you think?" I asked.

"It's more than we need," said Annie, again responding as I'd learned to expect her to respond. "But I like it, and I like the woods out back, too."

"How about you, Bee?" I asked.

And she nodded and smiled at Annie.

"So do I," I said. "So here's what I'm thinking.

"You two could take two of the upstairs bedrooms while I take the downstairs one. We could furnish the other upstairs bedroom as a guestroom and put the bookshelves and your piano and the map and the Buddha in the study. We could leave the rest of the study's floorspace clear for *Taijiquan*."

And then Bee grinned.

"So I could do my *Taijiquan* at home," she said as Annie smiled at her grin.

"And our Mustang would have walls on its house," said Annie. "Instead of only the carport roof and those poles holding it up. And getting our bikes in and out of the garage would be easier than getting mine out of our shed too. We'll have a lot of new exploring to do here. When we're not too busy with school."

So I offered twenty percent less than the asking price, and we settled at about ten percent less, and bought the house.

"We love it," said Bee at the closing.

"Thank you," said Annie.

And the agent smiled at them, told them they were welcome, and thanked them also. So, instead of flying to another country for Annie's fifteenth birthday, we moved into our new home. But we furnished each of the upstairs bedrooms much as I'd furnished Annie's room in Albion.

When I asked Annie and Bee how they'd like to furnish their rooms, Annie said she liked her furniture in Albion and would like to keep it, and Bee said she also liked Annie's furniture. But, because of changes in availability in the years since I furnished Annie's room in Albion, we needed to select some variance in colors and patterns for Bee's room. And Bee enjoyed making those selections and, immediately after the first time she made her new bed, did a snow angel on it.

And she and Annie selected the variations for the guestroom together, showing that Annie's choosing to keep her furniture didn't indicate a shift from her ordinary openness, as also did her initial remark on her new neighborhood.

"Looks like we might have some trick-or-treaters here," she said smiling as she stood in our new front yard surveying the other houses on our new block, three of which had bicycles on the walks leading to their front doors.

And she and Bee found themselves welcome in that neighborhood. But, with none of our new near neighbors college students, the main social interaction in our home remained the study group. And, less than two weeks after we moved there, the study group began its college classes.

But college was different from high school for them in many ways. And one way was that, because they selected among them a total of six major and minor courses of study, they had fewer classes together. Annie's major and minor were international relations and political science, while Suzy's and Bobby's were English and French, while Bee's were dance and music.

But none of that surprised me. I knew well Annie's interests and concerns, and I'd heard some of the conversations of the four with one another, both directly and indirectly pertinent to their deciding what to study. And I'd seen some indications of their particular talents before I heard them speak of them.

One winter, before I found Annie, as I looked from what became our front window at several inches of snow that had fallen that afternoon, Bee was walking home from the school bus stop with her father. She stopped in their driveway, stepped to a side of it and lay on her back in the snow on the grass, and made a snow angel. And then she stood and did a pirouette.

Her father brushed the snow from her and carried her into their house. But, as he carried her up their driveway and onto their front porch, she kept her arms in a circle above her head. She didn't lower them until he carried her through their front door.

So, for several reasons, Bee's choice not only didn't surprise me but also pleased me. It reminded me not only of that pirouette and snow angel but also of Annie's making the snow angel motions on her bed the day we became housemates. And it reminded me of my sister Peggy teaching me to make snow angels when she was about the age Annie was on the day we became friends. So it reminded me of the reason I gave Miss Walker when she asked me why I was thinking of becoming a foster parent. And it made me think I was right in that reasoning.

The snow angels seemed to me to be of the spirit of Peggy and Annie and Bee and also of Suzy and Bobby. Every moment I was with the four of them confirmed my suspicion in that regard. And nothing they did seemed to me to be an exception to it.

So, whatever they studied and whatever differences may have been in anything they did, they seemed to me to be of the spirit that made me wish to be sure they had the freedom to be what they were.

But, particularly regarding Bee, I also remembered seeing her way of climbing out of her mother's car, turning around and pushing the car door to close it, continuing the turn another 180 degrees, skipping up the steps to their porch, and opening their storm door, all in one continuous flow, as one motion.

And, of course, I also remembered her attention to our keyboard the first time she was in our house and her smile as she listened to the Rachmaninoff CD Annie gave her for Christmas. So neither did her response to my suggesting reserving space for *Taijiquan* in the study of our new home surprise me. It seemed to me to be simply how she was.

So an additional joy in our home in Ann Arbor was seeing her live up to her name by flitting about the house letting her study of ballet integrate into her ordinary actuality, producing a pleasant counterpoint to Annie's ordinarily even quietude, as each easily incorporated herself into all around them.

And Suzy and Bobby similarly validated their study focus. While all four of them read books beyond the books in the extracurricular project they organized, Suzy and Bobby read more fiction and talked more about methods of writing and authors' intentions, and they treated as a question of both conscience and craftsmanship Annie's question of whether most authors apply what *A Handbook to Literature* describes. Yet they didn't let their academic considerations distract them from their direct sense of what they read.

"I've never ridden a train," said Bobby of the rhythm in *Of Time and the River*. "But reading that book felt to me like the sound of the Amtrak trains clattering through Albion when they don't stop. I felt like, instead of me reading the book, the book was carrying me along for the ride."

And they carried their considerations across the full spectrum of literary purposes and effects.

"I didn't want to close the book when I came to its end," said Suzy of *Vanity Fair*. "I felt that the characters were my friends and that I'd known them all that time. So I was afraid I was going to miss them when I was gone."

Yet, while all those qualifications and considerations and specializations were what some might call differences, I never knew any of the four of them to give any indication that they thought or felt they were different from one another in any important way.

And other conversations of theirs told me the four's unity was part of why they'd need three years to earn their baccalaureate degrees. Having earned their first year of college credit through the College Level Examination Program, they easily could have received their degrees in three years with no summer classes, and they planned to carry a full courseload summers. But, to have a reason to continue their study group, they also decided to take together in each term one course in an area beyond the major or minor concentration of any of them.

And another reason they'd need three years was that their reading had told them the four centuries from the Norman Conquest through the Hundred Years War had made the French language about half of the English language and that it was also the language of diplomacy and ballet.

So Bee, both for ballet and to keep up with Suzy and Bobby and catch up with Annie, added a minor in French to her concentrations. So the others, both for that additional common fluency and to make that additional concentration easier for Bee, worked with her on it at our house and spoke it there enough for me also to became fluent in it. So that also required of all four some deliberate effort and time.

And another reason they'd need three years was that, to prepare for their move to New York City to enter Columbia in the autumn, they decided to graduate in the spring. And, of course, all of that required adjusting their schedule from what it was in high school. And transportation was another factor.

The university didn't send school buses to neighborhoods, and our house was in a suburb about three miles from the campus, and our Mustang didn't have seats for four passengers. So I considered buying a bigger car, but I enjoyed the open air and agility of our Mustang, and we all liked it for its aura of freedom. But that problem was easy to solve.

Suzy's and Bobby's parents readily volunteered. On each of their workdays, one or the other of them drove the four to campus before work and picked them up after work to drive them to our house, for their more direct learning together. And that also gave them time before and after classes to do much of their homework at the university's main library.

So, to do at our house as much as they could of their academic work they could do together, they did as much as they could of their academic reading at the library. So, as in Albion, my share of transporting them was only to drive Suzy and Bobby home for supper. But the transportation requirement changed in their first term.

"I made a new friend," said Annie at supper a few days after they aced their first midterm examinations. "He's majoring in international relations too. So he's in two of my classes, and I like the questions he asks in class, and his name's Maitri. So, after our afternoon class together yesterday, I asked him whether his parents named him for the Maitri in the *Maitri Upanishad*. And he said they did.

"But he said he's more of a Buddhist than a Hindu. So I told him I'm more of a Buddhist too but that, except for the part about the castes, I like the *Maitri Upanishad*. And he said the castes are part of why he's more of a Buddhist.

"But, anyway, I like him. So would it be OK if I ask him to supper some night? Maybe Friday?"

"It's OK with me," I said. "If it's OK with Bee."

"It's OK with me," said Bee. "I like him too. He had lunch with us today. He asked what the dance we do in front of the library sometimes is.

"And Annie told him it's *Taijiquan*. But she also said it's a Chinese way of feeling everything's everything. And he said it sounds Buddhist.

"So Suzy told him about Bodhidharma. He said he knew about Bodhidharma and Zen but didn't know about *Taijiquan*.. So Bobby told him about Zheng Sanfeng and why people call it *Taijiquan* now. And he asked us if we'd teach it to him. So we started after lunch."

"Bee," I said, "I don't think I've ever heard you say that much, all at once.

"It was a nice lunch," she said shrugging.

And that Friday evening was a nice supper.

"I brought some *gaajar ka halava*," said Maitri when Annie answered our doorbell. "I hope you like it."

And during supper he told us he was from Gaya and that his parents taught international relations and economics at Mogadh University in Bodhgaya.

"That's how I'm at UofM," he said. "They were able to arrange the grants I needed to study international relations and economics here. That sort of thing works differently in India from how it works here."

And, after complimenting my cooking, he commented on it further.

"And no meat," he said. "Is that for me, because I'm Buddhist?"

"No," said Annie. "It's because we wouldn't want a cow or a turkey or a fish to eat us."

And Maitri laughed, snickered and shook his head, and then laughed again.

"So much is in that answer," he said.

And all of us smiled at the *gaajar ka halava*.

"This is great!" said Bee. "What is it?"

"*Gaajar ka halava*," said Maitri. "That's Hindi for 'sweet of carrot'. It's carrots, cashews and almonds and sometimes other nuts, milk and butter, and cardamom. But this is from the Indian restaurant on Main Street. So I don't know what else is in it.

"I would have made it myself, but they don't let us cook in the dorm."

"Well, thanks for it, anyway," I said. "It's great."

"Thanks for inviting me," replied Maitri. "I've been at UofM since last year, but I don't have many friends here. Most of the students seem to me to care more about football than about their classes, and Annie's the only person here who's asked me about my name. That was a big surprise.

"And I like her friends too.

"They're teaching me *Taijiquan*. Annie told me its name and that it's a Chinese way of feeling what I think Buddhism is, and Suzy and Bobby told me some of its history and why it's both Buddhist and Daoist, both Indian and Chinese. And Bee told me it's a way of knowing and showing how thinking we're different only keeps us from being ourself.

"And that's all I understand Buddhism to be. So together they've made me feel at home, here in the United States, for the first time. And now I feel welcome in your home."

"Well we like you too," said Bee.

"And you *are* welcome here," said Annie.

"That's good to hear," said Maitri. "I'd like to come back sometime, and bring the groceries and cook for you three, and for Suzy and Bobby too if that's alright."

And Bee grinned at that, and Annie smiled, and I spoke.

"Next Friday?" I asked.

And then Maitri grinned.

"I'm thinking you probably know your name means 'friendship' in Sanskrit," I said.

"Yes," he said. "So I try to live up to it."

"Did you know that, Annie?" I asked.

"Yes," she said. "When I read the *Maitri Upanishad*, I looked it up in the Sanskrit dictionary on your Kindle account. I mean our Kindle account."

And, after that Friday, Maitri's visits increased their frequency, until he said he could drive the study group to our house after classes every day if we wished, and the four agreed to that. So that left Suzy's and Bobby's parents needing to take them to the campus only before classes mornings. And that also involved his making supper for all of us once or twice a week.

And, whether or not Suzy and Bobby stayed for supper, he also drove them home. So Maitri became a member of the study group to the extent that I didn't need to drive Suzy and Bobby anywhere. So, at supper the Saturday after the group's next midterm examinations, I asked a question I thought Annie and Bee may have been thinking. And they proved me correct.

"Why doesn't Maitri just move in with us?" I asked. "We have that room up there we're not using. And we know he doesn't much like living in the dorm."

"I don't know," said Bee. "I guess maybe it's because nobody's asked him."

"So let's ask him," said Annie.

So then neither did Suzy's and Bobby's parents need to take the group to the campus mornings. And Maitri parked his car in the side of our garage in which I didn't park our Mustang. But that changed that summer.

That was Annie's sixteenth summer. So I arranged for her and the other original members of the study group to take the driver training they ordinarily would have received in their sophomore year of high school. And I decided to buy Annie a car.

But buying the car was a little difficult. I wished both to surprise her and to be sure what I bought was what she'd buy for herself. And I also wished to keep my policy of not keeping secrets from her.

So I followed her example. I managed the process somewhat as she'd managed her purchases of Christmas gifts for the study group for our first Christmas together. I told her all I could of my plan while not telling her I was buying the car for her.

"I'm thinking of buying a new car," I said. "What do you think we should buy?"

"I don't know," she said. "I like our Mustang. I like the way it looks, and I like that it's a convertible, because of all that openness. But sometimes it's not big enough for us now. So maybe an SUV?"

And a few days later she gave me more details.

"I saw an Explorer I like," she said. "They're Fords like our Mustang, and they're big enough, and I like exploring.

"So I looked them up on the Web. They come in a gray color Ford calls stone. So, if we bought one that color outside and black inside, it would be like our Mustang but the other way around. I mean its outside would be about the color of our Mustang's inside, and its inside would be the color of our Mustang's outside, and I like stones."

Then she shrugged.

"Just thinking," she said.

But by saying what she thought, as she always did in reply to any question, she solved my problem for me. So then I found a Ford dealership and ordered the car. And the rest was easy.

On the morning of her sixteenth birthday, Maitri drove her and Suzy and Bobby to the nearest Michigan Secretary of State branch for their drivers licenses.

Fifteen-year-old Bee also rode along, for them to do all they could together, but the reasons he drove them there were more than the seating problem. The driver training teacher didn't train them to operate the Mustang's six-speed manual transmission. So they'd used Maitri's car for their learners permit practice. So his car would be easier for their driving test.

But, when they returned to our house with their three new drivers licenses, I drove Annie to the Ann Arbor Ford dealership.

The reasons both of us needed to go there were that I wanted her name on the car's title and that the dealer needed my permission for that before she was eighteen.

"Feel like going for another ride, little friend?" I asked her when she stepped out of Maitri's driver seat after driving the study group home with her new license. "I'd like to show you something I think you might like."

She replied to that with a questioning look, but then she gave me a nod with a little smile and didn't ask the question, unless it was the question she asked with a grin when we drove onto the lot of the Ford dealership.

"You bought the new car?" she asked.

"Not officially yet," I said. "I wanted to be sure you like it before we fill out the paperwork."

"It's what I told you I liked," she said seeing it, just outside the front entrance to the showroom.

"So you do like it?" I asked.

"Yes!" she said, looking through its driver window, and then she looked up and stood up and jumped up to see its roof.

"A sunroof!" she said. "It has a sunroof! I didn't see on the website that Ford makes them with sunroofs!"

So then, with her grin continuing from that, we went inside and found the salesman.

"You need to sign here," he said to me.

Then, after I signed, he turned to Annie.

"And you need to sign several places," he said.

"Why do I need to sign?" she asked.

"For it to be officially yours," I said. "I only needed to sign to give him permission for that. It's a birthday present."

Then she looked at me. But that time she didn't grin. She shook her head with a kind of kind and wondering smile and put a hand on my arm nearest to her. And suddenly I had to admit that she'd become an adult. And the salesman didn't help.

"Happy birthday, young lady," he said.

But, as she signed the papers, she grinned. And then the salesman grinned at Annie's grinning. So then I knew she hadn't stopped being Annie.

And that wasn't the last of her grinning that day. The salesman walked us to her Explorer, showed her what the buttons on the keys did and opened the driver door for her, and handed her the keys. Then he walked around to the other side of the car and climbed into its front passenger seat to show her how its cameras worked and how to use its GPS to find her way home. Our 2012 Mustang had no GPS or any of the cameras that then were standard. But she asked the salesman but one question.

"How do we open the sunroof," she asked.

Then she grinned as she opened it, was grinning as I pulled into our driveway behind Maitri's car and walked around to her, and kept the grin as she turned off the engine of her new vehicle, stepped out of it and closed its driver door, and turned to me.

But then she turned back, looked with no grin at her new Explorer, and stood silent for a few seconds.

And then she smiled.

"Vaucouleurs," she said. "I'm almost as old now as Jehanne was when the people of Vaucouleurs gave her the first horse she rode. And she's still in my heart, but I hope I never have to fight in a war, and I hope I can keep others from having to. And I think she'd be happy about that."

But then, as her comrades in peace came out of our house grinning, she grinned again. So then she took them for a ride in her new Explorer, and more evidence of the success of that selection process was what she did with it, for the remainder of her time at the University of Michigan. She drove it everywhere she went.

So, because Bee and Maitri went nearly everywhere she went and because Annie also began driving all of her study group to campus mornings and driving Suzy and Bobby home after their study together at our house, Maitri nearly never drove his car other than to move it out of my way or out of hers after he gladly relinquished his space in our garage to her. So, after their next midterm examinations, he sold his car. But, before doing that, he told Annie.

"It's only in the way now," he said, "now that you're driving all of us to campus and back and driving Suzy and Bobby home at night. And I nearly never go anywhere you don't go and can call an Uber when I do. So I'd like to pay for your gasoline.

"But I know your Explorer uses it only when its charge is low. So, when we go grocery shopping together, I'd also like to pay for the groceries you buy. The only reason I haven't asked you that before is that I'm afraid you wouldn't buy as much if I paid. But I don't know what I can do about that. Except to tell you I hope you will.

"And Billy isn't letting me pay rent either. He thanks me when I mow the grass or mulch the leaves or blow the snow, but I don't think he'd let me do that either if I hadn't figured out how to use the machines, to do it on my own. And, anyway, I'd like to pay for something.

"So will that be alright?"

When he said all that, he and Annie were sitting at the study table working together on an international relations class project, while I sat in my reading chair reading. So, when he said that about the rent and the grass and leaves and snow, he looked at me and smiled. But, though I also smiled, I didn't interrupt their conversation.

"I guess so," then said Annie, shaking her head but grinning at him. "I see what you mean. But you know we like having you around."

"I like being around," said Maitri. "So we're even on that."

And Annie also smiled at that. So that conversation went as I might have expected it to go, and I appreciated both that Maitri wished to earn his keep and that he wished to be open about everything, but I was also happy that Bee was in our study practicing her piano when he said that. And I had no doubt that Maitri considered that when he decided when to say it.

My thought in that regard was that hearing it may have made Bee feel she should pay something to live with us. And I was also happy that she seemed to me to feel as much at home with us as we felt at home with her. So I had no wish to change that.

But Annie's Explorer's shifting responsibility to her also ended a family tradition we established the summer we went to Jehanne's house.

"I think we should take a trip to Target," I said to her the week before we flew to France. "You're growing, and some of your clothes are fraying a little, and I think Target may have a little more variety than Walmart has. And, for France, I think we might make your *couture* a little more *haute*. So what do you think?"

"I don't want my *couture* to be too *haute*," she said shrugging. "I don't want people to feel sorry for me, but I don't want them to think I'm trying to be better than they are either. I just want to get along with people."

But then, with another shrug, she smiled and then grinned.

"But that would be a way to see more of what other people buy," she said,. "I mean we'd see stuff Walmart doesn't have. So I guess it would be like another kind of exploring. Maybe."

And, on our trip to Target for our trip to China, she looked at the tags to see if anything she liked was from there. But, with the mobility her Explorer gave her, she could take herself to Target and other stores as she took Maitri grocery shopping. And, before she entered college, we also established her financial freedom.

Before her graduation from high school, expecting her to need a social security number to request scholarships, we obtained one for her. So, after she obtained her scholarships, we used her social security card to open savings and checking accounts for her at my bank. And we funded them with her money.

I transferred to her savings account the cash from the account I'd used for the stipend the State of Michigan paid me for her before we changed the legal status of our relationship from fostering one another to adopting one another.

And, to fund her checking account, I set up a weekly transfer to it of her allowance. I'd inflated it at the annual rate the Web article suggesting its original amount said was ordinary. And I'd also inflated it at the United States' economy's rate of inflation.

And she set up direct deposits to her checking account of her scholarship reimbursements and cost of living stipends.

And, using her computer, she also taught herself how to reconcile her accounts. She and Bee and Suzy and Bobby taught themselves Microsoft Word to use it for their seventh grade English assignments. And, in high school, she stepped them into Excel.

"What's that?" she asked one evening looking at the computer screen in front us while I reconciled my bank accounts while we watched news.

"Excel," I said.

"What's Excel?" she asked.

"It's a computer application for calculating and tracking how numbers relate to one another," I said.

"What are those papers?" she asked.

"Bank statements," I said. "I use Excel to keep track of our money. When the statements come in the mail, I compare them to this Excel workbook and make any corrections or other changes the statements show."

"How does it work?" she asked.

So I showed her some of the basic functions for calculation and display and establishing relationships among the cells.

"So it's another way of seeing how everything fits together," she said. "I mean like what Bee said about numbers and letters and music. Is it on my computer?"

"Yes," I said. "Do you want me to show you?"

But, instead of answering, she went to her computer.

"There it is," she said, and then she pinned a shortcut to it to beside her Word shortcut on her taskbar, and after that the study group used it for their high school mathematics homework.

So, the evening of the day she received her first bank statements, she created a workbook to track her accounts. So, when she needed to step from her debit card to a credit card to facilitate her exploring with her Explorer, she was ready. And, selecting her credit card, she asked but two questions.

And both regarded how to make it a revenue producer and not an interest expender.

"Is this APR like when the bank pays me interest on my savings account?" she asked.

"Yes," I said. "It's for you to use your credit card to use the bank's money for your purposes for a while, as it uses your money for its purposes while you leave it in your savings account."

"Economists call that the time value of money," said Maitri.

He was sitting beside me on our sofa watching the news, while Annie sat at the study table comparing credit cards on our bank's website, while Bee practiced her music or dance in our study. Our house, for all its young inhabitants to accomplish all they wished to accomplish, was an easy place to be. We were always easily interruptible or easily not interrupting.

"I should have left that question to our resident economist," I said, and Annie smiled at that, but next she asked the second question with no smile.

"So I'd have to pay to use the credit card?" she asked.

"Not if you pay the full statement balance by its due date every month," said Maitri.

So then she smiled again, and she said nothing more, until she'd formed a hypothesis.

"Cash back, I think," she said after a few more minutes of searching the website. I don't think I'd do much of that stuff you have to do for points. And you can calculate the cash back and see what they're doing. And you get it on everything you buy."

Then she looked up again. But both Maitri and I smiled. So she didn't make that a question. She selected the card that paid the highest percentage of cash back. And, when she received her first credit card statement, she built reconciling it into her Excel checking and savings account reconciliation workbook. And she set up automatic monthly payoff of it from her checking account.

And using her credit card was the most substantial change in her way of living from her sixteenth birthday until her study group graduated from college.

15

Diamonds and Forever

    But the next year Bobby finished reading the *Qu'ran*. And that made him the last of the four original members of the study group to finish reading the definitive scriptures of each of the six most popular religions. So, on Christmas day 2025, in our living room after Bee and Suzy and Bobby spent most of the day with their parents, all six of us talked of all six of those religions, and Bobby began the discussion.

    "I don't understand the connection between Jesus and Judaism," he said. "Not even the genetic connection if the word 'Judaic' means 'descendent from Judah'. I mean, with the Bible saying Jesus' mother was a cousin of John the Baptist's and that both of John the Baptist's parents were Levites, I don't understand how Christians can believe both that Jesus descended from David and that Mary was a virgin when she conceived him. I mean with the Bible saying David was Judaic and that Joseph descended from David but that Jesus' parents were Mary and God.

    "And, with Jesus promoting peace and love in most of the Gospels, I don't understand why it also says he said he didn't come to bring peace but to bring a sword to divide us against each other. I mean that dividing seems to me to be consistent with the Judaic part of the Bible, with the Israelites' killing other people for their land, and killing each other for power. But I don't see how anyone can agree with both that bellicosity and the Beatitudes.

"And the same with the *Qur'an*. I mean, with the *Qur'an* forbidding killing for any reason other than for defense against oppression, I don't see why people calling themselves Muslims are about as murderous and divisive as that Israelite stuff. But, even with that, I don't see why Christians call Muslims terrorists, while they don't call Israelis terrorists, whatever they do."

"I don't either," said Suzy. "And, except the sword, that part about Jesus dividing us against one another is in both Matthew's Gospel and Luke's, and both of those Gospels also say Jesus said nothing's more important than loving God and loving our neighbors, and Matthew's Gospel says Jesus said those two are like one another."

"That last part sounds like Hinduism and Buddhism to me," said Maitri. "I mean with Hindus and Buddhists basically believing everything's God because God's everything. That's basically believing loving your neighbors is like loving God because your neighbors *are* God. But Hindu scripture promotes some dividing too. So the problem isn't all Abrahamic."

"I think Paul's the problem with Christianity," said Annie. "The Gospels say Jesus told his disciples to beware of the doctrine of the Pharisees. But Paul was a Pharisee, and putting pieces of the Bible together suggests that what made the Pharisees different from other Judaic people was how the Pharisees interpreted the prophesies that God would anoint a descendent of David's to resurrect the kingdom of Judah, that the Pharisees say they mean he'll resurrect not only the kingdom and the temple but also every member of the kingdom who either never violated Mosaic law or repented violating it. And a big piece is that the Book of Acts says the Pharisees believed in that but that the Sadducees didn't.

"It also says Paul's tribe was Benjamin and not Judah, but doesn't his being a Pharisee say he had an interest in saying Jesus was the descendent of David's the Judaic part of the Bible calls the messiah, whether or not his tribe was Judah?

"And another thing is that none of Paul's epistles mentions any of the four Gospels, and something else is that two of the authors of the four Gospels were Paul's apostles but not Jesus' disciples, and neither of the other two Gospels mentions either of those two. And no Gospel says either of them ever met or saw Jesus, and another thing is that the Book of Acts doesn't name more than three or four of Jesus's disciples, and Paul's epistles mention none of them other than three of the ones the Book of Acts names. And, like Luke with his Gospel, the author of the Book of Acts addresses it to someone he calls Theophilus.

"'Theophilus' is from Greek for 'loving God'. So I guess he may have been addressing it to anyone who loves God, but that word isn't anywhere else in the King James translation of the Bible, and Lucas is a Greek name. And Luke or Lucas was one of those two evangels no evangel says ever met Jesus.

"So I think he may have called Paul Theophilus and written both books. The language of the whole New Testament, or at least its oldest manuscripts, is Greek. But, unless, like Christ, Theophilus is a sort of name, why don't translators translate it?

"And 'christ' is Greek for 'anointed', and 'messiah' is Hebrew for 'anointed', as in anointing a king. And some of what Paul says in his epistle to the Galatians adds up to saying he wrote it at least fourteen years after the crucifixion. So I think Paul may have founded Christianity as a doctrine of the Pharisees and couldn't talk most of Jesus' disciples into it. But I don't understand why the Christian part of the Bible contradicts itself either. I mean if Paul supervised the writing of the Gospels.

"But I think a possibility may be that the reason he didn't leave out the most loving and peaceful things the Gospels say Jesus said, and especially the things he said that sound Buddhist, is that he didn't understand them."

And then, after that long departure from her usual quietness, Annie shrugged and sat back in her chair. But her friends, after listing to all that as all of the study group always listened to one another, continued the conversation from there. And, of course, Annie listened to them as they'd listened to her.

"That makes sense to me," said Suzy. "But I wonder how many Christians have read the Bible. The preacher at Bobby's mom's church quotes Paul and the Judaic part of the Bible a lot more often than he quotes Jesus. He hardly ever quotes Jesus, but the congregation wouldn't know that, if they haven't read the Bible. And he calls the Bible the word of God too. But the Bible doesn't."

"And," said Bobby, "how about Luke's saying in his Book of Acts that God killed a husband and wife for selling a piece of property and keeping some of the proceeds for their living expenses instead of turning all of it over to Peter? And Paul says in his epistle to the Hebrews that, when David said in one of his psalms that God told him he was a priest in the order of Melchizedek, God was talking to Jesus! In the Judaic part of the Bible, Melchizedek is the first person to collect tithes, and it says he collected them from Abraham from spoils of war.

"And Luke also acted as Paul's scribe for his epistle to the Corinthians that's mostly a fundraising letter. So I think that, besides being pharisaical, Paul and Luke may have been trying to serve mammon instead of God. That part of the Book of Acts is after it says the apostles consolidated their funds for central administration and before it says Paul took over the church. And neither do any of Paul's epistles mention any part of the Book of Acts. So doesn't that say Luke wrote it after the writing of the epistles too?"

"And," said Suzy, "In Paul's epistle telling Timothy how to be a bishop, he tells him to avoid foolish and unlearned questions! I mean, isn't any honest question an unlearned question, an effort to learn? So how is any question foolish?"

"Yes," said Annie. "And that would take curiosity out of the three C's."

And then she smiled at me, as the others gave her a curious look, and then she answered their question.

"The day Billy found me," she said, "some foster parents called me a troublemaker for refusing to go to Sunday school and took me back to the child protective services office in Marshall. That's why I was there when Billy went there.

"And they dumped me there with nearly nothing. So, the same day, he took me shopping at the Walmart in Jackson. And he watched me and asked me questions, to be sure I liked what we bought for me, clothes and groceries and other things. So, when we put the clothes on my bed in our house in Albion, I started crying. I didn't know why anyone would do that for me.

"So Billy knelt on both knees and took both of my hands and asked me what was the matter. So I told him I never had so much stuff before. I didn't know how else to say it.

"But he knew what to say. He said that must have been either because no one knew what I was worth or because nobody who did had a way to give me what I deserved. So I asked him what I was worth.

"And then he told me the three C's.

"Courage, curiosity, and compassion.

"And he said I had all three, and he said no one could be better than I as long as that was true, if I did the best I could."

Then, for a moment, she seemed to me to be about to begin weeping again, but instead she looked at me again and shrugged with another smile, and Maitri was the first to reply to that.

"Why did you refuse to go to Sunday school?" he asked.

"The Sunday school teacher told me I was going to hell no matter what I did," said Annie. "If I didn't accept Christ as my personal savior. And, when I asked her who Christ was, she said I'd find out soon enough. If I wasn't careful.

"And I didn't think any of that was fair."

And then she shrugged and smiled again.

"That's all three," said Maitri. "Trying to understand and standing up for fairness are curiosity and courage. And your sense of fairness shows your compassion. And you still always do the best you can."

"With plenty of help from my friends," said Annie, in the Chinese tradition of deflecting praise.

And then Suzy showed what she was worth.

"And how can we be compassionate," she said, "if we don't care enough to try to understand how one another are?"

"Yes," replied Bobby, also showing what he was worth. "And Paul must have been afraid Timothy might not be able to obfuscate Paul's mammon worship as pharisaically as Paul did! How courageous would that be?"

And then Bee, showing what she was worth, extended all of that into terms special to her but also common to all of them.

"All of that makes sense to me," she said. "And Paul, or Saul of Tarsus or whoever he was, also says in his epistles that slaves should obey their masters as they obey Christ. And he says that, because Christians are slaves of Christ, slaves shouldn't care if they're slaves to men. And he also says in his epistles that women talking in church is a shame. He says we should ask our husbands at home if we want to learn.

"That's like Solomon blaming women for his philandering and other troubles and preaching that parents should beat kids into being like them. If he treated his children that way, he should have expected the son of his who succeeded him to do what he did to divide Israel against itself, instead of calling all that stuff wisdom and preaching that everything's vanity. The vanity seems to me to be Solomon's.

"And what Maitri said is why I like music and dance and *Taijiquan*. They're all ways of feeling our sharing of air and space to understand that we're all really everything. I think that, whatever we call God, that must be how everything is.

"And I like the *Dao De Jing* because its only doctrine is accepting how we'd know things are if we'd stop trying to think some of us are better or worse than others.

"And Luke's Gospel also says Jesus said that, because the kingdom of God is inside of us, we shouldn't look in different places for it.

"And the *Dao De Jing* says that of the way of the sky."

And then Maitri, showing what he was worth, further proved his membership in the group.

"That's Buddhist too," he said. "But, anyway, I'm glad we're celebrating Jesus' birthday today and not anyone's misrepresenting him."

But my particular wonder that afternoon was how, in my seven decades of imagining this world before I found Annie, I never knew anyone to be as thoughtful and conscientious as I found those five young people to be.

But wonder had become ordinary in our household. And two especially wonderful changes in the way of life of the study group occurred between its receiving its baccalaureate degrees and its beginning its graduate work. And the first was mainly with Suzy and Bobby.

"We're getting married," said Suzy that summer, showing us the diamond engagement ring Bobby had bought for her with cash he was able to save from his scholarship cost of living stipends by living at home.

Of course, when Suzy showed us the ring, Bobby was standing grinning behind her. And, while the rest of us were thinking of something to say, he spoke. And that gave Annie something to say.

"I thought you might have expected it," he said to her. "When I said you were stupid, I did it to get Suzy's attention. I knew that was stupid, but I was afraid she'd just tell me to go away if I tried to be nice to her, and you responded perfectly. So I thought you might have figured it out."

"I considered that possibility after I said it," said Annie. "But I think I'd have said what I said anyway. And I've been glad I did ever since. And I'm more glad now."

"Well," said Bobby, "I felt that a door to all possibilities had suddenly opened to me."

"And," said Suzy, "his answer told me I was right about him, that his bluster was only the bleating of a lost but lovely little lamb."

And she reached her hand with the ring behind her to pull him up beside her.

"And talking with either of you is already like talking with both of you," said Annie beaming.

"Yeah," said Bee smiling and shaking her head. "So this isn't a huge surprise."

And Maitri just stood there grinning at his friends.

So all of us were glad and were also glad to attend the ceremony.

For Bobby's mom, it was at the church she'd found in Ann Arbor, and its minister officiated. But Suzy and Bobby constructed their vows from English translations of wedding vows from various denominations of Christianity. They omitted the word "obey", any reference to the dichotomy of sickness and health, and any mention of parting or death. But, of course, they included the words "love" and "honor" and "cherish". And the minister didn't ask them their reasons for any of that..

"He just said we didn't leave any room for any failure of faith," said Suzy. "And then Bobby looked at me and grinned. And then so did the pastor."

No guests attended the ceremony other than Suzy's and Bobby's parents and their parents' parents, an aunt and uncle of

Suzy's and an aunt of Bobby's and some of their cousins, the other members of the study group, Miss Walker and Mrs. Meredith, and Corinthia and I. But Miss Walker and Mrs. Meredith sat together and beamed through the whole ceremony like a couple of favorite aunts. And Corinthia and I were the official witnesses.

Bobby was in a dark blue suit he bought for the occasion. And Suzy was in a simple but elegant white gown Bobby's mother took her to buy with Annie and Bee along to help Suzy decide. And Annie told me Suzy's selection criterion was to keep it simple but elegant enough to please Bobby.

But, though Bobby smiled at Suzy all day, I thought the dress wasn't all that pleased him.

My wedding gift to them was bridal accommodations on a paddlewheel riverboat cruise down the Mississippi from Hannibal to New Orleans. I thought that, because of the affection they shared for both French and American literature, that would be appropriate. And they said they thought so too.

But, remembering what Bobby said of *Of Time and the River*, I also bought them Amtrak tickets to Hannibal. And I also booked for them a hotel room in Hannibal for the night before the cruise's departure and three nights at the Royal Orleans Hotel. And I also bought them airline tickets home.

"Wait 'til you see the clouds from above with the sun shining on them," said Annie.

"Yes," said Maitri. "That's what I enjoy most when I'm flying too."

"We saw the Kirov Ballet while we were in New Orleans," said Suzy when they returned. "They were doing a sort of exhibition at the Saenger Theatre."

"And we went to the New Orleans Museum of Art while we were there too," said Bobby. "It has Degas' *Dancer in Green*. And the museum's at the end of the street with Degas' New Orleans house on it. So we went there too."

"So you got a head start on New York," said Bee, smiling at the Kirov program Suzy gave her as she spoke of the performance..

"Yes," said Suzy. "We'll be saving programs from your performances soon, but it wasn't all like New York. Before we got on the boat in Hannibal, we went to Mark Twain's house."

"Yeah," said Bobby. "We saw his typewriter. And, Annie, a copy of that gold statue of Jehanne, the one in Paris in a picture you showed us, is in New Orleans. It's in the French Quarter where two streets join after they pass what they call the French Market. I don't know if you knew that."

"And, yes," said Suzy after Annie shook her head to that but smiled. "The clouds in the sun from above are . . . . I don't know. They're way beyond words."

And the next major change in the group's way of living was later that summer after Maitri made an exception to his habit of going everywhere Annie went.

"We're going to go see what Suzy and Bobby are up to," said Bee, coming out of the study with Annie, after playing piano with her during some of the extraordinary amount of unscheduled time they had that summer. "You coming, Maitri?"

"Not this time," said Maitri, who was spending that time watching cable news as I sat in my reading chair reading. "I want to talk with Billy about something."

And, after they left, he turned off the TV. Then he looked at me, looked down at the coffee table, and looked up at me again. Then he looked down again, looked ahead taking a deep breath, and looked at me again.

And then he spoke.

"I know it isn't customary in the United States anymore," he said. "But it still is in India. And I know how important you and Annie are to one other."

Then he looked down again and up again and took another deep breath before looking at me again and continuing.

"So I want to ask you for your blessing," he said. "For Annie to marry me. She's become more important to me than anything. It's like everything belongs in her hands, and I should do all I can to be that way for her, anything I can.

"I've felt that way since the first time I saw her, and then heard her questions in class, before she asked me about my name.

"So, well, I'm asking."

But I didn't need to take a deep breath.

"Well," I said. "That's how I feel about her too. And I'm glad you asked, and you have my blessing for everything else, but I never try to tell Annie what to do. So you have my blessing for that only if you have hers."

"I think I do," he said. "But I wanted to ask you before I ask her. So I'll ask her tomorrow. Thank you."

"You're welcome, Maitri," I said. "You've been welcome to me since Annie first mentioned you to me."

So, the next morning, while Bee was in the study alone, after closing the door to practice her music or dance during some of the time she regularly scheduled for that for that summer, Maitri told Annie he'd like to show her something at the library.

"It won't take long," he said when she looked at the study door, and then she looked at him but asked no question, and I went out to our deck to wait for them.

So, when they returned, Annie found me there, joined me at our patio table, and showed me the ring.

"He asked me in the library quadrangle," she said. "We've spent more time in that library together than we've spent together anywhere else, except here. I hoped he would someday, and I knew he liked me the first time we talked, but I didn't know how much. He's so quiet most of the time."

"Did he tell you he asked me first?" I asked taking her other hand.

"Yes," she said. "And I'm glad he did. It shows he knows how important you are to me. But I already knew he cares about how important everything is to everyone. That's what I liked about the questions he asked in class. It's why I talked to him that day."

And then her smile broadened a little.

"He asked me if he could kiss me too," she said. "After I got down on my knees to where he was and hugged him because I couldn't help it.

"That was nice. That touching, feeling like we're all mixed together, as I know we are anyway. I guess we'll do a lot more of that kind of being together now. I can hardly wait until we're married. To use the rest of me like that."

And then she grinned and looked down at her hands.

But their wedding ceremony wasn't in a church.

They used the vows Suzy and Bobby used. But a resident priest of the Zen Buddhist Temple in Ann Arbor officiated. Maitri had introduced Annie to her early in his and Annie's friendship.

And their ceremony was in our backyard.

Maitri's suit was nearly the color of Bobby's. But I supposed he selected it to accord with the customs of Annie's country. And, though Annie's dress was also similar to Suzy's, I supposed that was also mainly to please Maitri.

But Suzy and Bee went with her to buy it. I went with them also but only to be sure I paid for it. So I spoke only when they asked me what I thought. And I tried to accord my replies with how I felt they felt. Their other talk told me how to do that.

We didn't flood our backyard with flowers. But the roses I planted around our deck the year we bought the house hadn't yet ended that summer's blooming of theirs. And the celebration bloomed of itself like lilies of the field.

Excepting Suzy's and Bobby's grandparents and aunts and uncle and cousins, all who attended their wedding ceremony also attended Annie's and Maitri's, but Suzy and Bobby were the official witnesses with Bee the maid of honor.

And two others were there. Maitri's parents flew from India. They arrived two days before the ceremony and slept in Maitri's room while Maitri slept on our sofa. So for those three days, however comfortably Maitri slept, our house was more full of glee than it ordinarily was. And Maitri's parents also fell in love with Annie.

"Thank you for welcoming our son," said his mother to me before the ceremony. "And thank you for giving him such a lovely wife. I couldn't be happier."

"Thank you for sharing your son with us," I said.

And Maitri's father and I had a similar exchange after the ceremony, as we all stood about on our deck, talking and eating wedding cake.

"Are you next?" Corinthia asked Bee while we did that.

"I'm in no hurry," Bee replied shrugging, and still she didn't seem to me to feel behind.

And, a few days later, we returned to our plans..

The ceremony was the day after Annie's eighteenth birthday, the day after she and Maitri obtained their marriage license, and Maitri's parents returned to Gaya two days later. And the day after they left, Annie and Maitri left for a wedding gift of mine to them, three nights in the bridal suite of the Grand Hotel on Mackinac Island. They didn't have time to take a longer trip and be in New York in time to begin graduate school.

"What's it like up there?" asked Annie.

"I don't know," I said. "I've never been there. So I guess we'll have to get another color of tack for our map. I know nearly nothing about it, other than that they sell a lot of taffy and fudge up there, and that they don't let cars on the island."

"What'll I do with my Explorer?" she asked.

"They have parking where you board the boat to go to the island," I said. "I just thought you and Maitri might enjoy some quiet time together before you go to New York. And I think Maitri might like to see a less busy piece of the United States."

And they brought back a load of taffy and fudge.

And the next week, after their final preparations for their move to New York, they made that move in Annie's Explorer and a U-Haul truck.

But I didn't go. Annie was old enough to take care of herself, and she and Maitri and Suzy and Bobby were old enough to do for seventeen-year-old Bee whatever Bee couldn't do legally for herself, and all five were more responsible than I knew any persons calling themselves adults to be. And they already had made one trip to New York together.

In the week before the week of Annie's wedding, she drove them there in her Explorer, to rent an apartment in Chinatown.

"Where are we going to live in New York?" asked Suzy earlier that summer.

"I've been looking at Manhattan apartments on the Web," said Maitri. "They're expensive, but I found some three-bedroom apartments in Chinatown I think we may be able to afford, and I know Annie likes China."

"Yes," said Annie. "And Billy and I went to that Chinatown on our trip to New York for my eighth birthday. Those bowls are from there. I'd love that."

"So would I," said Bee. "We'd have *Taijiquan* neighbors."

"But wouldn't we have to pay more than a month's rent to move in?" asked Bobby. "I mean wouldn't they ask for a security deposit, or both the first month's rent and the last month's rent, or something like that? I've been looking into apartments there too. And we'd have to buy furniture."

"How about if I pay whatever it costs to move in?" I asked. "We can call that a graduation gift. And I don't need the furniture in your bedrooms here. And I'd like to buy you some living room furniture too, as a wedding gift, or whatever.

"And you five are using our dining table and chairs a lot more than I am. So I'd like you to have that anyway. So you won't forget me."

"There's no way we'll ever forget you," said Maitri, as smiles and then grins spread across the faces of all five of them.

So, after I basked a moment in the glow of their grins, we sat together around Annie's computer and continued their search for an apartment in New York's Chinatown, and extended it into looking for living room furniture, from anywhere on the World Wide Web..

But I did none of that deciding. Over the next few days they narrowed their apartment selection to three apartments and made appointments to see them. And then Annie drove them to the appointments.

"The landlord of the apartment we liked the most is Chinese," said Bobby on their return when I asked them how the trip went. "He said he was a little worried about renting to people so young. But he said Annie's speaking Chinese so well helped."

"And Bee told him we do *Taijiquan*," said Suzy. "So then he said we're quite a group. And Annie said she'd be eighteen and married to Maitri when we move in."

"Then he grinned and congratulated them," said Bee. "So then everything was fine."

And, with the financial skills Annie developed and proved in college, I was sure she'd be as safe financially in the big city as she'd be with her friends in every other way, and Maitri's minor in economics made that more of a certainty, for all of them.

But none of that made me happy to see them go. So I took one more step to be sure Annie and I would think of one another pleasantly while she was in New York while I was in Ann Arbor. I went on the Web and found another copy of our Buddha statuette.

"Here," I said to her when she came downstairs with her teddy bear the day of their departure, after they loaded the U-Haul truck they rented. "This is for you."

So she set her teddy bear in my reading chair and accepted the Chinese cardboard box I handed her, but she looked into the box for several seconds, before she spoke.

"What about you?" she asked when she looked up.

"I found another copy of it on the Web," I said. "That's how I had the box for it. I wanted a way to make us feel together while I'm here while you're in New York. And that one's become more yours than mine."

Then she touched her right index finger to the statuette's *ushnisha* for a few seconds. And then she closed the box, tucked it beneath her right arm, and picked up her teddy bear from my reading chair. But she said nothing more until after I followed her out to our garage and opened the driver door of her Explorer.

Then, after climbing into her driver seat, she set the box with the Buddha on the console between the front seats, set the teddy bear in front of it and leaning against it, and turned the key.

But still she didn't speak or start the car. She pushed the buttons to lower her driver side window and unlock the doors for Maitri to climb into the front passenger seat while Bee climbed into the front backseat. And, as I closed the driver door, Bee was the next to speak.

"We don't want them to fall off of there," she said, reaching between the front seats to take the Buddha and the teddy bear back with her. "I can buckle them in back here."

Then Annie grinned and started her Explorer. But then, with neither a grin nor a smile, she turned again to me. And then she spoke.

"Don't forget I'm your little friend," she said.

"No chance of that," I said. "And I'll come there in a few weeks, to see how you're doing."

"Good," she said, smiling at that, but she didn't smile as she turned away and put her Explorer into gear.

Suzy and Bobby were in the U-Haul outside. And Annie took the garage door remote control from the driver door pocket where she kept it and opened the garage door. But then, still not smiling, she looked at the remote control and looked at me again.

"I think you'd better keep that," I said. "I hope you'll need it again, from time to time."

And then she smiled again. But, as she turned to back out of the garage, she stopped smiling again before backing out of our driveway and into the street, where Suzy and Bobby were waiting in the U-Haul. And then, after following Annie's Explorer out of the garage, I didn't know what to do.

All of us waved, as they drove away, but I don't know what to call the looks on their faces as they did that. They were something like smiles, but they were full of both sadness and happiness, and other things I couldn't measure. Yet, while I couldn't name or measure them, I felt them as clearly as I feel anything.

So, looking in the direction in which they'd gone, I stood in our driveway with all that in my heart. Until several minutes after I could no longer see Annie's Explorer, and then I sat on our front steps for more than an hour, with my head in my hands. For more than a decade, Annie had filled my heart, and then it overflowed.

My memories of those ten years and more, from the summer I found her sitting alone in that corner to near the end of another summer, flowed and ebbed and flowed into the limitless possibilities for her and her friends for the future.

And then I went inside and ate a bowl of Froot Loops.

So such thoughts were most of my thoughts through the next few weeks. But, wishing not to interrupt their studies, I waited until the last Wednesday before that Thanksgiving before flying to New York to see how they were doing. I thought of waiting until the Christmas break, but I hoped all of them would come home for that, and I didn't wish to wait that long.

But Annie changed that plan somewhat.

"Can you stay through Monday?" she asked when I called to tell her when I'd be there. "I'd like us to do something together that I don't think we can do during the break. And I think I can miss one day of classes."

She didn't tell me then what she'd planned. But, having no reluctance to spending an extra day with her, I didn't ask her. So, Wednesday afternoon, I checked into a hotel in Chinatown and found my way to the study group's apartment only happy to be there.

And, immediately upon entering the apartment, I saw what they'd done with Annie's Buddha. They'd printed and framed the ten stanzas of the *Metta Sutta*, each stanza in a separate frame, in both English and Pali. And beneath the *Metta Sutta*, on a bonsai stand with carving of cherry blossoms in its wood, was Annie's Buddha.

Most essentially the *Metta Sutta* says one should live simply and honestly and harmoniously, mindfully cultivating boundless thoughts of benevolence for all that breathe or ever shall, as a mother would protect her only child with all her being.

So then I remembered that "*metta*" is Pali for "*maitri*".

And on the opposite side of the room, at the center of the sill of a window overlooking the street, was a bonsai Chinese juniper on a stand identical to the Buddha's.

And, between the Juniper and the Buddha, was the study group's study and dining table.

"Who trims the juniper?" I asked the next afternoon during our Thanksgiving dinner Maitri had shaped around requests and assistance from his housemates.

"Bobby does," said Suzy smiling at him. "He says it's like helping a story tell itself."

"I learned that from her," said Bobby returning Suzy's smile. "It's how she treats me."

And in my five days there then, Annie reintroduced me to that Chinatown, her new neighborhood.

Her building had a laundry room with coin washers and dryers. But, to befriend her new neighbors beyond that building, she did her laundry at a laundromat across the street. So she took me to the laundromat to introduce me to some of her new friends.

And she and Bee took me to a public outdoor basketball court two blocks from their apartment and introduced me to some people with whom they practiced the *Taijiquan* sequence there.

But Annie didn't tell me until Sunday what she'd planned for us to do on Monday.

16

Closing some Circles

"Can we go see George tomorrow?" she asked as we shared a lunch of vegetable eggrolls and fried rice with *suān méi zhī* at a small restaurant more new friends of hers to whom she introduced me owned near her apartment. "That's why I asked you to stay through Monday. I think I might be able to find his office, but we haven't seen him since that first day I was in New York, and also I want to ask you something. You never told me how you and he became friends."

"He was my editor for a book I wrote," I said.

"You wrote a book?" she said. "Why didn't I know you wrote a book? What's it about?"

"It's a sort of comparison of those scriptures you read," I said.

"Why didn't you tell me?" she asked. "And why wasn't it on our shelves?"

"A copy of it's in the credenza we were using as a TV stand," I said. "But I thought you needed to figure that stuff out for yourself, and I think you have, excellently. And now our friendship has made me think that book's at best a little trivial."

"Is it still in print?" she asked.

"Yes, little friend," I said. "Columbia's main bookstore probably stocks it."

"Good," she said. "Then, after we see George, we can go see if we can find a copy, and then you can write me a nice little note in it, for another way to help me think of you, like our Buddha.

"I mean if we can go see George. I should have asked you when you called whether we can. But, if we can't, I'm still glad you'll be here for another day."

But we did go see George. He took us to lunch, during which he nearly constantly smiled at Annie as though he'd never seen anyone so wonderful, and then Annie and I took a subway up to Columbia's main campus, where she showed me around a little, after we found the book. But, during lunch, George's conversation showed he felt what his smiling said he felt.

"What are you studying?" he asked.

"International relations," said Annie.

"Oh," he said, and he briefly looked down at his plate, and then he looked up at her again with his eyes glistening nearly into tears. "Then I think arranging that tour for you may be the best thing I've ever done."

And, riding uptown on the subway, Annie once again showed me how wonderful she is.

"Where's your Explorer?" I asked.

"I keep it uptown," she said. "The subway's easier, and parking's less expensive up there. And I still like to see all the people living their lives, and so do the others. We all love the city, all the things to see and hear and learn and how they seem to be different, while they also seem to fit together into one big thing. It's like the five of us and you not really being other than one another, like what Bee said of the piano and letters and numbers, like what you told me the Buddha said. So here we use my Explorer mainly for shopping when we need it to bring things home. But it's still a way for us to be together. And to feel like you're nearby."

And with my heart still full, after supper with her in her friends' restaurant, I flew back to Ann Arbor.

That visit told me she and her friends who found their way to New York with her would continue to excel wherever they went. But I was already certain of that. And they did.

Annie did her graduate work in international political relations while Maitri did his in international economic relations. And, of course, Suzy and Bobby did theirs in literature in English. But Bee didn't enroll in Columbia.

The New York City Ballet, offering apprenticeships to excellent dancers younger than eighteen years, readily welcomed seventeen-year-old Bee with her *summa cum laude* baccalaureate degree in dance and music. So, instead of enrolling at Columbia, she enrolled in the New York City Ballet's School of American Ballet. And her excellence exceeded the school's expectations.

She'd learned through *Taijiquan* the relationship between the space inside her and the space outside her that included the space others also occupied. So, with everyone at the school feeling her feeling that, she finished her apprenticeship and joined the permanent company in less than three months. And she didn't begin in the *corps de ballet* but as a ballerina.

And Annie advanced quickly beyond Columbia. She'd kept the card George gave us for the tour of the United Nations. And, calling the number on it and finding that Uma had become a career State Department analyst in the District of Columbia, she obtained her number there.

So she called it, and Uma remembered her also, and immediately proved herself the friend Annie thought she was. She told Annie that, when she gave us that tour, she was an intern in the office of the United States' Ambassador to the United Nations. And she came to New York to see Annie and arranged the same summer internship for her.

And she also extended that friendship to Maitri. Maitri used his marriage to Annie to obtain United States citizenship. So Uma also arranged an internship for him in that office.

And there Annie and Maitri made many friends. They made so many that, immediately upon finishing their doctoral coursework, they went to work for our State Department. So then they moved to the District of Columbia.

But, partly by teaching English at the University of Michigan, Suzy and Bobby put their excellence to work back in Ann Arbor. So all the other members of the study group, from wherever their careers took them through the years, annually spent a week with Suzy and Bobby in Ann Arbor. But, for Annie and Maitri, that required crossing oceans.

Annie wrote her doctoral dissertation on the relevance of religion to the Palestinian problem and its repercussions to relations among nations not only within the region ancient Romans called the levant, because going there from Rome required crossing the Mediterranean in the direction of the levitating sun, but also all around Earth. Maitri wrote his on the relevance of religion to the secession of Pakistan and Bangladesh from India and the economic impact of the residual strife among those three nations and beyond. And they converted both dissertations into books.

My friend George who had become Annie's friend became Maitri's friend also and advised both of them on how to make their dissertations generally marketable. So, after they took most of his advice, Scribner's published both books and promoted them. And Annie's rose to the top of the *New York Times* Best Seller list. Maitri's, though not at the top and not as long, was also on that list. And, of course, all that was relevant to the careers of both.

But, partly for reasons more people bought Annie's book than bought Maitri's, her diplomatic career blossomed before his. Those reasons were that Judaism and Christianity and Islam were all Abrahamic religions, that a huge majority of the population of the United States called itself Christian, and that most of the Bible is Judaic scripture. So, though most of the people of the United

States cared more about Christianity than about Judaism, most hardly knew or cared anything about Hinduism.

And 9/11 brought the strife between Muslims and Jews to the United States. So the politics of all that had extended into the government of the United States' joining the Judaic side of the strife between Jews and Muslims, what the people of the United States and their government and news media called a war on terror, while Muslims called it a struggle. So, of course, neither was the situation in the Far East as important as the situation in the Middle East to Annie's and Maitri's State Department friends..

So the first diplomatic assignment recommendation from the Secretary of State for either Annie or Maitri was that the President appoint Annie to be Ambassador to Israel. And, because of the popularity of Annie's book, the President invited her to the Oval Office. But Annie took Maitri with her.

"You're cleared," said the guard to Annie when she and Maitri arrived in her Explorer at the gate to the White House grounds for official visitors. "But he isn't."

"Then I guess I'll have to postpone the appointment," said Annie. "Unless you can call someone."

So the guard frowned. But then he called someone. And then he grinned and waved them through. And, in the interview, the President proved herself more broadly attentive than politicians often prove themselves to be. And she proved it relevantly and materially.

"That was impressive," she said grinning at Annie, "what you did at the gate. And I've looked into your dissertation on India too, Maitri. So it's also serendipitous.

"Along with reassigning our current Ambassador to Israel from Jerusalem to Damascus, I'm sending her DCM to Amman to be Ambassador there.

"So do think you might care to be Annie's Deputy Chief of Mission?"

"We work well together, Madam President," said Maitri.

"And we're a team anyway," said Annie. "Always."

"I could tell that from your books," said the President. "So I'm going to send copies of both books with my letter introducing you to the Israeli Prime Minister. Thanks for accepting the positions."

Of course, never forgetting a friend, Annie introduced Maitri to all she could find of those she made in her previous time in that land. And, also of course, they were of little official help to her and Maitri. But, also of course, she quickly made many more.

So, in three years, they solved the Palestinian problem. And they did it while arguing with no one and threatening no one and with no bargaining or treaties or secrecy or subtlety. Their method was to treat no one like a kid.

That is, in their conversations with the various leaders in the region, they asked them what they thought. And they replied to assertions they found incomprehensible not by preaching but by asking for clarification. But the road was rocky all the way.

"Why are we here?" asked Annie.

"To make peace," replied the Prime Minister of Israel.

"How?" asked the Chairman of the Palestine Liberation Organization. "I've read your scripture, and it makes plain that the Israeli idea of peace is subjugating your neighbors. And, to build more settlements on land international law says doesn't belong to you, you've violated every agreement between us. You've made that a habit since the United Nations called you a nation in 1948."

"The settlements are for our security," said the Prime Minister. "And, as soon as we gave you Gaza, you made of it a base for launching ballistic missiles against us! So what would happen if we had an Islamic state on three sides of us?"

"You didn't give us Gaza," said the Chairman. "We were Philistines the Egyptians pushed into Gaza three millennia ago, when we migrated to Egypt from the Greek side of the

Mediterranean, and we aren't inherently Islamic as you're inherently Judaic. And we have no intention of creating an Islamic state. And you must know all that."

"How is that migration relevant now?" asked Annie.

"They make it relevant," said the Chairman. "With all that talk of God giving them the land three millennia ago. And part of the craziness of that is that their scripture says they couldn't get along with themselves. All that war between Saul and David, and then between the Kingdom of Judah and the Kingdom of Israel, between Jerusalem and Samaria. And now they're proving that overweening absurdity by calling Israel a Judaic state. Why don't they make Samaria their capital?"

"You think I haven't read your scripture?" asked the Prime Minister. "It says it confirms both our scripture and Christian scripture! But it lies about our scripture and ridicules the Christian version of the Judaic prophesy of a messiah."

"The *Qur'an* doesn't lie about what I just said," said the Chairman. "And its only complaint against the Christian notion of a messiah is the notion that Jesus was God. And you also deny that, and the *Torah* disagrees with itself, in many ways. It makes lies about its story of the Midianite Balaam a sort of *leitmotif*."

"The story of Balaam is about what we've learned to expect from our enemies," interrupted the Prime Minister. "He tried to curse the Israelites before they fought for the land you say God didn't give us. But God turned his curse into a blessing."

"That depends on which parts of your scripture you believe," interrupted the Chairman. "The *Torah*, in the Book of Numbers, says Balaam told the people who asked him to curse Israel that he'd ask God and couldn't say anything God didn't tell him to say, and it says he willingly behaved accordingly. But later the same book says Moses ordered twelve thousand Israelites to kill all the Midianites, and it says he told the Israelites his reason was what happened on Mount Peor, where Balaam proved his promise, by blessing Israel, after asking God. And, in that story, Moses doesn't order that slaughter until after an Israelite brings a daughter of a prince of Midian to the Tabernacle of the Covenant.

"And that's after the *Torah* says Moses married a daughter of a priest of Midian. And the Book of Numbers also says the twelve thousand let the women and children live but that Moses told them to go back and kill all of them who weren't virgin girls. And it says he told them to take half of those 32 thousand girls for themselves, give all but 32 of the other half to the other Israelites, and give the 32 to the priests for God.

"And the Book of Genesis says Midian was one of Abraham's sons and that God promised the land to all the descendants of Abraham before he changed his mind for a reason that's invalid if the descendance from the sons of Israel's wives' maidservants' is valid. And together the Book of Genesis and the Book of Numbers also say the people who asked Balaam to curse Israel weren't Midianites but descendants by incest of one of Abraham's nephew Lot's daughters with her father. And, after the Book of Numbers, your scripture says others of your people also said Balaam tried to curse Israel.

"So how can anyone reasonably respond to that?"

"Well, anyway," said the Prime Minister, "whatever any scripture says, Muslims are beheading people now, only for not being Muslims. And, whatever you say, most Palestinians are Muslims."

"Anyone can call himself anything," said the Chairman. "And more than eighty beheadings are in your scripture. And most of them are Israelites' beheading other Israelites, and one of them is David's beheading the Palestinian Goliath with Goliath's sword, after knocking him unconscious and perhaps dead. And no beheadings are in the *Qur'an*.

"And, also regarding anyone calling himself anything, consider the term 'anti-Semitic'. Both Hebrews and Arabs are

Semitic, but both Jews and Christians use that term only to mean 'anti-Judaic', and that denies the existence of four hundred million Arabs while you seven million Judaic people calling yourselves Israelis demand that all of Earth recognize your right to exist and call yourselves that. And that's also relevant to right now.

"But, considering the genocidal racist blasphemy of your scriptures' claim that God commanded your predecessors not only to take the land but also to annihilate nine or ten of the races inhabiting it, that shouldn't surprise anyone

"And also relevant to now is that the Philistines weren't one of the nine or ten races it names in that.

"And your scripture also says the dividing of the kingdom of Israel into two kingdoms was because a son of the Judaic king Solomon threatened to be more cruel to the Israelites than Solomon was. It says he did that when the elders of Israel told him they'd serve him if he wouldn't be as oppressive as Solomon was, that he told them he'd chastise them with scorpions after Solomon chastised them with whips, and it also says Solomon told his son that not beating children spoils them. And it also says he blamed all his troubles on women.

"And it says he said all women are stupid. And, while it's saying all that, it calls Solomon wise and says he called himself wise! Is Solomon's misogyny and child abuse or other cruelty and preaching of cruelty the Judaic notion of wisdom?"

"What about your Sharia law?" asked the Prime Minister. "The stoning of women and other oppression of them in that! And what about Sunnis and Shiites killing each other? You have no room to talk."

"As anyone can say he's Islamic," said the Chairman, "Sharia can be any religion's law. And what people are calling Sharia law now isn't in the *Qur'an*. It's an emulation of the Mosaic law in your scripture. Mosaic law commands stoning for adultery. No stoning is in the *Qur'an* either.

"And, whatever Sunnis and Shiites may do, the *Qur'an* forbids Muslims' dividing into factions. And, as Palestinians aren't inherently Muslims, neither are they inherently either Sunni or Shiite. And you're calling the Kingdom of Israel lost tribes. A remnant of it remains in Samaria. Or at least did in Jesus' time."

And, whether or not Annie remembered asking me in Jerusalem when she was eleven years old the question of why the Israelis called Israel a Jewish state if the kingdoms of Israel and Judah were separate kingdoms, all of those concerns were in her book. And she knew the Chairman was also correct in everything else he said of Judaic and Islamic scripture, but she asked the question prompting that exchange only to let both of them air whatever they wished to air, and next she cleared the air. And she did it simply by rephrasing the question.

"So there's no way either of you can get past the past?" she asked, and both of them laughed at that and smirked at each other and started afresh, and Annie calmly persisted in her questions.

Annie's advantage in those conversations was that, while also having read both the *Miqra* and the *Qur'an*, she had no cultural bias for or against either. And, suspecting that most people taking sides in the United States had read little of either, neither did she have any bias toward taking sides with either side. Her only interest in any social interaction was common decency.

She was also aware that many people of each of the three Abrahamic religions persisted in calling traditions Judaic or Christian or Islamic while they had no basis in any scripture. But, leaving the other participants in those conversations to raise those questions, she based her references to the scriptures only on what they said. And she based her questions only on how they were relevant to what the participants said and did.

"The *Qur'an* says Jews don't keep their promises to anyone not Jewish," she said speaking slowly with her hands open in front of her as though she were trying to find the physical shape of her thoughts. "And, while the *Miqra* says one law shall be for both Israelites and what it calls strangers among them, it makes plain that it's referring to constraints but not to privileges. And the *Qur'an* says the trouble between Muslims and Jews began when Jews allied with pagans against the Muslims and broke a treaty with the Muslims to do it. So what can we expect now?

"I mean, considering the Israelis' scriptural claim to the land, including the *Miqra*'s basing that claim partly on its assertion that Philistines worshiped inanimate idols, while the *Qur'an* says idolators are worse than anyone not an idolator, how can we separate the wheat from the chaff, and how can we have any trust in one another, if we don't?"

"Basically," said the Prime Minister, "circumstances here haven't changed since the events of the *Torah*. The violence the *Miqra* sanctions was for our peace and prosperity in the land God promised us. And, whether or not Palestinians worship Dagon or are Muslims, look at Hezbollah and its Gaza faction Hamas?"

"Hezbollah and Hamas are extensions of Iranian militance in Lebanon," said the Chairman. "And Iranians aren't Palestinian or either Arabic or Hebraic. They're Persian."

"Then why have you allied yourselves with Hamas?" asked the Prime Minister.

"We need them for defense against your militance," said the Chairman.

"How have they done that?" asked Annie. "I mean how have they done anything in your respect other than draw fire on you in Gaza and everywhere else and justify Israel in the eyes of most of humanity?"

And she responded to the scowls of both the Prime Minister and the Chairman by asking another question she asked me more than a decade earlier.

"And isn't the land here enough for Israelis and Palestinians to share?" she asked, and economist Maitri was present in that meeting and took that question a step further.

"And what does any of the aggression do for the prosperity of anyone not in the Hezbollah business?" he asked. "Does anyone remember what Lebanon was like before Hezbollah drew Yasser Arafat into supporting the Lebanese National Movement when King Hussein asked him to leave Jordan? People all over Earth were calling Beirut the Paris of the Middle East."

And, in other meetings he attended, he raised more questions regarding the economic benefits of peace in the region. And both he and Annie raised questions more specific to both economics and politics in regard to sharing the land and the general welfare. But neither made any pompous speeches.

So, in that way, they drew all parties first into recognizing the components of the problem, next into recognizing the core of the problem, and finally into admitting that recognition.

A political question they asked when it was pertinent to the flow of a conversation was how many Palestinians would live in Israel if Palestine were a state. And a reason they asked that was that it was relevant to the question of how many Palestinians would participate in the Israeli government if Palestine were a state and Israel a democracy and not a theocracy. And, of course, the answer to both questions was that nearly none would.

So, through such, question by question, while not articulating all of the details of the desperate disparity, all the participants on the two sides recognized them and eventually agreed on solutions and behaved accordingly.

So Israel would remain effectually a theocracy, but its being a theocracy would no longer be a threat to the Palestinians, and those two factors comprised the fundamental dynamic of the situation. If the Israelis and the Palestinians weren't a threat to one another, neither would any of the Semitic Muslims have a rationale to be a threat to the Semitic Israelis, and then the Israelis would have no secular rationale for being a threat to anyone. So that left the Israeli settlements outside Israel's United Nations mandate the only remaining component of the problem.

So the final compromise was that, in exchange for the Israelis' agreeing to stop developing such settlements and stop excluding anyone not Israeli from residing in those already in place, the Palestinians agreed to let stand those already in place. And part of the hope from both sides for that compromise was that Palestinians might move from Israel to Palestine while Israelis moved from the settlements to land that was legitimately Israeli. So verbiage in the official agreement specifically encouraged both.

Of course a problem with all of that was that both the Israelis and the Palestinians had violated every agreement they'd made since before the ratification of the United Nations mandate that made Israel a state.

But the President of the United States solved that problem.

A reason she agreed with her Secretary of State to appoint Annie Ambassador and appointed Maitri to help her was that she not only had read their books but also understood them. So, not being as diplomatic as Annie and Maitri, she told the Prime Minister of Israel that any violation of the agreement on the Israelis' part while the Palestinians abided by it would result in withdrawal of any United States support for Israel. And she also reiterated that the Israelis had violated many more agreements before the Palestinians did than the Palestinians had violated before the Israelis did.

And she also pointed out that the Israelis hadn't produced the constitution they promised in the May 1948 Declaration of the Establishment of the State of Israel and that they'd promised to all of humanity that they'd do that by October of that year.

And, not excepting the condition of not being the first to violate the agreement they then were developing, she said nothing either to the Israelis or to the Palestinians that she didn't say to both. And, on the conditions that both Israel and the new Palestinian nation ratify a constitution within a year and that both constitutions include a proscription against oppressing any religious principle not contrary to common decency, she promised equal support for Israel and Palestine as long as they remained at peace. And she expressed none of that as though it were questions.

But, in a meeting at the United States Embassy in Jerusalem with the President and both the Prime Minister and the Chairman present, Annie set the tone for the final agreement.

"With peace in the lands," she said, "do you think this complex would be big enough for both our embassy to Israel and our embassy to Palestine? I mean do you children know of any reason you won't be able to smile on one another when you accidentally encounter one another in your coming and going?"

The President, knowing Annie, to conceal how she felt hearing that, looked down at her agenda on the table in front of her, and both the Prime Minister and the Chairman initially scowled at her, but then they looked at one another and grinned.

"We'll be neighbors anyway," said the Prime Minister, "with Jerusalem the capital of both of our nations."

"And think of how much more easily we'll all breathe," said the Chairman.

And then the President looked up and revealed her grin.

And that healed the abrasion the Palestinian in the wheelchair in Jerusalem mentioned to me as Annie listened, in reference to the President of the United States of that time, the day after Annie's eleventh birthday.

And the United Nations Security Council resolved unanimously that the United States and Israel and the new Palestinian nation comply with the agreements. And, after the Israelis and the Palestinians signed them, the Secretary-General of the United Nations read them in a public session of the General

Assembly. So, three years after Annie became an Ambassador, Palestine became a state under those agreements.

And the President of the United States and the Prime Minister of Israel and the President of Palestine jointly received the Nobel Peace Prize. And, three years later, the peace from those agreements had grown to prevail throughout the region. And so had prosperity.

But, by then, Annie and Maitri weren't in that region. Upon the ratification of the agreements, they asked the President and the Secretary of State to reassign them to India, for them to do for Bangladesh and Pakistan and India what they'd done for Palestine and Israel. But in that region, because Maitri was from India, the President appointed him Ambassador and appointed Annie his Deputy Chief of Mission.

But they didn't change their methods, and their main questions on the Indian subcontinent also regarded religion, and again they succeeded in three years.

They asked how the *Qur'an*'s precept that oppression is worse than killing is fundamentally different from the assertions in the *Upanishad*s and the *Sutta*s and *Sutra*s that happiness depends on extinguishing the illusion of differences and that accordingly both peace and prosperity for anyone require sharing with all.

Maitri's main economic question was how that region, with its wealth of natural and intellectual resources, was so poor monetarily. And he and Annie also asked whether the answer to that question might also be the disunity that each of the three religions most popular in that region decried. So the main political dynamic in that region was much the same as had been the main political dynamic in the region between that region and what people of both of those regions called the West.

So a result of that focus on unity was unification of India and Pakistan and Bangladesh into a relationship similar to the European Union but focusing more on common economic development than on commercial trade. And, when those three nations signed that agreement, their Presidents also shared the Nobel Peace Prize. And Annie and Maitri moved on again.

But that move was by invitation. The five of the six Nobel Peace Prize winners who both owed that honor to Annie and Maitri and were heads of state of nations that were members of the United Nations but weren't permanent members of the Security Council lobbied the Security Council to recommend to the General Assembly that it appoint Annie Secretary-General. And, of course, the President of the United States, the other head of state owing Annie and Maitri for that honor, supported that effort.

All six had become Annie's friends beyond gratitude and into personal affection. But their supporting Annie for that position was most dynamically because of what she'd done for their countries' international political stature and the effect of that on their countries' domestic economies. All six also had become friends of Maitri's, and they also recognized his contribution to that, but Annie's official leadership in solving the Palestinian problem gave her more stature internationally.

A problem was that the United Nations proscribed citizens of the five nations that were permanent members of the Security Council from being Secretary-General. But Annie had used her marriage to Maitri to become also a citizen of India, and she had substantial assurances from many world leaders that the General Assembly would approve the Security Council's recommendation, if she weren't a citizen of the United States. So, while no one could deny that Annie had proven herself a citizen of everywhere, she officially but congenially relinquished her United States citizenship.

So, in that sequence of events, little more than two decades after the day after she and Bee became friends, the day I asked her whether she'd considered becoming Secretary-General of the United Nations, Annie was that.

17

And Opening More

And Annie and Maitri asked their friend the President of the United States to appoint Maitri Ambassador to the United Nations. So he and Annie rejoined Bee in New York, where Bee had remained since she went there with the study group, while the others went other ways. And Bee was also thriving.

In her second year with the New York City Ballet she married a ballerina whose name was Giselle.

They became inseparable when Giselle danced Odile to Bee's Odette in *Swan Lake*, and the study group readily welcomed Giselle into their Chinatown apartment and into the study group, from the first time Bee invited her there for supper.

"That's how everyone would be if everyone knew what's good for everyone," said Giselle as she read the *Metta Sutta* from the apartment's living room wall, and then she placed a fingertip on the tip of the Buddha's *ushnisha*.

So, after she and Bee married, she shared the apartment with the group until the other four went other ways. And, the year after that, she and Bee bought a house on Long Island, and the year after that they adopted two seven-year-old boys, orphans of the strife in the Congo. Giselle suggested that when she heard how Annie and I became friends.

"Why don't we adopt some orphans of the chaos in the Congo," she asked Bee. "I mean when we've established our dancing more firmly."

And they learned Lingala. Both already were fluent in French, and they learned quickly in their research for the adoption that French was an official language on both sides of the river, but they wished that the children they'd adopt feel at home in the United States as soon as possible. And they also learned that not everyone's language there was French, and their learning Lingala proved serendipitous, beyond the possibilities they considered.

Their search ended in their adopting one boy from the Democratic Republic of the Congo and one from the Republic of the Congo, and Lingala was the primary language of the homes of both, during their first seven years of life. And, when Annie and Maitri returned to New York, the boys were in high school and talking of majoring in political science at Columbia to return to the Congo to end the strife within and between their two countries on the two sides of the river they shared. So their continuing to speak Lingala on Long Island helped with that plan.

And, during all that, Suzy gave birth to two children. After three years of her and Bobby's teaching at the University of Michigan, the university offered full professorships to both of them, and Bobby accepted. But Suzy decided she wished to be a mother, and she gave birth to a daughter the next year, and a son the next.

But she continued in her academic profession. She and Bobby wrote novels about people of little promise who achieved success by befriending people of little promise with whom they learned one another's possibilities and outperformed anyone's hope for them. And they wrote the books under the *nom de plume* Suzanne Robert, and my friend George did for them what he'd done for me and Annie and Maitri, and many more people read Suzy's and Bobby's books than read Annie's or Maitri's or mine.

But, in that time with the United Nations, Annie and Maitri also increased their renown. The renown they earned in Israel and India gave them the respect they needed to use their United

Nations positions to help the people of Tibet. And they used the same methods there.

The Chinese government, while calling Tibet an autonomous region, was permitting little autonomy there. But, with Tibet having nearly nothing to contribute to China's economy and being no political threat to anyone, China had no reason for the cost of ruling it. So that was a factor in many of the questions Annie and Maitri asked, and another factor was that sharing is a fundamental tenet of both communism and Buddhism, and that Buddhism derived that tenet from Hinduism was also a factor in solving the problem that one of the horns of the Tibet dilemma was that China had relinquished some of western Tibet to India.

So, while Annie's fluency in Chinese helped them with the Chinese government, what she and Maitri had done in India and Maitri's being a native of where the Buddha taught gave them more influence in India than they had in China. And, while the main political weight in China was economic, religion had more political weight in India. But Tibet's peacefulness influenced all.

So largely by promise of a buffer between nuclear powers, in Annie's and Maitri's third year of working directly with the United Nations, Tibet became an entirely autonomous region.

It became an independent nation with its President sharing the Nobel Peace Prize with the heads of state of China and India.

But, of course, Annie had other responsibilities in her United Nations position, and one of the trips she made was to the Congo, to understand attitudes there. And, by then, the boys Bee and Giselle adopted were sophomores at Columbia majoring in political science and minoring in economics and international relations. So Annie took them with her on her trip to the Congo. She also invited Bee and Giselle. But they stayed at home.

"Do you want to go too?" she asked. "To see your boys in diplomatic action?"

"I don't think so," said Bee. "Not this time."

"No," said Giselle. "We don't want to distract them from their official duties."

And they more than met their mothers' and their Aunt Annie's expectations. Annie's French helped her, but so did the boys' continuing fluency in Lingala, and they'd also kept track of what was happening in the Congo. So they contributed materially to the mission, partly by the credibility their friendship with Annie gave her, but also largely by the questions they asked.

They showed the influence of Bee's example, the approach to problems that she and Annie and the others of the study group shared, the attitude that became the basis for both Annie's and Maitri's diplomacy and Bee's and Giselle's parenting.

So they laid much groundwork for more work there.

So that visit and what Annie and Maitri did for Tibet, and also their success in eliciting Islamic support from Islamabad to Cairo for the Afghan insurgency that eventually absorbed the Taliban, substantially augmented the reputation Annie and Maitri earned in Israel and India.

Annie didn't solve all of Earth's political problems. Such as the Pyongyang government's generations of dedication to the cruelty of arrogance and lies had built some hardly penetrable barriers between some governments and the common decency of honest conversation. But Annie's friends in Beijing agreed to make their support for Pyongyang contingent on deliverability of international aid to the Korean people, and Annie's and Maitri's connections to both the United Nations and the United States made relatively easy ending the three quarters of a century of the United States' government's punishing the people of both Cuba and the United States for the behavior of Castro and Kennedy and the also defunct Soviet Union, and that had become largely economic.

So the work Annie and Maitri did directly with the United Nations removed all doubt that the committee responsible for awarding the Nobel Peace Prize may have had of the importance of their peace-making abilities and accomplishments.

So, in the third December of that work with the United Nations, they received the Nobel Peace Prize together.

"We've only tried to be everyone's friend," said Annie, accepting the prize in Oslo with Maitri standing behind her while the other members of the study group sat in the audience in front of them, with the past and present heads of state owing their nine Peace Prize sharings to her and Maitri. "And our way of doing that has been by trying to help others understand the importance of their doing that, both for themselves, and for us all. That's all."

And, of course, Maitri's proud parents were among the leaders and study group members in the audience, and so were Miss Walker and Mrs. Meredith, and George and Uma.

But Annie also spoke to the purpose of the Nobel Committee.

"Of course we all know," she said, "that Alfred Nobel endowed the Nobel prizes with funds he acquired by developing and marketing explosives for war. I've read that he suffered from heart disease in his later years and expressed gratitude that the nitroglycerine he'd marketed for weapons somewhat alleviated that. But I haven't heard he repented the bellicose uses of the explosives he developed and sold.

"And I've read that he was Judaic, and Judaic scripture suggests that the Judaic notion of peace isn't befriending neighbors not Judaic, but subjugating them. But Maitri and I have learned all around this earth we all inevitably share that, if anyone congenially but persistently asks any of us to explain what they're doing and why, they'll find their own way to relinquish willingly their oldest and most deliberate habits of kicking against the prick. So we welcomed the opportunity to come here and express to the Committee here our gratitude for its prizes for repentance.

"I mean for any who've repented or led or inspired repentance of the wars of our world, whether or not Nobel did and whether or not he recognized the need to beat our swords into plowshares, and not subjugate others to do that for us.

"And Maitri, my loving economist husband, has told me that professors of economics have told him their business is to study how to distribute a scarcity of goods. But he's also pointed out to anyone he's found willing to listen that the scarcity is artificial, that the problem is our fear of sharing the wealth of our largely green earth, and that the basis for both that and much of the war is irrational greed. So we're also here for that.

"Courage, curiosity, compassion.

"Are we afraid to ask one another how we feel? Are we afraid of common decency being common? Or do we lack it?

"Those questions are why we came.

"We came here to ask those questions on this world stage, in hope that all of us will ask them both of what we call others, and of ourself."

But, after that speech, Annie and Maitri moved on again.

"I've been thinking of being a mother," she said to him at supper at home the day after that return of theirs from Oslo. "I still miss how my mom was with me when I was littler, and I'd like to have the chance to be the mom she never had a chance to be for me, and I'd like to be sure a couple more kids have the opportunities I've had, instead of what might have happened to me, if Billy hadn't found me."

And Maitri looked up from his plate and grinned a grin as wide as anyone ever grins.

"I was trying to think of a way to ask you if you wanted that," he said, and the grin Annie grinned then wasn't into space but at Maitri.

But then Maitri's grin changed into something as hopeful but less certain.

"And I never intended to stay in the United States this long," he said after looking down at his plate and up again. "So I've also been thinking of going home. I'm grateful for our visits during our assignment to India. And I'm glad we were able to go there for my grandparents' funerals. But still I miss my mom too."

And Annie smiled. And the grin returned to Maitri's face. And they resigned their positions with the United Nations.

Annie and I had flown west to Tibet together when she was nine. When she was 29, completing her circumnavigation of Earth, she and Maitri flew east to Tibet together. And three years later she made that side of Earth her home.

She and Maitri bought a house in Bodhgaya. And, officially, they never again worked for any government. For income, to be parents of the daughter and son to whom Annie gave birth in the next two years, they wrote books about what they did in Israel and India and Tibet and how they did it and why they did it that way. So their books clarified and propagated happiness all around Earth. They told how all could be happy.

Annie's relinquishing her United States citizenship wasn't an abdication. All she'd done for the United States' Department of State increased the stature of the United States, not as a city on a hill but as a member of the society of all of our world, a sharing participant. So people in other countries came to expect from and give to United States tourists congeniality that hardly had been possible since before the publication of the novel *The Ugly American* at the end of the Eisenhower administration.

But, in India, Annie's life was mainly family life.

She was a mother and a wife. And, by being a wife, she also was again a daughter. And, through Maitri's parents' siblings, she also became a cousin and a niece and an aunt.

Maitri's relatives welcomed her into their homeland as they welcomed his return, and she responded in kind to that welcome at least as easily as she'd befriended Bee and Suzy and Bobby, and she and Maitri also treated their children as they'd always tried to treat everyone everywhere.

They asked them what they thought and never tried to tell them what to think or what to do.

And Maitri's parents treated their grandchildren as grandparents ordinarily treat grandchildren. And Maitri's mother not only enjoyed her grandchildren but also treated Annie as the daughter she'd never had, and Annie responded in kind to that, also welcoming it. Happily, while keeping her first mother in her heart, she found her also in Maitri's mother's smiles.

So, while also enjoying all those aunts and uncles and cousins, Annie's and Maitri's children excelled as had Annie.

Occasionally, heads and secretaries of state called Annie and Maitri, to ask them to accompany them on visits for particular diplomatic purposes. And, after their children began school, Annie and Maitri acceded to those requests when they could take their children with them on those trips. And, for their children's birthdays, they took them anywhere on Earth they wished to go.

But, excepting for that and other opportunities their relative affluence and openness permitted, their children grew up through secondary school among and as ordinary Indian children.

And then, having excelled in the Indian system of academic advancement by examination, they entered Mogadh University at about the ages the study group entered the University of Michigan. So, when they began studying international relations and economics and politics there, readily and willingly accepting the example their parents and grandparents provided by simply being what they were, Annie and Maitri accepted the professorships Maitri's parents left to complete their marriage, in the expanse of all unity beyond sky's below. And three years later, when their children went to Columbia for doctoral work in international relations, Annie and Maitri accepted professorships there.

And Suzy and Bobby followed a similar course.

Bobby didn't bully their kids into following in his and Suzy's footsteps. But, as Annie's and Maitri's children followed in their footsteps with no bullying, Suzy's and Bobby's children enrolled at the University of Michigan to study English and French literature, and then Suzy accepted a full professorship there as had Bobby. And, when their two children went to Columbia for doctoral work in literature in English, Suzy and Bobby solicited and received professorships there.

So, eventually, buying homes on Long Island, the study group came together again, in Bee's and Giselle's neighborhood.

And, during that time in New York, Suzanne Robert wrote what literary critics would call a *roman à clef*. But all their books were that, novels with characters who are fictional representations of actual people, but Suzanne Robert's books didn't have the flaw that made "*roman à clef*" a pejorative term. They weren't libelous gossip but monuments to their friends.

Suzy wrote her doctoral dissertation on the role of character in historical novels. And Bobby wrote his on the role of the zeitgeist in autobiographical novels. So they applied those considerations in each of their novels.

The principal protagonist of their first novel was an orphan of the Siberian GULAG who danced her way to the Bolshoi Ballet and from there to becoming President of Russia and cleaning up the corruption that was consuming that country's economy.

But, in that novel, they didn't present communism as the perversion into the sort of feudal capitalism people had come to call communism. Instead, they presented it in terms of its original ideal of sharing, and so they not only received a Pulitzer prize for it but also received an invitation to the Kremlin from the President of Russia. They suspected his motive was to use them as a sort of propaganda tool, but they accepted the invitation with the motive of letting that visit serve the purpose of their novels, to tell anyone who would listen how they felt.

"Reform isn't easy," said the President at a private lunch in the Kremlin with his wife and Suzy and Bobby. "But I hope you're right about a journey of a thousand miles beginning beneath one's feet. Isn't that what the mother of that little girl in your book told her daughter before she died, before her daughter danced her way to Moscow? I read the *Dao De Jing* to try to figure out how to deal with the Chinese. But both we and they have a long history of bullying."

"Do you know the founders of Hinduism immigrated to India from the Caucasus?" asked Suzy.

"No," said the President. "I haven't read that."

"They initially settled in the Indus valley," continued Suzy after shrugging and smiling. "But, during the next few centuries, they spread into the Ganges valley. And, while they were doing that, other Caucasians migrated west as far as what we now call the English Channel, and that was the basis for Hitler's propaganda about Aryans, calling them the German master race. The swastika was a symbol of auspiciousness for Hindus millennia before it was a symbol of Nazi racism. And those immigrants to India also called themselves Aryans. '*Arya*' means 'noble' in Sanskrit.

"But the Aryans never mastered the Europeans. And the reason they were able to master the Indians in those valleys was that, because their understanding of agriculture was obviously economically beneficial, the Indians welcomed that mastery. So eventually the Aryans assimilated into both societies."

"That's a lot of thousands of miles of steps," said the President. "And I agree that Stalin and others made a lot of mistakes besides the failure of trying to bully our people into the futility of all those five-year agricultural plans."

"You know, I used to be a bully," then said Bobby. "Until I met Suzy in the third grade. She understood the *Dao De Jing* before she read it. And it worked on me."

"What's the third grade?" asked the President.

"It's the level of education of most eight-year-olds in the United States," replied Bobby.

"By now," then said the First Lady of Russia, "that must be more than a thousand miles of steps."

"And hand in hand," said Suzy, "since our wedding a decade later."

But what made the first novel Suzy and Bobby wrote in New York different from the others was that it was a key to knowing that each of their other novels was also a *roman à clef*. Its title was *Prospectus*, and its main characters were four children of misfortune who found fortune in one another, and then found ways to extend that fortune to unfortunate persons all over Earth. And that story had no ending.

And, while the Nobel committee responsible for evaluating literature recognized that it was a *roman à clef*, it didn't hold that against its authors but awarded them the Nobel Prize for literature.

"We've written only about friendship," said Suzy as Bobby stood behind her as their parents and their children and the other members of the study group and their children and Miss Walker and Mrs. Meredith and their first Manhattan friend sat before them in the center of the front row of their audience in Stockholm. "And all we've written has been in hope of everyone being everyone's friend as we've tried to be."

Bee and Giselle never received a Nobel prize. But that may be only because the Nobel Committee offered no prize for dance. After they retired from performing on stages, they reduced the rivalry among dancers by teaching their *Taijiquan* approach to dance, for the School of American Ballet. And the dancers learning it from them extended that sense of harmony to their audiences in New York, across the United States, and all around Earth.

And the young men Bee and Giselle adopted from the Congo earned baccalaureate and doctoral degrees at Columbia and fulfilled their high school goal.

And, of course, their interaction with their aunts Annie and Suzy and their uncles Bobby and Maitri began long before they enrolled in Columbia for anything. It began the day they arrived in the United States, and they came to know them through the annual reunions in Ann Arbor and at other times and in other places, before their return to the Congo with Annie. So that was partly how they decided their major and minor courses of baccalaureate study and their focus for their doctoral degrees.

They learned of the study group's educating one another in one another's courses of study. And that was especially reasonable to them, through their becoming both friends and brothers in the United States, beyond sharing their goal for their original homelands. And Annie helped them in ways beyond the trip to the Congo and asking them what they thought.

While they were in graduate school, she helped them into State Department internships at the United Nations, and their performance at school and in their internships earned them more permanent employment with the State Department, and Annie's recommendation and their performance in their first year in the District of Columbia earned them appointments to be United States Ambassadors to the Congo, to each of their homelands there.

And, in those positions, they used Annie's methods of diplomacy to befriend leaders of both governments and of the main striving factions. So, at the end of a year of that, they resigned from our State Department and successfully ran for election to the Presidencies of their two nations. And, of course, they then extended Annie's peace-making method into their presiding.

So, in effect, they became both ambassadors from the United States to their original homelands and ambassadors from their original homelands to the United States, and in the same way they also became ambassadors to and from one another's original homelands, and that dynamic made possible what otherwise might have been impossible.

They asked the leaders of the factions what their strife was doing for anyone, what they thought working together might do for them as well as for everyone around them, and what ending the strife might do for both their countries' economies and their personal prosperity

And then they used their connections with the United States and the United Nations to solicit successfully international aid to develop their two countries' agriculture and education systems.

So the factions stopped fighting, and the two nations united into an economic union they modeled on the European Union, and that union quickly became the fastest-growing emerging market in the global economy.

So the Nobel Peace Prize Committee awarded those two nations' Presidents the prize for the peace that immediately followed the chartering of the Congo Economic Union.

"Our methods were how our African American mothers taught us to dance," they said in unison as Bee and Giselle and their parents and the other members of the study group and their children sat before them in their audience in Oslo. "They taught us to move, whenever we can and as well as we can, always with and never against all around us."

And, as had Suzy and Annie, they delivered their acceptance speech in the language of Jehanne of Domremy, the language of diplomacy and ballet, of *fraternité, liberté, égalité.*

And all the other children of the study group also found productive paths to peace by way of their parents and friends of their parents and friends they made along their way helping assure no one kept them from finding their way.

So, like their parents, all became only what they were.

18

Beyond

And that wasn't the only way that wasn't the end of the study group's story.

One sunny fourth Thursday in November, when the study group had become what people call senior citizens, they were enjoying blueberry pie *à la mode* at their study table at Bee's and Giselle's house.

For various reasons all their children were celebrating Thanksgiving in their spouses' parents' homes or in their own homes in other cities.

Bobby had baked the pie. Maitri had churned the ice cream. And Annie was grinning as she ate both.

Though the table was there because Bee and Giselle were the last of them to leave the study group's Chinatown apartment, my Buddha was at Suzy's and Bobby's house, and Suzy had an idea.

"I have a question," she said. "Now that we have plenty of money and time, with our kids off making us proud and letting our grandchildren be as wonderful as they are too, I'm thinking we might do for some other kids what Billy did for Annie, what Bee and Giselle did for their boys. I mean hasn't the time come for us to refill our nests?"

"Oh, yes!" said Annie. "I think so! And that's exactly what Billy did! Before he went looking for me and found me sitting alone in that corner, he waited until he had all the time and money I needed, and there I was."

"What do you think, Maitri?" asked Giselle. "Oh you of the *Metta Sutta*."

"I think we should look in corners beyond this county's Child Protective Services office," he said. "As you and Bee did."

"And," said Bobby, "with two adults in each of our homes and plenty of room, we could have two kids in each, not but one Annie."

"And the time and money we all have now will also make it easier for all of us," said Bee, "than it was for Giselle and me."

"So should I call our United Nations friends to find out who needs us most?" asked Annie.

So, after nods and grins all around, she did. And those friends connected them with UNICEF, and the UNICEF connections told them in which half dozen countries children most desperately needed their help and also connected them with responsible agencies in those countries, and then the study group made a few more trips outside the United States. So, by the next Thanksgiving, their Long Island neighborhood was a kind of united nations of children.

Those three pairs of parents could have done that more quickly. Logistically, adopting six children from six countries on three continents was quite complex, but Bee's and Giselle's experience and Annie's and Maitri's connections and international reputation for making no kind of trouble made many steps in the process easier for them. But, wishing to make the process easy and pleasant for the children, they did it carefully and methodically.

And they looked for the loneliest children, and they began in the most difficult place, Pyongyang. And, for all of them to learn from Bee's and Giselle's experience from the beginning of the process, all of them flew there. And, to assure the children that they wouldn't desert them, the adopting parents of each child stayed in the country where they found the child until the child could leave the country with them.

And, before meeting each child, they learned how to introduce themselves to the child in the child's language, how to ask the child his or her name, and how to ask one more question.

"Will you help us learn your language?" they asked.

And, to avoid any compulsion or presuppositions, they tried to be sure no one told any child to expect the first meeting. And, for each introduction, whether the child was sitting or standing, for their eyes to be on the level of the child's, they knelt on both knees to introduce themselves. And, while the expressions on the children's faces ranged from a questioning gaze to a big grin, each replied affirmatively to that request.

And, as children sometimes say thinkers go first, Suzy was the first of them to do all that. In Pyongyang, in a big room full of little children, she went directly to a little girl sitting alone in a corner. And she and that little girl left that room hand in hand.

So, a few months later, that child was officially Suzy's and Bobby's daughter. And then, grinning while eating airline food when she wasn't grinning while gazing through the window beside her at the shining clouds below her, she flew with her new friends to Phnom Penh to find her a brother. And neither could nor would her three pairs of traveling companions stop grinning with her.

"Now, you can fly, little friend," thought Annie. "And you'll never be hungry again."

But, while Cambodia was about as poor as North Korea, it wasn't nearly as dangerous or politically paranoid. So, after Annie and Maitri introduced Suzy and Bobby to the people there to whom their UNICEF connections referred them, Annie and Maitri flew on to Mogadishu and Khartoum while Bee and Giselle flew on to Caracas and Bogota. So, in a total of less than three times the amount of time they spent in Pyongyang, the three pairs of parents were together at home again with their half dozen new little friends.

And, with their three homes a short walk from one another, each of the six children they found quickly had five new friends, beyond the six members of the adult study group, who had always been their friends.

So, when those half dozen little friends weren't busy teaching their new parents their languages and otherwise being happy, they were busy helping one another learn one another's languages and the language of their new homeland.

And their new parents tried to consider all possibilities for them. They tried to be sure they weren't taking them long out of touch with anyone they wished not to leave. And they knew they couldn't rely on the governments of those desperate countries to give them complete or accurate information in that regard.

So, as soon as they could, they asked the children for that information. And they did all they could to assure the children that they'd do all they could for them in that regard and any other. And, of course, they kept their word.

And, much as had Annie in India, the children found that suddenly they had a huge family of six brothers and sisters in addition to the five in their immediate neighborhood and many nephews and nieces of various ages.

None of that further extension of their family resided on Long Island. But all of them both came to visit occasionally and happily relinquished to its new occupants their space in their parents' or grandparents' homes. And, partly because Bee's and Giselle's boys missed the snow, they and their families flew there from the Congo every December. And those men of three homelands became especially close to their new little friends.

They, of course, understood the children's situations better than any of the others there could. So they did all they could to be sure the children were conscious of their possibilities and that they understood that having a new homeland could also produce new possibilities for the old one. And, of course, the similarity of situations made their efforts especially credible to the children.

And, also of course, Bee's and Giselle's new son and daughter had encouraging stories to tell their young Long Island friends when they returned from visits to their Congo brothers and their families for their Congo brothers' birthdays each year.

And, of course, each of the three homes had a piano.

So, to remind themselves of who they were, as they rode their bicycles exploring the varieties of life and culture and commerce around the neighborhood they shared in their new hometown, those girls and boys from all over Earth composed a mantra, to the melody of "Twinkle Twinkle Little Star": "*Yīn* and *yáng* and up and down, black and white and all around; each in all and all in each, nothing is beyond our reach."

The first book all of them read was *The Jungle Books*.

And their other neighbors called them what they were.

"There they go," they said as the six rode past on their bicycles. "The little united nations of Little Neck."

But, by then, I was gone, beyond. And my departure point was in our home in Ann Arbor. Annie, after graduate school, gave the house to Suzy and Bobby. So the six members of the study group had their reunions in it from then until Suzy and Bobby returned to New York with their children. But my departure was before those reunions.

I was sitting in a chair I'd put in our study to meditate with a view of the Michigan maples behind our backyard. So, with my hands in the *dhyana mudra* as were Annie's the moment I found her, I was enjoying the view through the window of the study into sunlight on snow in the trees. And quietly it all came together, the sun and the snow and the trees, and all the memories and promises within and beyond. All came together.

The year was the 81ˢᵗ of my imagining this world, and the day was the ninth of that year's second month, the day of my birth on Earth in that time. 81 is the number of parts of the *Dao De Jing*, and nine to its second power is 81 while 8+1=9, and 3^4=81 while 3+1=4, but 1x1=1. So one to all of its powers is always one.

But all came together in a bright sweet smile, in the place where all is anyway, in a warm small hand.

In a world of desperate disparity, the refrains "reaching out" and "unconditional love" are often clichés conditioning groping and grasping, but they also ultimately dissolve and resolve in the infinitely large and small and numberless lotus of the genuine heart.

And I had learned that one is always the first power of one's acceptance. And I learned that largely by seeing how those children lived their lives. They only did the best they could.

So all is only as absolute as Annie.

Beginning

never

ends

∞

Books
by
Billy Lee Harman

Dust
a novel
2005

Ashes
some memories
2015

Angels
summaries of scripture
2020

Dao De Jing
a literal translation
2021

Tai Ji Quan
(fundamentally)
2021

Annie
(how children are)
2021

Space and Light
2023

Made in the USA
Columbia, SC
17 October 2023